She was lounging against one side of the open doorway, her cheek pressed languidly against the frame.

He saw her in the mirror, before he'd had time to turn. Then, having seen her there, her reflection seemed to hold him fast, like some hypnotic apparition, so that he was no longer able to turn.

His hands dropped away from his tie, as though they'd withered and died up there, and dangled lifeless at his sides, no longer volatile; dead things still fastened to him by their own tendons.

She peeled her cheek from the doorframe and came in a little further. He hadn't moved. He couldn't.

A cord at the side of his neck whipped up, and, as though it were a rusted hinge, he emitted a grating sound. "Get out of here."

"This is the last time, Press," she said.

His mouth twisted at one extremity. "Each time it's the last time. Then each time there's another time that comes after it."

He picked up the checkbook from the top of the dresser. His hand was shaking too much. The pen point regurgitated a great glossy blot, left it behind as it swept on.

She took the check, folded it carefully, and opening her handbag, put it inside.

"Now go to your wedding," she said, with an inflection almost of fondness. She surveyed him with a sort of kindly interest. "You make a good-looking groom. Wait, your tie ends aren't straight. I wonder why it is men can never— Do you want me to fix it for you before I go? That'll be my wedding present to you, Press, a nice even tie."

She set her cigarette down against the rim of the table, and came around it to his side.

Her hands reached toward his tie.

She shouldn't have come so close to him...

FRIGHT

by Cornell Woolrich

A HARD CASE CRIME NOVEL

A HARD CASE CRIME BOOK
(HCC-034)
August 2007

Published by

Dorchester Publishing Co., Inc.
200 Madison Avenue
New York, NY 10016

in collaboration with Winterfall LLC

*This book is a work of fiction. Names, characters, places, and
incidents either are the products of the author's imagination or
are used fictitiously, and any resemblance to actual events or
persons, living or dead, is entirely coincidental.*

ISBN 0-8439-5774-3
ISBN-13 978-0-8439-5774-7

Cover design by Cooley Design Lab
Typeset by Swordsmith Productions

The name "Hard Case Crime" and the Hard Case Crime logo
are trademarks of Winterfall LLC. Hard Case Crime books
are selected and edited by Charles Ardai and printed in
the United States of America.

Visit us on the web at www.HardCaseCrime.com

Nor God nor man will tell you now
What you must do, or when, or how—
There's no retreat that must be won to,
No one except yourself to run to.
SARA HENDERSON HAY

One
New York

1

He was twenty-five that year, 1915, and his name was
Prescott Marshall. He had already been living in New
York for three years, and for one of those, now, he had
known Marjorie Worth. And for a good part of that one,
now, he had loved her. He worked in a stock brokerage
office at Number Two, Wall Street, and he didn't make
very much money. But he was young, he presented a
good appearance, he had a certain indefinable appeal for
wealthy elderly ladies who were clients of his firm, and
that would take care of itself in due course. The fact that
he didn't make very much money as yet.

He had obtained the position through a girl he had
known the first year he was in New York. She had spoken
of the opening, she had told him whom to see, she had
spoken to whom he was to see before he did. She was
gone from his life now, but the position remained. Pro-
viding a rather illuminating commentary on the relative
staying powers of physical attraction as against self-
advancement in the average life.

This first foothold, this niche that he had secured,
that he still clung to so precariously, would broaden,
would expand with the passage of years, would become
a platform of security, and at last a pedestal of success.
But he needed her help to make it that: Marjorie. For
she would bring to him the very things he needed most
in this particular, highly selective career he had chosen
for himself. She had money and money attracts other
money; she had impeccable social standing, and social

standing attracts confidence; she had friends who had money and social standing, and through being her friends they would eventually and in due course become his clients; through being his clients, they would attract friends of their own. It was an ever-widening circle, working to his advantage.

And so he was going to ask her to marry him. And waiting to do so until he was sure that she would consent, for he wasn't a gambler. He didn't believe in gambling with his own future, he didn't believe in staking his own chances on a premature spin of the wheel.

He was ready, but he wanted to give her plenty of time to be ready too. He only bet on a sure thing.

Her beauty was what had first attracted him, tangoing at tea-time at the Plaza in a long slit skirt, and made him ask them who she was, and made him urge, "Take me over there, I've got to meet her." She had a lot of it. That had held him fast past the original introduction and the first few chance meetings after. She was an extremely lovely brunette, tall and graceful of carriage. The styles were lovely that year, they seemed to have been invented just for her. They were dressing like ladies for almost the last time. He soon enough found that she was what a later generation would have called good publicity. She was prestige-enhancing to take out. She wore well on the arm. She made heads turn, and when they turned, he was the man who was with her. The boy from a New Hampshire hamlet was on his way in the big city.

Then later, when the impetus that had carried him this far might have begun to slow, had come the insight into her family's wealth and social position to dazzle him, sweep him up again, just as he was about to drop off and let her go by. She was Money, she was Family.

His original interest had by now kindled a reciprocal

interest on her part. She was a stage behind him all the way, but following the same path he was.

Then had come his self-taken decision to marry her.

All that remained now was the asking.

2

Her boxed corsage, violets ringing a gardenia, had been duly sent off. The tickets were in his pocket. They were for Madge Kennedy in *Fair and Warmer* at the Eltinge. And quite expensive too as tickets went those days; two-fifty apiece for seats in the orchestra.

He was sitting waiting in the fabulous corridor that ran through the Waldorf-Astoria, from Thirty-fourth to Thirty-third Street, "Peacock Alley."

There were two places that were de rigueur for meeting anyone, in New York in the Nineteen Teens. If you were meeting a man, you made it the Knickerbocker Bar, on Forty-second. If you were meeting a lady—Peacock Alley.

"Paging Mr. Marshall."

He failed to connect the name to himself the first time he heard it. He wasn't used to being paged at the Waldorf-Astoria.

"Paging Mr. Prescott Marshall."

He sat up straighter, beckoned, and the boy came over.

"There's a lady on the telephone, sir. I'll show you the way."

He wasn't sure if you were supposed to give them something for that. He hesitated, finally gave the boy a dime. The hesitation had spoiled it, though. The boy thanked him, but with constraint.

It was she, of course. She was the only lady in his life.

"Press," she said, "we've just had bad news up here."

Although she wasn't crying, there was a tearful tinge to her voice, a melancholy undertone, that he'd never heard before.

"What…?" he said with bated quickness.

"They're both gone. We just received word from the American consul at Queenstown. The cablegram got here about fifteen minutes ago. I was all dressed and ready to leave when it arrived." She stopped a moment, then she went on, "It's an official confirmation. The bodies have been recovered and identified."

"Good God," he breathed. "Your Uncle Ben and your Aunt Nelly, both."

The *Lusitania*. Her mother's only sister and the latter's husband had been on it when it had gone down, at two o'clock Greenwich time the afternoon before, to a world-wide gasp of horror and incredulity.

He didn't know what to say. What was there you could say, at such a time, to such a thing? He never was very good at emergencies, anyway. In the end, she was the one who had to go on talking.

"I can't leave Mother right now," she said wanly. "*You* understand, don't you, Press?"

"Don't think of it," he urged. "Of course I understand. Will you give your mother my deepest sympathy?"

"Thank you, Press," she said gratefully. "I will."

"And I'll call you tomorrow."

He left the hotel by the Thirty-fourth Street side, and walked over to Herald Square, past the watchful bronze guardian-owls along the cornice of James Gordon Bennett's wedge-of-pie-shaped Herald Building, and then on up Broadway; the entire evening was now disappointingly back on his hands, before it had even had a chance to begin, and with no one or nothing to help him pass it.

Which at twenty-five can be not only a major dislocation but even a considerable danger.

3

He'd been drunk for some time now, and steadily getting drunker. It had happened more by accident than deliberately. He'd just incautiously gone past the point of being able to stop any more, before realizing it himself.

The lights kept spinning, spinning, like the exposed magnified works inside a jeweled watch. Sometimes a crazy alphabet of letters seemed to shoot out from them, like sparks, and form signs all around him, and at all angles, against the sky. New Amsterdam — *Watch Your Step;* Liberty — *The Birth of a Nation* — Mae Marsh; Geo. M. Cohan Theatre — *It Pays to Advertise;* Globe — Montgomery and Stone in *Chin Chin;* Shanley's; Hippodrome — Strand —

Sometimes they were like pinwheels, revolving around a single colored center. The bright red cherry of a Manhattan. He must have been looking straight down into his own glass when that happened. He was on Manhattans.

He'd never been so drunk at any time before in his whole life.

All at once there was a woman with him. She'd been with him for just a few minutes, she'd been with him for long, endless nights at a time. She kept changing her dress at intervals. And even her hair and face to go with it. First she was in pink. Then suddenly she was in light green. As though a gelatin slide had revolved and cast a different tint over her.

"You changed your dress," he accused her.

Interlude of more coruscating pinwheels, again like the oversized works of a watch, all flashing and tinseled and rotating at once, but in counter directions.

This time she was in yellow.

"Can't you stay in one dress?" he complained querulously.

The bars were very unreliable tonight. They looked nice and steady, but he'd lean on them too heavily, or something. They'd tilt way up on one side, and slope all the way down on the other. It was like trying to drink from off the top of a see-saw.

The pinwheels were dimming now, they weren't nearly so bright.

The bars gave place to a sidewalk. A sidewalk that was straight up and down in front of his face, like a rule measure held to his nose.

The toecaps of shoes made patterns on the surface of it. Sometimes they'd stand around formed into a semicircle. Then this would break up, they'd all resume going this way and that once more. Then a new semicircle would form, adding to itself pair by pair, until it was all ranged around him again complete.

Presently a couple of diminutive pointed vamps ventured forth out of this background row of shoes and poised themselves tentatively close up alongside him.

He split in two at this point. *He* went on, but memory stopped where it was, didn't accompany him any further.

4

And now the time had come, the night had come. For asking her.

She had caught up with him. There was nothing further to wait for. In fact, delay might even have been dangerous. She must be caught where she was, at the outskirts, and drawn all the way into love. Bound to him by a formal declaration. Otherwise, a reverse current might set in that would carry her away from him.

You could not stand still in love. It was a moving stream. You floated together, or you drifted apart. It had to be one or the other. There was no such thing as a fixed position. There were no life rafts on these tricky seas.

And so, this never-to-be-forgotten night in both their lives, when "both their lives" became "their lives"; this fateful date, this turning point, this Saturday of May in Nineteen Fifteen.

She was in pale blue satin, the pale blue that lies within the depths of ice, or when moonlight strikes on burnished steel. And at her waist she wore pink roses, his pink roses. And long afterwards, looking back, he could remember her as she was this night. As a man should.

It was so easy to be in love with her, so easy to want to make her your own. Even if she'd been poor, even if her family had lacked all standing, he still would have wanted her, the way she was tonight. She was too much for him, she gave his poor heart amorous indigestion.

An intermission came on, and they left their seats and went out to the foyer.

"I have something to say to you," he said out there.

"And I can't hold it back any longer. I've tried, and I can't."

She smiled. I know, that said, I understand.

"And if we go back in there again, I'm afraid I'll come out with it right there, with people sitting all around us hearing every word."

She nodded. I know, that said, I understand.

"Shall we clear out of here?"

She didn't have to smile or nod or anything else; he knew, he understood.

They never went back to their seats again. They got into a carriage there at the theatre entrance and were driven uptown and into the park at Fifty-ninth Street. There they slowly coursed along the driveway, now a silver-plated lake beside them, now an arbor of trees in lush new leaf closing over their heads for awhile, now a twinkling line of apple-green gas lamps striking off along some walk; the drowsy clop-clop of their horse the only sound to break the magic stillness of the night. There he kissed her, and she met his kiss. There he told her what he had brought her there to say to her.

"Marjorie, I love you. Will you marry me and be my wife?"

The words that are the oldest in the world, the words that are always new again each time. The words that are so short in speaking, the words that last for so long.

"Yes," she said quite simply, "I will."

His arms and his lips thanked her.

"I'll be a good husband, Marjorie, for the rest of my days."

As simple as that. And as irrevocable.

They had joined their lives, from now on until death.

5

The next day was Sunday.

He always took it easy Sundays. Lazed around and read the papers. He was going up to Marjorie's house for supper later. That wouldn't be until toward eight.

But then, sometime around five, just as he was applying the lather to his face, there was a knock on the door.

He wasn't sure he'd heard it at first. He silenced the flow of water and listened a moment. It came again. He wiped his hands off and came out and stopped before the door and called, "Who is it?"

The answer was voiceless, a repetition of the knock.

The maneuver frustrated him, just as it might have been intended to. He opened the door, and he was face to face with an unknown young woman, a girl really, looking at him with a sort of demure insistency.

He recoiled an inch behind the shelter of the door, and said "Oh, excuse me." In 1915 a man's undershirt, if not shocking, was at least still reason enough for apology between the sexes.

She kept looking at him with that air of childlike fixity; he could find no other description for it in his own mind.

She was quite young; twenty-two or -four at the utmost. She was quite pretty, but in a run-of-the-mill sort of way. It was not a lifelong beauty of feature and formation such as Marjorie had; it was a transient coloration lent her by the fact of her youth alone, that would disappear with that again some day. She was slim and small; she looked as though she could not have weighed more than a hundred and ten pounds. She was dressed neatly and with a sort of youthful freshness, that avoided being rakish.

She kept looking at him in such an innocently questioning way, as one who has had no previous experience at all with men, particularly at such close quarters, and whose eyes seem to say: "*You* wouldn't hurt me, now, would you?"

He gave her a smile meant to be reassuring. "I guess you have the wrong door."

"No, it's you I want to see," she said in a small, almost babyish voice.

He was taken back. "Me? About what? Are you sure?"

Her lips formed into a little smiling pout of rue. "You don't remember me, do you?"

He simply looked at her blankly. "No, I—I—" Trying to place her, failing completely. Some long-forgotten friend from his old home town?

"I can see you don't. Doesn't my face come back to you at all?"

She took a step forward. He took a step back, to avoid having his undershirt and his lathered jowls brush against her. She took a second step forward. She was in now.

She touched the door lightly with her hand, and it closed. "There," she said, with the elfin, nose-crinkling grin of a mischievous child.

"But do you think you should come here like this?" he expostulated.

"I was in here the other time," she said, with a defiant little perk of her chin. She sat down primly, carefully tucking her skirt about her and removing one of his discarded news-sheets from behind her back. "*Now* do you remember?"

She drew a long pin out of her hat, took that off. "Try me now, this way." She touched at the puff of hair that was worn over each ear, covering the entire ear.

She waited a moment. The effects must have been visible all over his face. "I see you do now," she said. "I didn't mean to startle you. I thought surely you'd…Don't you remember Leona Harris? I even gave you my name."

That came back too now, at the sound of it.

"I didn't really—" he said lamely.

"But it is my right name. Look, I'll show you." She opened a patent-leather pouch she had carried tucked under one arm.

He made a dissuading motion of his hand toward her. "It's all right, I believe you."

"And after all, I *did* come back here with you." It was said inattentively. She was looking into her bag for something, and not at him, as she spoke.

He could feel a slight pull at the lining of both his cheeks, as though they had grown taut for a moment. "Oh, no," he said quietly, "aren't you mistaken about that?"

"But I *did*," she said with innocent trustfulness, her eyes on him now almost reproachfully. "You *know* I did. Didn't you find my hairpins on the dresser the next day? Didn't you find my little stick of lip rouge lying around somewhere the next day? I know I must have left it here."

"How did you know I'd find those things?" he asked her.

"Because I left them here. You'd have to find them; who else would if you didn't?"

"Did you leave them purposely for me to…?" He checked himself. He rubbed the back of one hand against the hollow of the other, as though it troubled him a little, itched perhaps. Then belatedly he felt for the evaporating stickiness on his face. "Will you excuse me a second?"

He went into the bathroom and hurriedly wiped his face off on a towel. Then he put on his shirt and buttoned it and thrust it under his belt.

When he came out she was still sitting there, in a sort
of amiable quiescence. Not looking toward the doorway
through which he had gone. She was holding a cigarette
in her hand now. A skein of silky smoke threaded its way
upward, bisecting her face.

She saw the startled look he gave. "I have to steal the
chance whenever I can get it," she said apologetically.
"We women haven't as much freedom as you men."

He went over and selected a tie and began to do it up
before the glass. His hand wasn't quite steady at it; he
had to begin the knot over. "Well, it was nice of you to
drop by," he said.

"I don't hold anything against anyone," she said.

He picked up his watch and glanced at it as he did so.
"It's after six already," he said.

She took a puff of her cigarette.

He ran a brush sketchily over his hair. He took his
jacket out, and shook it a couple of times, and put it on.
She took another puff of her cigarette. He turned toward
her, prodding a fresh handkerchief down into his breast
pocket. "Will you excuse me now? I've got to go out."

"No."

The flatness of it startled him, threw him off balance,
out of key, for a moment.

She must have wanted that, that was why she'd toned
it that way. A man off balance is a man easier to over-
throw.

He stood there looking at her for a minute before he
was able to bring out anything. Then finally, "What is it
you want?" he blurted out.

She smiled again, in that demure, abashed way. "I'm
glad you asked. I was hoping you'd ask me that. I've been
waiting for it."

"Well, now I have."

There was something a little frightening about her

protracted smile, Marshall thought, and he wondered what it was. But he couldn't tell.

"And now I'm going to answer you," she replied.

But she didn't.

There was a silence, a lapse, while he stood looking at her expectantly. Nothing more came, only the smile was there. He found himself becoming uneasy, at a loss. The smile did something to his poise. She seemed to want it to, the way she prolonged it.

"You really can't guess?" she asked.

"No, I can't," he said shortly.

"I want some money, for the other night."

The smile hadn't left her face, as she said it. It was only the text of the remark itself that was completely at variance with her attitude of friendly, quiescent ease; nothing else; neither the inflection of her voice, nor the expression of her eyes and face, nor the posture of her body. There was neither tautness nor hardness nor anything else; it was almost a wistful drawl.

"I don't get you."

She chose to take it literally; that he hadn't heard her clearly, rather than that he didn't understand. "I said I want some money, for the other night."

"And I said I don't get you."

She was still smiling that way. That slow, sticky, glutinous way.

The smile was working at last, simply by dint of being worn so long. She wanted him to understand it.

"The other night, in the café?"

"The part after the café part." She waited a moment, then she added: "The café part is paid up."

The shock was cataclysmic. It was like having a basinful of filthy water flung unexpectedly into his face. It was like suddenly seeing worms crawl out of the eyes of a beautiful porcelain doll.

His mouth opened and he jarred a step back.

For a moment rage and disgust gave him back his self-possession, his command of the situation. Even if fleetingly.

"Why, you brazen little…! With an innocent face like yours, and to come out with such a thing!"

"I'm glad you used that word, innocent," she mused.

"You little liar! Get out of here! Go on, get out of here before I…!"

She didn't move. The smile had left her face, that was all. She looked up at him with the grave mien of a child, weathering an adult storm of temper without even knowing what it was about, content to sit it out.

"You know what that is, don't you? Blackmail. Do you know that I could have you arrested for that?"

To his surprise, she nodded acquiescently. "Yes, I thought of that before I came up here. You could." It threw him a little; he'd expected counterrecrimination, not assent.

"I told you to get out of here. Go on now, get out."

She shook her head. "No, I won't. You'll have to pick me up and carry me out, if you want me to go."

"Well, I can do that too!" He made a sudden lunge toward her with both arms extended, then stopped short.

"Don't you think it's better to keep the conversation in here, in your room, than to carry it outside, to the hall? Don't you think it's better to keep it just between ourselves?" She shrugged. "I don't care. It's up to you."

"Well, I know the quickest way to settle this!" he said wrathfully. "I'm going to call the police."

She nodded. "Go ahead. There's the phone."

He wrenched it up, then took the receiver off the hook. "Central, give me the Police Department, please."

She crossed her legs. Then didn't forget to modestly lower her skirt. She even let her torso sink down somewhat into a slumped position, as a person does who expects to have to wait for some time. She opened her purse and peered into it, presumably into a mirror berthed in it, for he saw her touch at her hair once or twice, in fastidious adjustment.

She closed the purse again, done with her primping. Her gaze roamed idly about the room, as if in search of entertainment to while away the time. The way people will pick up a magazine to leaf through while waiting in a doctor's anteroom.

"That's your fiancée's picture over there, isn't it?"

The phone came down an inch, from his lips and ear. "Take your eyes off that!"

"Her name is Marjorie Worth."

The phone came down two inches more, both sections of it together.

"Shut up, I said."

"She lives at Nineteen East Seventy-ninth Street."

The phone dropped down to waist-level. He could feel the skin around the corners of his eyes drawn back tight, the way a cat's ears are pulled flat when it's at bay.

"Her telephone number is Regent 1200," she said softly.

His breathing seemed to interfere with his speech.

She went ahead looking at the picture. She gestured with her cigarette. "Well, why don't you finish your call?"

He didn't answer.

"*She'll* believe you," she said reassuringly. "She's bound to. She's engaged to you. She won't believe me. Is that what you're worried about?"

He still didn't answer, didn't move.

"She'll have to hear of it, of course," she went on. "That's something else again. You can't have people arrested without…Is *that* what's worrying you?"

He brought the phone up again, stopped a moment.

Then he said into it, "I'm sorry Central. Never mind that call." He bracketed it together and put it down.

"You don't seem to know what you want to do. First it's one thing, then the other."

He came over toward her slowly. He stood over her. He put one hand out finally to the top of the chair she was sitting in.

"I've never hit a woman yet in my life, but if you don't get up out of there and start over to that door…"

She didn't even cringe or draw her head away.

"When you hit someone there are some screams and a commotion, the whole house'll be attracted, and that brings us back again to where we were."

She looked up at him. Her eyes never wavered, never blinked. They were those of a belle listening to compliments being directed toward her by a hovering admirer, on a settee at some dance.

"All I want is fifty dollars," she said brightly.

"All you want is fifty dollars. Well, the answer is still get out."

Suddenly, to his surprise, and when he least expected it, she had risen accommodatingly to her feet, was standing before him. "All right, I will. I've asked, and you've refused, and there's nothing else to be done…"

She moved toward the door.

"*Here,*" she finished softly.

She opened the door, and stepped outside. Then and only then she turned and looked back at him, smiling again—now in affable farewell. It was as though a pleasant, though totally unimportant, little call were being concluded.

"What'd you mean just then?" he said sharply, still standing by the now-empty chair where she'd left him.

"Well, I have to get it *some*where," she said disarmingly. "I can't go to an absolute stranger for it. There are only three of us involved." Her eyes flicked briefly toward the photograph, far offside within the room. She moved toward the head of the stairs, beyond, in the hall.

"You wouldn't dare!" he exclaimed, ripples of shock spreading outward from the pit of his stomach as though somebody had lunged at him there.

She didn't answer.

"You'll be thrown out faster than—!"

He couldn't see her any more from where he was.

"But not until at least they have heard what their reason is for throwing me out," he heard her say.

He took a quick step after her. She had reached the head of the stairs, was about to descend.

"Do you think she'd take any stock in such a thing?" he said hoarsely.

"She won't believe me. I don't expect her to. But those little things are so hard to get out of your mind once they're put in. It'll stay with her. It'll always be there, hiding away somewhere. She'll always know it's there. You'll always know it's there."

His face was very white. "What good'll that do you?"

"None. But what good will it do you, either?"

He came out to the banister rail and leaned across it. She was on the third step down from the top now, passing below him on a descending plane. His breath made his stomach go up and down against the rail that pressed into it.

"Why should a girl go to her with such a story, if it isn't true?" she shrugged. "Why should a stranger look her up and tell her such a thing, out of a clear blue sky? About you, just you and no one else. How would the stranger know about you, know there *was* a you, in the first place?" She was halfway down the flight now.

He took a deep breath, inclined over the banister rail.

"Come back here, you," he surrendered in a low, smothered growl.

She didn't come back any faster than she'd gone. She sauntered up, just as she'd sauntered down, and then over to the doorway.

He motioned her into the room and closed the door, to bar their being overheard any further.

"I haven't got that much in ready cash, but…"

"A check will do," she said affably.

"What makes you think I—"

"You carry an account with the Colonial Bank, Fifty-fifth Street Branch. You've got eight hundred dollars in it and seventy-two cents."

He looked at her with almost a sort of grudging awe.

"You sure have been busy."

"I woke up earlier than you did that morning. I had nothing to do with myself. If things are left lying around…" She gave her wrist a little deprecatory twist.

She prodded a fingertip against the corner of her mouth in whimsical speculation. "What else, now? Let me see. You're employed by a brokerage house called Ritter, Pease and Elliott. Customer-accounts man. Your departmental chief is a Mr. Bruce. *They* wouldn't like it either, I suppose, if— Shall I go on?"

She didn't have to. He'd uncapped a fountain pen, seemed to be drawing the ink that flowed through it from his own vein, the one that stood out like a blue rope down the center of his forehead.

"To—?"

She smiled at the ingenuousness of that. "Bearer."

He gave the completed check a looped toss onto the table, without handing it directly to her. It seemed almost to fly up from there of its own accord and be sucked into her hand, so quickly did she grasp at it.

"Now get out of here!" he said wrathfully, from under

an obscuring handkerchief that he was pressing tight to his brow.

But even that paltry dismissal was robbed of whatever salve it might have had for his smarting self-respect. She already had.

6

The street door of his house swung open and he flung in through it. Coming-home time. Outside, the street was gold-plated with the late sunset, and some of the precious substance seemed to have been poured into him, he was so alight and glowing. He was filled with anticipations of the party they were going to tonight. A special dinner party in their honor, his and hers. The engaged couple, everybody's darlings these days.

He was in such exuberant haste he'd already doffed his topcoat in the short distance from taxi door to house entrance, and he was carrying it slung backward over one shoulder, the way a bather does a used towel. He had no time, no time for anything but joy. You were only young once. You were only in love once. You were only fêted like this the once that you were both young and in love. He had to get all togged out—dolled up, that was the jaunty new expression for it they were beginning to use these days—and then he had to dash right on again from here, go over to her house and pick her up. The steps flew by, meanwhile, four and five at a time under his avid, scissoring legs, and he had to grab the banister rail tightly at each turn of the stairs and hold on as he swung around it, to keep himself from flying off his trajectory and into the wall.

And then suddenly, sweeping around like that, he

floundered to an awkward, eddying stop, too short, that left him swaying and tipping almost face-downward with his own checked velocity.

She was sitting there on the topmost step. Just above him. Like an elfin small girl docilely waiting to be let in by one of her elders, since she is not of an age to be trusted with the key herself. Knees to chin, the way a child waits on a stair, skirts demurely tucked close about her ankles, arms in turn clasped about them to hold them in place.

"Hello," she said brightly. "You're home early tonight. I just got here myself."

7

A sudden shower had come up, one of those violent almost tropical affairs that sometimes belt New York in the warm season of the year. The precipitation was rigidly vertical, and so thick it had the look of a sheet of warped glass standing static before one's face. The lightning was so continuous it gave the darkness the effect of wearing spangles that kept coruscating.

The subway kiosk—they still had the enclosed domed kind later removed as traffic hazards—was like a little glass casket imprisoning a pack of tightly wedged upright corpses. Some kind of fluid running down all around outside it to preserve them. Their outlines peered swollen (as though decomposition had already set in) through the wire-meshed glass, lighted from within.

He stood there in the front rank, at the very lip of the orifice, toecaps of his shoes and forward brim of his hat just impinging on the watery curtain, but unable to edge back because of the bodies jammed behind him. He was umbrellaless and cursing himself for not having been on the train just ahead of the one that had brought him. It had still been dry when he'd boarded it at the Wall Street station.

A furled umbrella suddenly slanted outward over his shoulder from somewhere just behind, flared open with a comfortable cottony pop. Somebody wanted to get through. He tried to crush himself sideward to allow the person to pass.

Instead, a hand undulated edgewise under his arm. He thought for a moment it was an honestly accidental entanglement, that the hand, seeking an outlet, had become caught between his arm and body. He tried to lift his arm. Instead, it fastened on it, hooked curled about it, the hand.

He swung half about, in a sort of shocked impersonal outrage, as when some anonymous member of a crowd has trodden on you or jostled you unwarrantedly.

Her face was there, close, smiling into his. The next face to his, the nearest of all.

"Coming?" she suggested familiarly.

He turned outward to the rain again, as though he hadn't seen or heard her. A moment later, no doubt because the continuing presence of her hand upon his arm interfered with this negation, he reached down, plucked it off, and cast it back where it belonged.

"No need to be standoffish about it," she continued in a slightly risible tone. "I have an umbrella, and we're both going the same way."

"Are we?" he said through clenched teeth, continuing to face the rain.

"You know we are," she answered indulgently. "Come on, be a good boy."

Faces, he knew, without having to turn his own, were all turned now to look at the two of them. Faces, he knew, were smiling, were amused. She wanted that, she enjoyed it. It strengthened her position; it did the reverse for his.

"Come on, don't be stubborn," she coaxed. "I'm offering you my umbrella."

Faces were grinning outright now; he could tell by the inchoate little sounds there were, still short of overt laughter, but that was on its way, and she was fanning it.

He extricated himself the way most men would have, being the unheroic creatures that they are, took a pull at his hatbrim to tighten his hat on his head, and suddenly plunged unprotected into the downpour, and away from her baiting.

He ran in sweeping strides, kicking up little silvery cuffs about his ankles. The rain drummed hollowly on the glass-studded pavement topping the subway in this immediate vicinity, for there was no fill below it, just the open track-well itself, but not loudly enough to drown the laughter of the crowd.

In a moment he became aware she was coming after him. "Hey, wait!" her voice came through the torrent, funneled to a foglike density.

He ran on full tilt, and around the corner, and into the side street that would lead him eventually to his own door, but only after a length of three maelstromlike blocks. The rain pellets seemed to be beating holes through his clothing, each one to let its successor a little further in in turn.

He had to stop, paste his oozing shoulders up against a doorway finally. It was impossible to cover the entire distance in this; it was like running through upended surf, it was only a little less dense than actual surf would have been. No one was abroad, no one (and he was the one felt he would have liked to have help, not she).

He stood there, chest flickering wetly under a shirt

soaked to the sheen of oil silk. His face was sweating rain-drops, as though he were crying all over, from his crown down.

A moment later she had run into the shallow shelter after him, ranged herself there alongside him, shoulder to shoulder, facing outward as he was. She had not suffered so; it was a windless perpendicular rain, and the umbrella had let her retain a core of dryness.

"Get out of here," he said, but too out of breath to put more than a whispered venom into it.

She ignored the imprecation, as if it were simply an understandable peevishness due to his uncomfortable bodily condition, and not his own real feelings toward her, that was speaking. "It's so foolish for the two of us to stand here like this," she argued comfortably. "What's the good of my having the umbrella with me at all?"

"You're even lucky in that, aren't you!" he spat out bitterly. "How'd you happen to have that with you, when a lot of *decent* people were caught on the streets without one?"

"It's been threatening since before five," she answered as evenly as if it were a courteous question. "I brought it with me when I came out. You see, I didn't know how long I might have to wait for you."

"And you've been standing waiting for me at the top of those subway steps since five?"

"They're the ones you use coming home every night," she said with matter-of-fact simplicity. "What other ones *would* you use? The next station's eight blocks too far up for you."

He choked down his discomfiture by breaking from the doorway, running on again, in a long, gradual loop that brought him in at last to another doorway further down.

Within minutes she had done the same thing, was

beside him again, breathing quickly in time to his own quick breathing.

He gave her a violent push out into the downpour. She staggered, but kept her footing. The umbrella, however, she lost for a moment, and it rolled circularly around on its own handle as an axis. She quickly retrieved it, backed up into the trough of dryness from which he had ejected her.

"I'm going to slap your head off, if you keep this up!" he threatened, his face pulled taut with rancor.

She smiled at her own thoughts. "You never slapped a woman in your life," she told him, almost contemptuously. "You're not the kind." Almost as if to say, You would have long ago, if you were going to.

"Get away from me," he said surlily, but already backing down from his own threat.

"You don't own the doorway. I can stand in it as well as you." He couldn't seem to shatter her equanimity. She had the complete calmness of superiority. Or the superiority of complete calmness.

"Then I'll get myself another." He loped out again, ran the greater part of the remaining distance, crossed the final intersection, and took refuge one final time, now on the self-same street that held his own door, but still at an appreciable distance up from it, and unable to negotiate that without one last sodden halt.

She didn't join him there. A sworl, a vaporized blur, hastening along on the opposite side of the street, showed she had not desisted and turned back, but she went on past him this time, and was blotted out in the borealislike conflagration of the rain. He knew that his own door was on that side. He knew that she did too.

A flash of the lightning, slackening now in its frequency, showed her to him ensconced in it, waiting for him. Like a black, mushroom-topped fungus, growing up from a crevice in it.

After awhile the rain petered out, came to an end. Pavements of spilled licorice, that caught every reflection and gave it back upside down, were left in its wake.

The two figures stood in the two doorways, on opposite sides of the street, watching each other. Almost detachedly gazing toward each other.

After awhile she collapsed her umbrella and took it down. There was no further need for it.

After another while, he lit a cigarette. The match flame was like a vivid poppy in front of his face for a minute, with his hands forming the petals.

Presently his waterlogged clothes had begun to feel clammy on him. He turned up the collar of his coat, around the back of his neck, held it tightly closed in front.

On he stood like that, for just a moment or two longer, beginning to quiver a little now with the dampness. All at once he flung his cigarette down, with a long over-hand shoulder-roll that had in it both exasperation and final, wearied capitulation. Even the paper of the cigarette had been a little soggy, made it difficult to draw on it satisfactorily.

Abruptly he struck out from the doorway, started walking the long diagonal toward his own doorway—and the figure waiting in it so complacently, so sure that in the end he would have to do just this.

8

It was late, it was past twelve at night. The street was empty, charcoal brushed with gloom, only the pin-point lights of an upper window or two, like open pores, to mar the evenness of its texture.

The empty taxi drove up to the curb, stopped.

Suddenly Marshall, as though until now he had been part of the doorway sediment piled up by the darkness, detached himself from the entryway without the door having opened behind him, and ran over to the cab, hatless.

"Are you the party called for a cab to be sent around to this number?" the driver asked him.

"Wait here a minute," Marshall said in a curiously bated voice, as though he were afraid of their being overheard. "I have two bags standing inside the door."

He returned to the shadowy entrance, this time a doorlatch clicked open, then a moment later crunched closed, and he reappeared with a heavy bag weighing down each arm. He launched them into the back of the cab and got in after them.

"Where'll I take you?" the driver asked him unhurriedly, without doing more than tip down his pennant.

"Don't stand here," Marshall hurried him. "I'll give you the address in a minute. But start moving."

He struck a match, cupped one hand around it, and with the other took out a newspaper folded to a one-column span. He ran the match down the edge of this, almost as though he were attempting to set fire to it. A perpendicular array of little fine-printed boxes lit up one after another, and then dimmed out again, as the thin yellow gleam went by. It stopped suddenly opposite one whose frame had been thickened at all four corners by diagonal pencil strokes. "Attractively furnished room, gentleman preferred—" That stayed in sight for a moment longer than its mates, then the match went out, and it was gone back into limbo.

"One-eight-four East Fifty-first," he told the driver. A moment later he'd thrown the newspaper out the window of the cab.

They coursed on uninterruptedly for several minutes, with nothing to stop for even at lightless four-ply crossings. Then, "Oh—my hat!" Marshall exclaimed suddenly, clapping a hand to the top of his head.

"Want me to take you back for it?" the driver offered. "We're only a couple blocks away yet."

"No!" Marshall said sharply. "Never mind, let it go. I'll do without it."

"Well, I don't suppose you need one this time of year," the driver observed philosophically.

"Not that badly, anyway," Marshall agreed grimly.

The new house was simply an east-side duplication of the one they had come from on the west side, just as one street was merely a numerical variant of the other. He paid the driver, carried his bags over to the door, found his new key and let himself in. Unchallenged, he carried them up the stairs to the door to his new room, found the key to that, and let himself in there.

He'd asked her, earlier in the day when he'd first called to inspect the room, if it would be all right for him to move in quite late that same night, instead of waiting for the daylight hours of the following day. "You see, I, er, have to work quite late, and it may be twelve or after before I can get my things together and bring them over here."

His signed receipt was waiting for him on the table now, left there during the interim. "Rec'd of Mr. William Prince…$15…for two weeks' rental," and then the new landlady's signature.

An admonishment she had given him during the course of their interview returned to him now.

"There's only one thing I must ask. No girls, now."

No, he agreed bitterly, you bet no girls!

He sprawled in a chair, lit a cigarette, and, as though savoring immunity for the first time in weeks, let his head

loll back almost to a breakneck position and aimed the
smoke from his nostrils ceilingward.

In a moment he had thought of something and was on
his feet again. He took out a plain white card, such as
they used down at the office, and with the same fountain
pen that had written those various checks, printed out
on it "Mr. William Prince." Then he reopened his room
door, went down the stairs, and in the entryway inserted
the card into the slot that corresponded to his room.

He came upstairs again, closed the door once more,
and turned and shook his fist at it with vindictive satisfaction.

"Now try it," he said savagely, "you little tart!"

9

On his wedding morning he woke up late, after the bach-
elor party of the night before.

He opened his eyes, and they met her face, in a frame,
on the dressertop, slanted so that it would look toward
his bed. Just as in her house, probably, his own face was
there to meet her eyes when they first opened of a
morning. Paper replicas, the need for which would come
to an end at five o'clock this evening.

At the bottom, where the shoulders paled into an
impersonalized background, she had inscribed: "Forever,
your Marjorie."

"And forever, your Prescott," he breathed in soft-voiced
answer.

He got up, and the moment of contemplation ended.
He set about his preparations for the day.

He went out for some coffee, and he called Lansing
up from the place where he was drinking it, since there

was no phone in the house where he was now rooming. Lansing was standing up for him as best man.

"How are you after last night?" Lansing asked him.

"Oh, boy," Marshall groaned.

"Same here."

"I've been packing for the trip. I'm about finished now."

"I'll be over and pick you up at about four-thirty," Lansing said.

"Hadn't you better make it a little earlier?" Marshall asked worriedly.

Lansing laughed. "I'll get you there on time," he promised. "The less time you have to spend hanging around waiting, the less you'll suffer. I know those things. Just leave everything to me."

"All right," Marshall said gratefully. "See you later."

"See you later."

He went back to his room again. There he laid out his wedding clothes and got into them, dressing slowly and carefully. He caught himself whistling. The song of that season, the new song that everyone was taken with just then. "Peg o' My Heart."

He stopped a moment to shrug. *I thought grooms were supposed to be nervous, or something. Funny; I don't feel that way.*

He went to work with his hairbrushes, stroking them on opposite sides of his head with as much meticulous care as though he were modeling something in moist clay between a pair of trowels.

He looked at his watch. A little past four. Lansing should have been here by now. He said he'd come earlier.

He had her picture still out, saving it to put away until the last. It stood on the table, ready to go into the valise. He stood still, to look at her.

When we were born, I didn't know you. And you didn't

know me. Last year on this very same day, in June of Nineteen Fourteen, I still didn't know you. You still didn't know me. Now we come together, in the closest way two living people can. Then when we die, and we both must die someday, the one of us who is left a little while longer will go back to that before, to that without-the-other stage. And then again it will be: I don't know you. And you don't know me. What a strange thing marriage is.

He was all ready now, just for the dress-tie and the coat. He looked at his watch again, good-naturedly. What's the matter with that Lansing? Am I going to have to send out a St. Bernard with a keg of brandy?

Then finally the summons came that he'd been expecting for so long. The buzzer sounded, as Lansing fingered the downstairs doorbell to his room. He released the latch to the downstairs door, to let him into the house, then stepped over to the room door and left it ajar for him, so that he wouldn't have to go back to it a second time. Then he went back to his own immediate task: the tie. He dipped his knees slightly, in his absorption, as he stood there before the glass struggling with it. One wing kept stubbornly projecting a fraction of an inch beyond the complement above it.

He could hear Lansing's tread coming up the outside stairs, now. He called out a raucously jovial greeting to him sight unseen from where he stood, without turning his head.

"You lazy hound! So you finally got here, did you? Well, it's about time!"

There was a smothered chuckle, and Leona Harris was lounging against one side of the open doorway, her cheek pressed languidly against the frame.

He saw her in the mirror, before he'd had time to turn. Then, having seen her there, her reflection seemed to hold him fast, like some hypnotic apparition, so that he was no longer able to turn. He kept looking at her that way, by indirection.

His hands dropped away from his tie, as though they'd withered and died up there, and dangled lifeless at his sides, no longer volatile; dead things still fastened to him by their own tendons.

She peeled her cheek from the doorframe and came in a little further. A dainty, mincing step or two, like a dancer pointing a delicate toe before her, feeling her way in some difficult *pas* she is not yet sure she has mastered.

He hadn't moved. He couldn't.

"So you're getting married today," she said affably. "So today's the great day. I thought I'd drop by and offer my congratulations."

A cord at the side of his neck whipped up, and, as though it were a rusted hinge, he emitted a grating sound. "Get out of here."

He was still looking into the mirror, frozen. The very position of his feet hadn't shifted. A man staring into a looking glass.

"I haven't got any present for you, but the least I can do is offer you my—"

The hinge jarred again. "How did you know?"

"It was in the papers. After all, she's a society girl. It was in all the morning editions."

"No. I mean how did you know...? My name isn't downstairs."

She nodded matter-of-factly. "I know. William Prince, isn't it? That was on my account, I suppose." She swung the loose end of a handkerchief about in one hand. "You moved in here on a Wednesday, I think, and I've known ever since the following Friday. After all, you *do* have to start home from the same place each night: Two Wall Street."

He made a peculiar hissing sound under his breath, as

when something hurts excruciatingly for an instant or two. His eyes shuttered themselves in accompaniment, then opened again.

She had moved closer to the table by now. Drifted, seemingly, without use of her feet at all. Now he wrenched himself from the glass at last, turned face-forward to her, sprang over there protectively. The table was between them.

She looked down at the train tickets. "Atlantic City," she murmured idly.

Her hand moved on a little. It didn't touch anything, just rode the surface of the table.

"Tiffany's," she mused. "It's beautiful. I saw you the day you were in there buying it."

"Get away from it!" he ordered harshly.

She withdrew her hand trailingly. Her fingertips left little steam-tracks on the polished surface which quickly cleared.

He was leaning toward her across the table, gripping it at its outer sides. His head was down, but the pupils of his eyes were sighted upward toward her, so that they were directed at her face instead of downward at the table, as they normally would have been given the tilt of his head.

"Look, I don't want to use force."

"I wouldn't," she said without inflection.

His fist crashed down on the table. "You're not human at all!" he screamed sobbingly at her. "You're a demon. I don't know what you are. You look like a girl. You've got a face like a baby, but— Haven't you ever slept with other men? Why don't you hound one of them?"

She backed her hand to her mouth. "Press," she said with shocked propriety. She went over to the door, softly closed it. "What things you say. They'll hear you out there."

He crashed his fist down on the table again. This time

he didn't say anything with it. His head went lower in accompaniment to the blow.

She ran two fingers back and forth across the frame of her handbag.

He was looking down, as if staring at his own reflection in the surface of the table. A tendril of his carefully brushed-back hair reversed itself and fell forward, down over his forehead, partially obscuring one eye.

"This is the last time, Press," she said soothingly.

His mouth twisted at one extremity. "Each time it's the last time. Then each time there's another time that comes after it."

They stayed motionless and silent for a moment after that, as if an unspoken contest of wills were taking place. They were not even looking at one another. His eyes were cast downward at the tabletop, sullenly immobile. Hers strayed, with an air of insouciant waiting; but never toward him.

"Press, why don't you let me go?" she urged at last. "It'll be over in a minute. It would have been over already by this time if you'd only…"

A drop of moisture peered through the hairs of his eyebrow, dammed there in its slow descent.

"Press, this is your wedding day," she reminded him, in the tone of someone seeking to restore a spoilsport to good humor.

"And if I don't, you'll go there to the very church itself, won't you?"

"I *would* like to see a real society wedding," she said almost contritely.

He was shaking all over.

"How much this time?" he said simply. He tried to turn from the table, and had to hold it for a moment to support himself. Then he turned from it and went over to the dresser.

"The same as last. Two-fifty."

He opened a drawer, looked in it, then closed it again, as if not seeing what he sought.

She pointed briefly. "It's up there, on top," she said.

He picked up the checkbook from the top of the dresser, and brought it over to the table. Then he turned and looked helplessly across his shoulder in search of something else. A slight impact on the tabletop brought his eyes back, and his fountain pen lay there uncapped, barrel toward him in readiness.

"It was clipped to your vest pocket, on the back of that chair over there," she said. "I saw it from here." She examined her fingers to make sure no trace of ink was on them.

His hand was shaking too much. The pen point regurgitated a great glossy blot, left it behind as it swept on.

He tore the check out of the folder, began again on the one below.

"Don't be so nervous, Press." There was a note of laughter in the observation, but it wasn't unkind laughter; it was rather the good-natured, indulgent kind apt to be exchanged between two close friends at times.

He didn't look up at her. He heard a match snap, and a thin panoply of smoke drifted horizontally past his nose.

He signed his name, and he had finished it.

He relaxed his thumb, and the pen slid from his hand and fell to the floor at his feet.

"It's a good thing it's *not* your rug," she said.

She took the check and made sure it was dry by blowing her breath along it, passing it back and forth below her lips as she did so, as if it were a harmonica. Then she folded it carefully, opening the handbag, put it inside.

He was still standing where he'd written it, quavering hands to the edge of the table, as if incapable of releasing it.

"Now go to your wedding," she said, with an inflection almost of fondness. She surveyed him with a sort of kindly interest. "You make a good-looking groom. Wait, your tie ends aren't straight. I wonder why it is men can never— Do you want me to fix it for you before I go? That'll be my wedding present to you, Press, a nice even tie."

She set her cigarette down against the rim of the table, and came around it to his side.

Her hands reached toward his tie, and she was right before him for a maddening moment.

She shouldn't have come so close to him.

He didn't see what happened next. Missed seeing it as completely as if he were outside the room, on the other side of the closed door. There was a singeing flash of six weeks of accumulated hate, fear, and torment, as blinding to his senses as a literal combustive explosion would have been. She disappeared completely behind it. He didn't feel anything, or know what any part of his body was doing. He heard a stifled scream come through from the other side of the sheet of fire, as though it were a visible thing that had shocked and seared her too, as well as himself.

Then it dimmed, and she peered through at him again. He could see her once more.

They were locked together in a serpentine double arm-clasp. Her throat was between his hands. They were turned inward, thumb-joint toward thumb-joint, pressing in upon the soft front part of it. Feeling it give, and circle, and try to swim away in ripples of flesh. While the firmer structure beneath held fast in columnar hollowness, a column that he was trying to cave in and crush closed.

He kept his face back beyond her reach. He had a longer arm-span than she, and her hands flickered helplessly upon his arms, like wriggling snakes trying to clamber up a pair of fallen tree trunks.

They were moving, but he couldn't feel it. Taking little steps, this way, that way, now forward, now back, like a pair of drunken dancers. And as in a conventional dance his steps—the man's—led, her steps—the woman's— followed. Whichever way he stepped, she stepped a moment later.

One time they were very near the door. Her mouth opened abortively, and closed, frustrated; opened again, then closed once more; and he could feel a little straining lump or sac come up in her throat, under his thumbs, and he squeezed it flat again.

Then the door moved past along the wall, and she was gone to the far end of the room. And still the silent music played, and still they rocked to it.

The bedstead came nosing toward them diagonally, one corner of it forward like the prow of a ship. Then like a ship that suddenly changes course, it too veered aside. But not quickly enough. The back of her heel must have struck the bottommost part of its leg, where its caster nosed the floor. The jar coursed through both of them, passing from her arms to his, and from them into his body, just as though it were he himself had struck the obstacle. There was a hollow, tubular ring from the bedpost, as when a faulty anvil is struck. Then suddenly she began to lean acutely away from him, and pull him violently downward after her with her whole weight, and it was only after the act had been half completed that he realized it was a bodily fall, involuntary.

He couldn't brace against it. The two of them went down together, still locked together at her neck. They fell crosswise, in the little clear space between the foot of the bed and the bulky steam radiator against the wall. She fell upon her back and he fell face forward. She fell uncushioned to the floor, and he fell partly upon her body, due to the overlap from their formerly vertical position. His face fell upon her breast, as if in amorous indolence.

And as the fall completed itself, again there was a hollow, knell-like ring, this time from the steam radiator. It ebbed and dwindled into silence, and they didn't move.

She was completely supine, except for her head, and that was tilted a bare inch or two by the radiator behind it. It was as though she were trying to look down her own length at the top of his head, nestled on her breast.

Their eyes met, in a strange stillness. His hands had burst open with the fall, but they still formed an unclosed half-circle toward her neck, and lying within its compass, like an overripe fruit, lay her silent inert head. Like a giant seedling of death, that had just burst free from its pod.

A little blood twinkled at the seam of her lips, like a new kind of rouge applied from the inside out. But over-applied, for it ran over at last, at one corner, and started tremulously down her chin, then stopped again and ran no more.

He flung his arms wide in sudden, explosive gesture of riddance, and her own fell off them like disengaged tendrils, lay sodden on the floor.

He shook her at the shoulders, then, and her arms moved; but when he stopped, they stopped, were still again.

He made spasmic squirming motions backward away from her, and reared on the points of his knees, on the floor beside her.

"You can have the money," he whispered. "Go ahead, take it, and get out of here."

He shook her urgently, this time by one shoulder alone, and she seemed to say "No," for her head went slightly from side to side.

"Come on, get up. Take the money, and get out."

He pulled at her, tried to draw her up toward him.

"Cut it out, do you hear me? Get up, will you?"

Her head came erect, and then overbalanced itself, came forward against the white front of his shirt, as if in a smothered kiss. He quickly pried it away and held it at a distance. It went over to the side, and lay thus, as if cocked at him in macabre quizzical interrogation.

He could do with her what he willed, move her any way and she obeyed; and now that he could, he didn't want to any more, he wanted her as she had been. And that was the one thing that he couldn't do with her, make her as she had been.

Dead. They called this being dead. This was what it was when they said someone was dead. He'd never seen anyone like this before. He'd seen them dead in coffins, stylized, prepared, but not like this, just *minutes* after. And—done by himself.

Four whimpered words escaped from him into bated sound.

"Christ, I've killed her."

It was very quiet, and he didn't move. It was as though he was given that one precious, gratuitous minute to rest upon, to gather himself together upon as best he could, for there would be no more, for the rest of his life, for the rest of all time.

And then the knock came at the door. The knock he'd once been expecting, and now had forgotten to expect any more. Of his best man, come to take him to his wedding, come to take him to his bride.

10

The next few moments were living horror.

The knock had caught him on his knees, in a peculiar double penitential position, holding her partly uprighted form at arm's length away from him. There was a blur. Then he was across the room, standing just inside the door. The bolt had just been drawn closed.

Another flurried blur. Like smoke swirling within a tumbler, unable to escape, repeating itself and repeating itself and repeating itself. He found himself by the door of his clothes closet now. The closet door stood wide. The row of clothes, on hangers, were all eddying a trifle in unison, as though something had been forced through their midst, parting them violently. On the floor, blatant, her legs stuck out, still projecting a little across the sill.

He dropped down, seized them both together by the one hand, and switched them over into a straight line that followed the back wall of the closet. She could not be seen from standing position now, but she could still be seen when the beholder was down low, as he was. He reared, and reached for a hanger, and swept its garment off it. It dropped deftly upon her, and covered up that section of her where her knees were. He swept another one off; that covered up her feet. Another; her waist. Two, three more, and her shoulders and her head went. There was just a pile of massed clothing now, strewn along the closet floor at the back, rising highest in the corner, for she had been propped sitting upright there, limp and dead.

He got the closet door closed.

He closed it not only with his hands and arms. He closed it agonizedly, expiringly, by pressing the side of his face against it as well. Letting his cheek lie flat upon it, exhaustedly, as though that would add to the security of its closure.

His heart was pounding on wood. No wonder it hurt, it was striking the door so hard, through his skin and shirt and all. Then he forced space between his breast and the panel, by stiffening his arms against it and thrusting himself back.

Talk to him, say something. Look around, make sure nothing of hers, left out.

Voice wouldn't come. He had to cough first and break the rigor in his throat. Then it flowed through, hoarse and scratchy.

"All right, Lance. All right."

Handbag exploded into his awareness, as though a small flashlight picture had just been taken of it, where it lay.

He went to it and got it, got it into a drawer, got the drawer closed.

A muffled voice came through; cheerful but remonstrative. Its effect for a moment was acute nervous shock, as though someone had spoken unexpectedly right into his ear.

"Come on, come on. That won't save you. I've got you cornered. Open up. You can't get out of it that easy."

My God! he thought, and the edge of his hand flew up and struck him just above the eyes. Then: No, he doesn't know, he can't. That was just badinage.

One more thing: the check. She had put it into the handbag, he had seen her do it, but that only came back to him now.

Then he was at the door. Then the bolt had been drawn. Then the door was back. His aloneness had ended. He

was looking into another man's eyes. Accordingly, enemy
eyes. The eyes of his best friend. Still—enemy eyes.

"Well, it's about time," Lansing expostulated, with
a broad yet perplexed grin. "What were you doing in
here, anyway?" He strode in, as one who has the right to
uninvited. "Who is she?" he demanded ribaldly. "Where
y' got her?"

Marshall could feel his heart give a single pained
afterbeat, like a postscript to the hurtful way it had been
throbbing just now.

He tried to produce a disclaiming smile, but it wasn't
on secure foundations, it soon lost its hold and slipped
off.

Imagine having killed someone, and then looking into
your friend's face like this, three or four minutes later, he
thought wryly. If he knew.

"You've got the funniest expression," Lansing chuckled.
"I wish you could see yourself."

"What'd you do, come over here to make it easier for
me?" His smiles wouldn't stay on long enough, there was
too much quivering underneath.

"I've seen them nervous, but man you've got them all
beat. I never saw them as nervous as you yet. You take
the cake."

"Here," Marshall said casually, to get him off the subject. "This is for you." He handed him the gift on the table.

"Well, that's a peach, that's dandy," Lansing said
enthusiastically. And then he threw in the current slang
catchword for good measure. "That's a bear."

He began to open and close it repeated times, as
people invariably do with such a sectional or hinged gift.
It made little sharp clicks.

"It works, it works—" Marshall pleaded, harassed, and
his hand went up toward his ear for an instant, although
he never quite completed the silencing gesture.

Lansing stopped short, peered at him. "You need a drink. And I mean a drink. Where's your liquor, Marsh?" Then he answered it for himself, out of old recollection. "Oh yes, in the closet."

And he stepped over to it, and put his hand out, and grasped the knob. He was so *springy,* Marshall protested to himself, expiringly. He said, "No—" And then, "Wait a—" And then, "I'll—" Without completing a phrase. And then finally got one out intact. "Here, let me. You get the glasses; there's a couple of them in the bathroom." And took a weaving step toward the door, to replace Lansing.

"Man, you act like you *had* a drink already," Lansing remarked appraisingly.

But he took his hand off the knob and went into the bathroom.

"Rinse them out a minute," Marshall called after him, to hold him in there a little longer.

"Particular," he heard Lansing comment drily.

He got the door open—the way it opened it was a barrier between him and Lansing—and dropped down to his heels. He wormed his arm into the sediment of clothes. He had to reach *behind* her to get the bottle out. It had been in the corner, originally, and she was now propped up against it.

He had to spade his hand behind her, feeling her all the way, until he found the neck of the bottle; and then he had to wrench it bodily free, and yet hold her back with his other hand, so she wouldn't come out along with it.

Bottle in hand, he got up on his feet again by clawing at the edge of the door. He let his forehead roll itself along the surface of the door, as though he had an intolerable headache and were seeking to ease it by such pressure.

Then he got the door closed, just as Lansing went striding by with the two glasses in his hand, saying jauntily, "Here we go!"

He followed Lansing over to the table, bringing the bottle.

Drinking this, he thought nauseatedly, Drinking this, after her body had been coddling it.

Lansing uncorked the bottle, and poured.

Lansing handed him his glass.

"Drink up, boy," he invited. "Last drink as a free man." Then he backed his head, drank. Then he righted it again, winked, saw fit to remark: "The condemned man drank hearty."

Marshall didn't think that was funny. "Condemned"; what a grisly expression to use. He contorted his face and emptied the liquor into his mouth.

Suddenly Lansing was holding a lighted cigarette in his hand; he hadn't had one a moment ago, as far as Marshall could recall. He was offering it to Marshall, mouth-part foremost.

"This yours?"

"No, throw it away!" he said with sudden stridency. It had been there on the edge of the table the whole time. From—from before.

"Well, you don't need to look so bilious about it." Lansing was looking at him askance. Humorously askance, but still askance, and he saw that he'd made a slip there. "What do you mean, no? It's here in the room with you. It's got to be yours, who else's could it be?"

"I meant—I meant, throw it away. I don't want it after it's been standing there on the edge of the table like that."

"Aw, don't be so fancy!" Lansing said with gruff raillery.

Before Marshall could guess the direction of his hand, it had speared forward, thrust the cigarette between his lips, left it there clinging to them of its own adhesion.

Fumes of death seemed to go up into his brain.

He retched violently, all but vomited. His hand flew to his stomach, to curb the inclination. The cigarette sprang to the floor, and he trapped it with his foot almost as though it were something alive, crushed it unmercifully.

"Well, for the love of…" the astounded Lansing cried, watching him incredulously.

"Caught my windpipe," Marshall said, backing his hand to his forehead.

Suddenly he pulled himself together with an excess of nervous energy, bunched his shoulders defensively, began to edge Lansing before him toward the door.

"Come on, let's go! Let's get out of here, will you? We'll be late. Let's get started, let's get over there."

"We're not late, we'll make it," Lansing tried to calm him. He gave him a whimsical look. "First you're in no kind of a hurry at all, you keep me standing outside the door ten whole minutes before you even let me in. Then all of a sudden you're in such a hurry you can't get out of the place fast enough!" He chuckled. "They talk about the bride being nervous. I think they've got the wrong party." He tried to dig his heels in, hold his ground against Marshall's jerky propulsion, even at the threshold.

"Well, what about the ring? Don't you think it'd be a good idea to take it with us, or are you going to leave it there on the table?"

Marshall turned back, scooped it up, came forward, jammed it into Lansing's pocket. "Come on. Let's go. Come on."

They were both on the outside of the door by now. He'd maneuvered Lansing to the outside of the door at last. He clawed at it to bring it closed after them. Lansing, perhaps because he was in the nearer position, finally was the one to close it, with a good plump impact.

"Close it good," Marshall pleaded harriedly. "Good and tight."

Lansing smiled, gave the knob an extra twist to test it. "What, are you afraid somebody'll get in?"

No, echoed Marshall in horror-stifled silence as he started down the stairs, I'm afraid somebody'll get out.

I I

He followed Lansing out of the vestry room. Moving close behind him, almost treading on his heels, the way some helpless, frightened, lost soul clings to the only familiar person, the only point of support, in a terrifying situation.

He even wanted to reach out and keep his hand firmly on Lansing's shoulder as they moved along, but he refrained with an effort.

They were in the chapel now. All those people seated out there. All staring his way. Row upon row of faces.

Lansing took up his stance. Marshall stopped behind him, wanted to stand there protectedly behind him, sheltered. Lansing had to motion unobtrusively to him, where to stand. They'd rehearsed all this yesterday, positions and all. But yesterday he wasn't a murderer.

He shifted over and stood there alongside Lansing.

Music swelled out. Hollowly, sepulchrally, he thought, echoing dismally within the cavernous interior of the church. It had never occurred to him before how similar the wedding march and the funeral march were. There was as much reason, today, for the one as for the other to be played. He winced at the horrid thought that this was a double ceremony, not just a single one.

Beautiful girls were coming down the aisle toward

him, by twos, with slow, stately grace. Dwelling on each
step, balancing on it a moment before taking the next.
Almost as in those musical shows that were becoming
popular, the Ziegfeld Follies and the Winter Garden
Passing Shows.

The first pair in lilac, the second in pink, the last in
azure. They fanned out and became motionless, in a
graceful half-circle.

She was coming down the aisle now, on her father's
arm. A snatch of ghostly tune seemed to lace through the
stately, sonorous music of actuality for an instant, that
strain that Lansing had been whistling in the cab coming
over, and he himself had been humming before that.
"Come be my own, come make your home in my heart."
Then it whisked itself away again, like the interloper
it was.

Satin white as new-fallen snow, a little girl behind her
to bear her long train. Veiling gossamer as mist. Orange
blossoms for purity, and a tiara of pearls no more lustrous
than all the rest of her.

His heart was wrung. We don't marry women, he
thought; we marry angels, and in this moment or two of
the marriage act, the scales fall from our eyes and we see
them as they really are, perhaps never to glimpse it again.

How lovely she is, how unearthly lovely.

And I'm so unclean. I have blood on me.

A shudder coursed through him.

She's coming toward a killer, step by step. She's about
to join herself in wedlock to a murderer. Oh, somebody
warn her while there's time, somebody stop her—

A knife-edged cry rang through the church.

"Marjorie! Don't! Turn around and go the other way,
quick!"

Who had screamed out like that? Who had cried that

terrible warning? His eyes darted this way and that. But step by unmoved step, she came on, steadily on.

No one had. His heart had, but not his lips. No one but he had heard it.

Lansing nudged him slightly. He moved forward mechanically, took her father's place at her side.

Those beautiful eyes, that even the veiling couldn't quench. Like topazes burning through snow.

She cast them down. The sonorous words began, the stately age-old words, bringing peace, bringing God's consent and blessing.

But they are not meant for me. I have no right to be here, let them be spoken over me. I killed a woman just now, but no one knows it but me. No one in the whole world knows it but me. But God knows it. I can fool my fellow men, but I can't fool God. I have no right to accept this sacrament before Him.

Too late. She sank to her knees beside him. Lansing tugged at his sleeve. He sank to his, beside her.

The sign of the cross was made over them. It seemed to leave a trace of fire in the air, and almost he quailed, almost he cringed away from it.

The crucifix was being offered to him. And as his lips touched it, a burning sensation seemed to course through them and run down into his heart.

"—in the name of the Father, and the Son, and of the Holy Ghost."

It's over, and she's married to a murderer.

"You may kiss the bride, my son."

The veil dissipated like morning haze lifting in the sunrise.

Her lips were so cool against his, he thought. So loyal. So trustful, more than anything else.

12

Now they were back at her house for the reception. Glittering electric lights in crystal chandeliers, women in evening dresses, a giddy hubbub of voices and laughter, the strains of the waltz and the hesitation played in an adjoining ballroom by a five-piece orchestra.

They were standing alone together for a moment, he and she. Alone in all that crowd. Champagne goblet in each one's hand.

She extended hers toward him. He extended his toward her. Their goblets met, with little silvery clink.

"Mrs. Prescott Marshall," she said softly, with grateful upraised eyes.

("Mrs. Murderer," he amended, unheard.)

Her eyes strayed to his bosom, suddenly stopped there.

"Ah, darling, you've hurt yourself. There's a tiny speck of blood on your shirt front."

His head went sharply downward, riveted.

"How was it? Where? Shaving?"

If she hadn't been a girl, she would have realized before speaking that couldn't have been; you shaved before, not after, your shirt was on. She would realize it in a moment anyway...

"Perhaps trimming my nails before," he said, with lack of full breath. "I was in a hurry." And defensively put one hand behind his back.

She kissed her own fingertip, then touched the place with it.

With sudden fierceness, he gulped down the rest of his champagne. His throat swelled with it as it forced its way down.

She slipped away a moment later, with a whispered, "I'm going up now. Nobody's looking, this is a good opportunity."

He stayed there by himself, where they'd been standing.

He stole a look down at it.

It was such a small speck, such a tiny one.

It was so *bright*, though. It shone so. You could see it all over the room.

His hand crept up to it, and stayed there, covering it.

But under his hand, he knew, it was still there.

13

Night scene, Atlantic City. Double life, on a honeymoon. Solitude, on a honeymoon. Secret thoughts.

In the bed, Marjorie sleeping, alone. Never so alone, not even before her marriage. For before their marriage, his thoughts at least were with her. Now she hasn't even those. Sleeping alone, in innocence, in trust, in confidence.

And at the floor-length windows, open to the June night, the watcher. Not seeing what is there to see, but watching something that is not there to see. Something that no one can see but the eyes of fear. His eyes.

Beautiful night, beautiful scene. Wasted, unseen. Rustle of silk, that is the surf. As if some superhuman dry-goods merchant were continually rolling, then unrolling, a gigantic bolt of the precious stuff, trying to sell it all along the shore.

Licorice-black sea, with a meshed trellis of silver running up it to the horizon line, aiming toward an unseen moon somewhere high above. As if put there for someone to climb. And below, like fogged pearls, the lights of the boardwalk, like the double strands of a necklace spread out along the shore.

And under that still, interrupting it at one point, at the one point where the windows are, the motionless inked-in outline of a head and shoulders. A head that sometimes breathes a little moonlit smoke. A head that watches the night slowly spend itself and be no more. A head that thinks and fears, and has no one, knows no one, to turn to.

Night scene, Atlantic City. Double life, within the very bridal suite. Secret thoughts. Hidden knowledge. The sleeper and the watcher.

14

Daybreak, Atlantic City. Secret life, on a honeymoon. Life apart.

In the background the towering Moorish hotel turrets, scarcely a light in all their multiple perforations. Somewhere behind one of these dark niches, a girl, sleeping alone. Guileless, in love with a chimera; in love with something that vanishes as her eyes drop shut, that only reappears again as they reopen. Alone, and not even knowing her own aloneness.

Nearer at hand, the elevated trestle of the Boardwalk, lights out now. Nothing moving along it as far as the eye can see, from down by the Inlet to up toward Ventnor, save a little empty paper bag, stirring and skipping and stopping again, in the dawn breeze.

Tiger-striped sky of daybreak; yellow, and gray, and

black stripes, rising up out of the somber lead-colored water.

And on the beach, a lone figure, sitting on its haunches, the only erect object for miles along the gray, deserted sand. Not seeing the sea, not seeing the sky, not seeing the day break. Head bowed between knees. As if mourning the irrevocable. Never stirring. Only a strand or two of his hair stirring now and again, lifted by the breeze. Live hair on a dead figure.

Beach scene, Atlantic City, dawn. Secret sorrows. Life apart.

15

He first met the other man on the hotel piazza, he coming in, the other man stationary by the rail.

He would have passed him by, but the other man spoke and claimed him. The other man was alone there, in all that long defile of regimented wicker chairs, and they were conspicuous to one another. It was six in the morning.

The other man was older than he, by a good deal, and he was benign, and no one to be wary of; he was just a little too prying, a little too observing, and—at the first only—a little boring. Then suddenly he wasn't boring any more, he had become the most compelling factor in Marshall's whole existence at the moment.

He was stoutish too, and he looked as such people usually do in their summer-vacation clothes. Which is to say, just a trifle too eager to appear jaunty.

"Good morning, there."

"Morning," Marshall said, without applying any adjective.

"Both of us early birds, I see."

Marshall kept trying to walk on in through the hotel entrance. "Yes, we are."

The man had extended his hand, as an invitation to shake with him, even from the distance at which they stood from one another. Then started to close it by moving over toward him. Marshall couldn't continue walking on in any more, after that. He had to wait for the hand to reach his own. It wasn't in him to be that ungracious. This would only take a moment, anyway.

"See you around. May as well get this over with. I've been trying to get around to it for several days now. Then we can go on from there. My name's Ponds. We're here from—" He mentioned some faraway town—"for a little rest, before the summer rush gets under way."

"Marshall. New York."

"That's the place, all right. Last summer we went over to Europe. Never again—not after the time we had getting back from there! They were sleeping on the open decks on the trip home, and lucky just to be on the ship, I can tell you. It was a madhouse. Germans were thirty miles from Paris, night we left there. Just had to pick Fourteen to go nosing around over there. From now on I stay where I belong."

He mopped his brow in recollection, even a year later.

"Not bad, this place down here, though. It's our first time down. We usually don't come this far east."

"Ours too."

"Honeymoon, right?"

Marshall nodded.

"We spotted that right away. So did everyone else, I guess. You know how it is. Everybody takes a proprietary interest, sort of. All the world loves a lover. Shouldn't let it embarrass you. Lovely little lady you've got there with you."

"I think so," said Marshall demurely.

"Saw you from my window just now, when I was getting dressed. All alone on the beach. You're not…?"

"Not what?"

"Nothing, none of my business."

"No, go ahead. Not what?"

The other man rallied him briefly by the arm. "Don't worry too much about—anything, son."

Marshall flashed him a taut look.

"Oh, *I* know. *I* know. I was a groom myself once. We all go through that. What you're going through right now. Every man jack of us. *They* don't know. They're not supposed to, anyway; wouldn't be right if they did. That's *our* part of the bargain. New responsibility, added expense. Wonders if he can make it. If his prospects are good already, wonders if they're good enough. If they're not so good, wonders how in the world he's going to better them."

Marshall let him think it was that. He nodded. The nod was one of relieved enlightenment, but he let it be taken for one of tacit confirmation: that the other man had correctly diagnosed what his trouble was.

"Look, son," Ponds said, putting a paternal hand to his arm for a minute. "I like you. I'm quick that way. Maybe too quick, Mother always says. I like you: maybe because you're newly married, and when I look at you I can see myself, just as I was twenty years ago. Or I dunno, maybe it's because I'm just a soft-hearted slob anyway; Mother's always telling me that too. But anyway, whatever it is, I'm going to make you a proposition here and now. Anytime you feel like coming out to—" he mentioned that faraway town again—"there's a job waiting for you in my office. Clerical work. Forty-five a week."

He was getting fifty in New York.

"Oh, I'm not risking anything," Ponds excused himself, as if hastening to avert a charge of undiluted sentimentality, though no such charge had been made, except by himself, perhaps unheard. "You must be all right. A girl like you've got yourself there *couldn't* have picked herself the wrong kind of a fellow. I've been watching her even more than I have you. You just take your time, think it over, and let me know before we leave here. Now go upstairs to her, where you belong. And just remember, from now on there's no more call for you to sit brooding on the beach by yourself at crack of dawn."

Forty-five a week, Marshall said to himself. In a faraway town. Far away from New York. Safe from New York.

He went in, noncommittal. But somehow, the other man had stopped being boring all at once.

16

"And not go back to New York?" she said.

There was something akin to fright in her voice. The first time he had ever heard it there. It must have been the first time, for it was he who had put it there.

"And not go back to New York," he answered.

They had the room dark. He'd wanted it to be that way when he told her. It made it easier for him that way. He hadn't wanted to see her face, see her eyes, when he told her. She was back there where the bed was, somewhere; standing by it, sitting on it. He was over here where the window was, looking the other way, looking out, keeping his back to her. Counting each wave below on the beach as it licked up onto the moon-gray sand. Counting, counting, to keep his mind from her, to keep his mind from giving in.

"But your job—"

"This is a better job. With this man I'll be somebody. You met him tonight at dinner, you saw how he likes both of us. There I'll just be a cipher, a blank."

"But the flat that's been picked out for us…the furniture that Father wanted to—"

"We'll have a flat wherever we are. Furniture wherever we are. Of our own, that nobody has to give us."

"But all my things…my wedding presents—"

"Wherever we are, they can be sent after us."

"But not even for a *day*? So sudden. He didn't say we *had* to do it that way. He said we could come on after."

"After may be too late. He may change his mind."

"But don't we *have* to go back anyway, to take the train from there?"

"We can go straight from here, through Philadelphia instead."

She's taking a long time. Will I win? Or will I lose?

Wave number seventy, fresh from the silversmith's, hammered and lustrous, delicately filigreed. Then, as he watched, already tarnishing into pewter dinginess, already crumbling and corroded and breaking into pieces all up and down the sand. That silversmith did poor work.

Wave number seventy-one, wave number seventy-two, wave number seventy-three.

"Is this the way you'd—rather do it?"

"This is the way I'd rather do it."

Wave number eighty.

Wave number eighty-one.

Wave number eighty-two.

She is coming toward me now. I can't hear it, but I can tell it; I know it without looking around.

I must have won, for she is coming toward me, I am not going toward her. Don't turn my head yet; one moment more, and I have won. There…

Her arms crept down his shoulders from behind, and linked, and held him in placative embrace.

"Then this is the way I'd rather do it too. Then—there isn't any other way than this. Whatever you want to do, that's the way I'd rather do it. Wherever you want to go, that's where I want to go too. Wherever you'd rather be, there is no other place in all this world for me to be. I am no other one, just you. I'm not even your wife, just you."

And her kisses of submission were scarcely cool upon his lips, than, somehow, still holding her to him, he already had the phone in place between them.

"Give me Mr. Ponds' room, please. He's in four-o-five. I know it's late, but he won't mind. I have to reach him tonight, he's leaving the first thing in the morning."

Two
Some Faraway Town

1

She took the head of the dishmop and squeezed it dry between her fingers. Then she stood it upside down, beside the water faucet. She sighed, and lowered her head a trifle, to an inclination of despondency. Her hand went through her hair, and coaxed it back, above the forehead. Then she sighed again; and looked about to see if there was more to do; and saw that there was no more to do. And sighed once more, almost as if she regretted that, rather than rejoiced in it.

Then, becoming aware that his eyes were on her, that he had been watching her all this while, everything she did, she smiled at him. She smiled for him.

It was just for him to see. It wasn't from the heart, it wasn't from joy. He could tell the difference.

He got up and went over closer to her. "What is it?" he said softly over her shoulder. "Are you tired?"

"I don't do enough for that."

"Are you lonely?"

"You're right here with me," she answered that.

"Are you blue?"

She shook her head, but the very act of negation was in the mood that she denied.

He nodded slightly, in confirmation to himself; unseen behind her. He went to the window. He looked at her appraisingly from there, a look she did not see. Then he began to talk for her benefit, as when you try to draw a person's attention to something they would not notice of themselves.

"It's beautiful out. You ought to see it. What a night.

The moonlight's all over the whole sky, like spilled milk. Shall we go out and see the town? Shall we go out and see what the town is like?"

She nodded. But she didn't go to the window to see for herself, as he had.

"I'll get your coat," he said.

He put it over her shoulders, leaving the armholes empty.

"That's good enough," he said. "Come on, just you and me together."

He put out the lights and locked the door, and they walked down the street side by side. Until they'd come to another. And then they followed that. Until they'd come to another. And then they followed that in turn. Slowly the lights grew more numerous, the walks more peopled. And presently they were in the very heartblood of the town, vivacious, virile.

"Shall I take you to a picture show?" He tried to tempt her. "Clara Kimball Young, or Eddie Polo, or Sessue Hayakawa? Or maybe a Max Linder funny?"

She shook her head. "They're just make-believe. They're just shadows on the wall, for little boys and girls. I'm too big a girl now."

"And a sad-hearted one," he murmured half audibly.

They walked on a little farther, like two lost souls, hand-linked, in the crowd.

They came to a busy intersection, and looked about.

"I wonder what that building is?"

She didn't say she wondered too.

They crossed to the opposite side.

"Shall we go down this way? See where this leads to?"

The grounds slowly dipped, so that they obtained a fuller perspective, out before them.

"Look," he said. "Look at the lights. Isn't that beautiful?"

"All towns are beautiful at night, when they're lit up," she said wistfully.

He laughed a little. "You almost sound as though we don't live here ourselves. As though—this were some place we were just passing through."

She didn't answer. But her eyes avoided his for a moment, a thing they rarely did.

They found a park, though they didn't know what it was called.

"Let's go in here and sit down," he suggested. "Break our walk before we start back."

They sat down upon a bench, and he circled his arm around her shoulders, as any husband would at such a time, in fondness and in oneness and in languid understanding.

In the moonlight, the clouds were like clotted cheese in the sky.

He saw her looking upward, and on her face was a haunted loneliness, a forlornness, that wrung his heart. Vacant, aching eyes, looking for something up there above that was not to be found down here.

"What are you looking for up there?" he whispered. "What? Tell me."

"I'm pretending that it's Central Park, down here where we're sitting," she breathed. "And while I keep my face up like this, I can see the little lake tucked in the corner where the Sherman statue is. And on that side, the lights of the Plaza Hotel against the sky. The Vanderbilt mansion is there, but much lower down, just edging out in back of it. And over on this other side, the tall thin Netherland Hotel, and then the Savoy. I'm sitting here with my best beau—no, it isn't you, it's poor old Lance, poor reliable old Lance—and I'm not much interested in *him*. But Papa and Mamma are up that way, just about that far, waiting for me at home, on

Seventy-ninth Street. And after awhile Lance'll walk me over—just to there, just that far—and we'll both get on one of the double-decker Fifth Avenue buses that keep running back and forth just over the park wall there, and he'll take me home.

"Home," she repeated softly. And then again, scarcely to be heard, "Home."

"But when I bring my face down again, to here, I only get this faraway town."

He tightened his arm about her in helpless consolation.

"Talk to me about it," she begged piteously. "I want to hear about it again."

"What'll I say?"

"I want to hear the names of it again. The names I used to know. The names of—home."

"I didn't know you—missed it so," he faltered.

"Everyone has to love *some*place," she said defiantly. "And that's the place I love. Oh, let them laugh and let them sneer, with their 'to visit but not to live there.' Oh, I know it's big, and it's supposed to be stony-hearted, and it's hard to think of it that way. For others maybe, not for me. It's the place I was born, it's the place I was raised; I'll always be a part of it, and it'll always be a part of me. It's my *home*town. It's my New York. There's no other place, in this whole wide world, that can ever take its place in my heart. New York—when I say it soft and low, it seems to bring it closer—New York. Just a whisper and it's here again—New York..."

"Sh-h-h-h," he tried to soothe her. "Close your eyes. I'll say the names that bring it back to you. I'll try to say the names you want to hear.

"Behind us—don't turn and look, or you'll make it go away—but over our shoulders, over that way, that's where Central Park West is. The Century Theatre. And the Columbus Circle. Reisenweber's. Then you come back along this way, toward where we are, that's Fifty-ninth Street. There are the Spanish Flats. Remember the Spanish Flats? Or if you keep going west, you come to the San Juan Hill district, the colored folks' district. Then there are the roofed stairs going up to the Ninth Avenue El. See them? One on each side of the street."

"Fifty-ninth Street," she murmured. "Forty-second, Thirty-fourth, Twenty-third. Madison Square, and the Madison Square Garden. Fourteenth Street. Union Square. Luchow's. The green crosstown cars. The red and yellow ones that run on Broadway and Third Avenue. The Second Avenue El, and the Third, and the Sixth. With that lonely spur that runs as far as Central Park, and then has no place further to go. (Does anyone ever use it?) The subway trains, packed with salesgirls and stenographers, and businessmen and workingmen and all the world. Always going so fast, but always going nowhere, I guess. Uptown, and down, and around, and back home again. The Bronx Express, the Van Cortlandt Park Express, the Sea Beach line to Coney..."

"Say the names of some of the stations over to me. Let me hear the way they sound again. There's a kind of poetry even in the names of the stations. The poetry of the familiar—and the faraway. And if you miss one, I'll try to help you put it in."

Litany of the dispossessed. "There's Battery Place, and then there's Rector Street. There's Cortlandt, and there's Chambers. There's Fourteenth, Pennsylvania—"

"You left out Franklin, you left out Canal."

"But those are for locals, I'm giving the expresses."

"Go back to Chambers and start over," she said wistfully. "Go more slowly. Don't make them go by so fast."

He started over. "I'll begin at Wall Street this time, that was the branch I always took. Wall Street, Fulton Street—"

She turned suddenly and hid her face against his breast, and her sobbing was so close and hot it shook his own frame as well.

"Don't," he tried to console her. "Don't. Come on, let's get up now. I'll take you home."

She shook her head despairingly, even while her sobs were slowly lessening. "No," she contradicted with infinite poignancy, "no you won't. You'll take me back to a furnished flat in a faraway town. But you won't, no, you won't—take me home."

2

He got a five-dollar advance in August. On the twentieth. And the same day that he came home and told her about the advance...

"I'm getting five dollars more a week, starting on Monday." He shrugged elaborately. "And I didn't even ask for it. What do you think of that? Ponds just happened to be going by, behind me, one time this morning, and I turned my head and gave him a great big smile. Not because it was him; that was the way I felt. I would have smiled at anybody who happened to be passing near me just then. He smiled back, and then all of a sudden he stopped and said, 'How much are you drawing again, Marshall?' Then when I told him, he let his hand come down on my shoulder for a minute and he said, 'Starting Monday it's fifty. I'm going to speak to the cashier.' "

"Oh, I'm so happy," she rejoiced.

"I am too," he seconded. "And isn't it funny? I bet if I'd asked for it myself, he would have refused."

Then when they'd crowed and exhilarated over this

for awhile, she in turn related: "Oh, here's something I nearly forgot to tell you—"

"What?" he beamed.

"There was a man here to see you this afternoon."

His face and his voice both dimmed. "A man?" he said slowly. "Here?" And then he said bleakly, "Who— was he?"

She was still out in the sunlight. "Some man. I don't know who he was. I haven't any idea."

"Well, didn't he—?"

"He didn't give me his name, from first to last. I couldn't get it out of him. When I asked him if he'd care to leave it, he mumbled something about—that you wouldn't know it anyway."

He shot her a swift look for a moment, from under his downcast eyelids. A look that was not at her nor meant for her, perhaps, but was produced by the phrase, 'you wouldn't know it anyway,' lodging itself in among his thoughts, pressing upon them, so that his eyes gave that little flicker.

He was speaking more quietly now, more slowly, than he had been before. "Then if I—wouldn't know his name, what would he want of me?"

"I waited for him to tell me that, but he didn't. So, as long as he didn't I didn't ask him. I didn't want him to think I was one of these women who meddle in their husband's affairs."

"But he did seem to know that I lived there."

"Well, he wasn't any too sure of that, in the beginning, I could tell."

"But afterwards he was," he prompted her with an undercurrent of bitterness.

"He asked me if you did, so of course I said you did."

"What did he look like?" he said dismally.

"Oh, I'm no good at that," she protested. "If it had been a woman— But it was just a man. How can you describe a man?"

He smiled mirthlessly at that. Friend or enemy, civilian or police official; that's how, he thought.

"He was young and stocky," she said. "He—well, he was very sure of himself. There was something a little aggressive about him, I thought."

A plain-clothesman would be sure of himself, a plain-clothesman would be aggressive.

He tried to read the future in the water at the bottom of his glass, but all he could see was the tablecloth through it, its damask pattern slightly magnified by the crystalline coating.

"Go over it again," he said. "Maybe I can get something out of it."

"You dwell on it so," she said lightly. Then she did as he had asked. "I heard the doorbell ring, and when I went to the door, he was standing out there. I remember he didn't tip his hat to me, and I didn't like that. He was holding something in his hand, and looking at that, not at me."

"What?" he said, looking steadily into his water tumbler as though her voice were coming out of there, and not out of her lips.

"Well, I couldn't see exactly, since he had the back of his hand up, like this, between us. Whatever it was, it was on the other side of his hand."

A badge of authority, that he was holding ready to have turned outward the other way, had it been I, instead of she, who answered the door?

"It was either one of these vest-pocket notebooks, or something that had your name on it, a card or a slip of paper, something like that. Because when he asked about you, I could tell he was reading it from there, he had it on there, by the way his eyes went down to it, instead of to my face, He said, 'Does a Mr. Prescott Marshall live here?' "

"He put in 'a' like that?"

"Yes, he put in 'a' like that.

"Then I told him yes, but that you weren't in. Then he took a pencil from his pocket, up in here, and put it to the other side of his hand, and made some mark or notch or check against whatever it was that he was holding there. Then he put both the pencil and the—whatever it was— away again, and that seemed to satisfy him, that seemed to be all he wanted. That was when I asked him if he'd care to leave his name, and he said that you wouldn't know it anyway. That was as far as I got; then before I could say another word, he'd already turned away and left me standing there high and dry. I called after him, 'Will you be back again?' "

He swallowed the water in his glass. "And what did he say to that?" he whispered half audibly.

"He didn't turn his head to look at me, but from over his shoulder he answered in a—in a most curious voice—"

"What was curious about it?"

"Well, it was so drily emphatic, as though that were the most needless question to ask."

"And what was it he did answer?"

"He answered, 'O-o-oh, yes indeed, lady! O-o-oh, yes indeed I will!' Twice, like that, and sort of drawled out slowly, as I've said, in sarcastic emphasis. I didn't like his whole tone or manner, and if there's one thing I hate, it's to be called 'lady.' I'm afraid I closed the door rather sharply."

She changed the subject, yet it was no change. "It's so close in here tonight. Just look at that, your whole forehead is moist, I can see it from here."

He dabbed at it with a sort of absent ruefulness. "I don't know anyone here in town," he said. "The only ones

I know are the men down in the office with me, and they were all down there today, no one was missing."

"Maybe he was somebody from somewhere else," she suggested.

Somebody, he agreed unheard, from New York.

She'd finished with it. That was all she said about it. That was all there was *to* be said about it.

She went on; or rather, back to where they'd been before, to the raise.

"Oh, I'm so happy," she reveled.

He didn't say that he was, any more.

3

Still life: their living room. A painter, had he attempted to do it, might have called it "Sudden Interruption," it was so eloquent of just that. No one in it. But the easy chair he habitually used drawn up close beside the reading lamp. On it, stretched from arm to arm, a collapsed newspaper, like an explosion of paper leaves, attaining such expanse and dishevelment only in one way: by being first held open at double arm-width and then abruptly deflated by the removal of both its supports. On the table by the lamp a little hurriedly scratched note: "Back in a minute, dear. Something I forgot at the grocer's. Just read your paper awhile. M."

But two things in the room were not altogether still, and might have eluded the painter had he tried to reproduce them with complete fidelity. One was the chain-pull of the lamp, which swayed ever so slightly, as from a recent violent jerk. The other was the struggling exhalations of a cigarette, suddenly put down and abandoned on the table's edge.

In the hallway outside the room, also a still life. And this one its would-be painter might have called, with equal appropriateness, "Concealment" or "At Bay."

On the rack, his hat and coat, Marshall's, in usual homecoming position, one over the other, as though they adorned a skeletal wooden man, without a face or arms. No motion, though; even less motion than inside in the room beyond. The curtained glass inset in the upper part of the door lighting the scene with a sort of pearly glow from the twilight outside. Looming against this, moleculized into dots by the very fine pores of the curtain, the blurred gloom of a head and shoulders. Not sharp enough to be called a silhouette, but rather more like a dark, watery stain against the curtain and the glass. Immobile.

And down below, up flush against the lower, wood-opaque section of the door, in tortured crouch, Marshall's back, and the back of his head, and the backs of his legs, one tightly compressed in folded support, the other spread out along the floor behind him in sort of dragging position. And the upturned soles of both his feet. And the backs of both his hands, opposite one another, one pressed flat against the door panel itself, the other flat against the door-frame, as though desperately trying to hold the two things closed. His immured face was where the keyhole was; that must have been directly before one eye.

And again, complete immobility. On both sides of the door alike.

Then suddenly the doorbell battery buzzed out angrily, like a split-open hive of hornets, stinging the stillness to death for a few moments. Then stopped again, wearied, as though it had done this many times before.

And again, complete immobility. The darkling puddle on the glass. The sprawled, half-prone figure crushed against the door.

Then, like dingy water running down off a surface too smooth to hold it, the glooming stain altered contour, swirled, evaporated and was gone. The glass became all an even twilight gray, a little lighter than it had been. A step sounded in withdrawal, giving strain to wood.

Then a tin slab chocked closed, out at a distance.

Then a car engine tried to revolve, and failed, and died again momentarily. Then tried once more, and this time exploded into successful operation, and pounded shatteringly away into the distance.

The inert figure slowly moved, a section at a time. First the leg that had been laid out far behind it drew in, to give it leverage. Then one of the supplicating palms crept up higher on the door. Then the other followed, over on its own side. Then the whole figure rose to its feet.

Then he turned, and staying sodden there in the crevice into which he had wedged himself, took out a handkerchief and calmed the saturation from his face.

When she returned some time later, paper bags crackling all about her, he was still standing there, like that, limply putting a handkerchief away into his back pocket.

Something snapped, and she'd suddenly drenched the two of them with an unbearably vivid silver-gilt glare, so that his eyes winced in repulsion for a moment. She only saw him then.

"Press!" she said. "Are you ill? You look so white. Why were you standing in the dark like that?"

"I had a headache," he said. "I wanted to rest my eyes for a minute or two. I'm all right now."

"Has anything happened here? You were standing there so strangely, when the lights first went on just now."

"Nothing's happened here," he assured her, with a fervent gratitude for being able to say so that she could not have guessed. "Nothing. I was on my way to put on the lights myself, just as you came in, and for a minute I couldn't find the switch in the gloom, that's why I was standing there flat up against the wall like that."

"I noticed the oddest thing, outside just now, as I was getting out my key," she related, as though in the belief she had changed the subject. "Someone made a chalk mark on the stonework facing our door. A sort of round thing, like a bulls-eye, I don't know what you'd call it. I'll have to go out there and take a damp cloth to it afterwards, see if I can get it off. Some mischievous little boy or other, I suppose."

Some mischievous little boy or other, he mused, with a quiet sardonic sort of horror.

4

The telephone rang two nights later. He got up as a matter of course and went to it to answer it. That was his privilege, his prerogative, as the man of the house, to answer the phone if it rang when he happened to be there; rather than hers. It was a mechanical instrument, it was an electrical thing, it was a thing of wires, it still fell more within the masculine domain than the feminine.

He took it up and he said, "Hello?"

There was no sound from it.

He said "Hello?" again.

There was still no sound.

He said "Hello! Hello! Hello!", his voice quickening in impatience.

No sound, no sound at all.

Irritated, he tapped the suspension hook repeatedly. "Hello!" he insisted. "Who is it? Who's there?"

Then he listened intently.

Faintly, as if in far-off echo of the brusque clicks he

had just perpetrated himself, there was a single, muffled, ghostly one somewhere at the other end of the line. He could barely catch it, but he did catch it, hard as it tried to dissemble itself.

He was gripping the instrument tautly now, staring at it frightenedly. Someone had been on there.

Suddenly he began manipulating the hook more feverishly than ever. "Central" got on.

"Central," he said. "Was that a mistake? You just called me here. Was that a mistake?"

"No, sir," Central answered soothingly. "A party asked for your number. I connected them with it just now. Didn't you receive the call?"

He didn't answer that. "Was it a—a man or a woman?"

"It was a man's voice, sir," Central told him.

He knew then. Knew as he quietly hung up. Knew all there was to know about this mystifying little occurrence. Knew what it was, and why it was, and who it was.

That was *he*.

He wanted to find out if I was here, first of all.

And now he has.

And now that he has, he's coming over.

I have to get her out of here. I have to get her out of here *first*. He didn't say to himself what was to follow that *first*. He didn't have to.

Suddenly he'd gone to the closet, come away again. He was holding four things, all on one arm, all in one hand. His coat, and hers as well; his hat, and hers as well.

Where, though? Where could he take her? Where could he leave her? No friends, no relatives, no— They were so alone, so cut off, in this faraway place.

It came to him then. He fumbled in his change pocket. Two twenty-five-cent pieces. That was enough, more than enough. He dropped them back in again. Then he took his wallet out of his jacket inside pocket, and without looking to see how much was in it, deliberately drew open the top bureau drawer, tossed it in there, and closed the drawer on it.

Then he strode forward to rejoin her. He stopped just short of the doorway, for an instant only, before going in to her. His expression was taut and grim with impending purpose, and it didn't suit the face he was about to show her. He put his free hand up to it, and drew his hand slowly downward across it. The way you do when you're wiping something off. Only instead of wiping something off, his hand left something behind it.

A smile. A carefree, lighthearted, totally lying smile.

5

The screen became an inky black square, as it did at intervals of every two or three minutes. Four intercrossed white lines, pencil-thin, were superimposed upon this to form a frame just a little smaller than the screen itself. Interrupting the bottom one of these lines, in white lettering, intruded the trade-mark "Essanay." Within the frame itself appeared two lines of white letters, upper case, beginning and ending with quotation marks.

"COME AWAY FROM HIM.
CAN YOU DOUBT THAT I LOVE YOU, DEAR?"

They, like the frame, like the trade-mark, vibrated slightly, but not enough to interfere with legibility.

A slight sibilance became audible as a minority of the audience, there was always such a minority, repeated the words to themselves, under their breaths, without realizing they were doing so. The elderly woman piano player, silhouetted against the lighted music rack buried deep down at foot of the screen, continued to play softly unobstrusive strains of "The Skater's Waltz."

Now, he thought. Now's the time, while this subtitle is on up there.

He stretched out his hand a little, gave his fingers a crisp snap so she would notice it.

She turned her head. "What's the matter?"

"I left my wallet on the dresser, back home."

"It'll be all right. We locked the door after us."

"I won't be able to enjoy the show. I'm going back for it a minute." He was already standing up.

"All the way there and back?" she protested.

"It's only a couple of blocks each way. I can make it in five minutes." He was already out in the aisle now, beyond reach of her deterring hand, had it occurred to her to use it, which it probably would not have. "Here, watch my seat for me. I'll leave my coat and hat on it."

"Will they let you in again?"

"I'll tell them at the door." He was already starting up the aisle, head turned backward to talk to her over his shoulder. Ordinary conversation, unless it became inordinately vociferous, was in itself no disturbance to others at a picture show; it was indulged in without hindrance at all times. "Watch the picture; I'll be back before you miss me."

She had no longer any way of stopping him, other than accompanying him out herself, and the admission had cost them forty cents, twenty apiece.

The screen brightened to silver, and the face of a young woman now occupied it, clown-white, eyes imbedded in glutinous black masses of mascara, treacly, Ubangi-thick lips fluttering in rapid, pantomimic speech. The swing door fluxed behind him and obliterated her.

He explained his situation to the ticket taker. The ticket taker remembered him well, because (a) he had asked him if there were two seats on the aisle available, when they went in just now; (b) he had asked him what time it was; (c) he had somehow managed to drop his tickets to the floor, in seeking to hand them over, and both of them, he and the ticker taker, had bent over together to retrieve them; and (d) he had complimented the ticket taker, who was actually on the elderly side, on his agility in bending, using the flattering expression "a young man like you," which had pleased the ticket taker to the point of brimming cordiality.

The ticket taker, still cordial, agreed to pass him through on simple sight alone, on his return.

The theatre canopy, with its spinning threads of alternately broken and resumed current, rippling liquidly against the night behind him, he broke into a quick jog that was only less than a headlong run.

He came back in sight of their place. He slowed, then stopped, just short of it. He looked around. There was no one in sight.

So I beat you back here, did I? he gloated grimly.

He keyed the door, let himself in, closed it after him.

Darkness, but he knew his way around by heart. He made sure all of the shades were down, first, on all of the windows. Down to the very bottom, to seal up any telltale gap, no matter how slender. They were blue; they didn't give out light, they kept it in. Then very sparingly he lit just two lights, one at the back of the hall, so that he could see him, take his measure, when he opened the door; the other a lamp in the front room. He moved this from where it habitually was, set it down by a certain chair, now dedicated, so that that particular chair received most of the benefit of it, the periphery of the room remained less clear, if still not actually shadowy.

Then he went to the back, and without lighting any

further lights, took from one of the kitchen hideaways by sense of touch alone a pocket battery-light which he owned. He used this instead to see his way around, poking it now into drawers, now into cupboards, in search of something.

It had apparently not yet taken definite form in his mind, for he picked up two totally dissimilar objects, half tentatively, then set them down again. One was a knife used for carving roasts, the other a flatiron of Marjorie's.

He found something finally, on the shelf of the broom closet, which in the act of finding became what he had sought. An ordinary household claw hammer. None too bulky, in fact with quite a slender shaft, but with a head weighted sufficiently at least to stun someone, render them senseless, so that they could be transported else-where for the more mortal assault.

He tried to slip its handle rearward up his coat sleeve, hold its head reversed in his cupped hand. That was too awkward, attracted attention to his hand by the stiff unusable way he was compelled to hold it.

He laid the hammer down flat finally, so that its shaft made a bridge between two height-differentials, crashed his foot down on it full force. The shaft fractured at about two-thirds length. There was enough left below the head for a good solid hand-grip, and that was all he wanted. He now put this part into his side jacket pocket, and that took it quite easily.

He discarded the pocket light, returned to the front room, sat down in the selected chair, and measured it for head-height. His own head extended well up over the back of it, and therefore so would anyone else's who was of average height.

On the wall opposite him, however, there was a long, slender, ornamental mirror panel. This revealed the sector behind the chair. He took that down, stood it off in a corner, face inward to the wall. The wall was now blank opposite the chair.

He moved the chair out a little, not much, so that there was a little more space behind it to move about in. To take a stance in, and swing your arm up and over in.

He looked dubiously down at the rug. Even if you upset a glass of water on it, it retained the stain (as he knew by experience), much less—something thicker. He got the evening newspaper he had brought home with him the first time, three hours ago, separated it into its component leaves, and made a mat of these all over the floor, forward of the chair, so that anyone falling face-forward would rest upon them. As spilled ink does upon a blotter.

He felt in his pockets now. He had a packet of cigarettes in them, a yellow lead pencil, not much else. The cigarettes would do. He went behind the chair and placed them upon a small three-legged tabouret or stand they had there, hugging the wall. He left them standing there.

Then he went outside, close up to the front door, and flattened himself against the sideward wall, right up against the door seam, and fell motionless and waited, hands crushed behind his body in a leashed attitude.

He waited for minutes that were hours; that fell as sluggishly, one by one, as drops of molten lead from a smelter, seeming never to part from it, stretching themselves out into elongated strings before they at last severed themselves and tumbled.

He took no count of them. Fear—and this was fear that had him, purely and simply—usually gives a mercurial restlessness, an instability. Yet paradoxically it can give a stoical patience too. He would have stayed there all night like that if he'd had to, feeling no ache, no stiffness, no constraint.

A car drew up and stopped. It just stood there for some moments, and no one got out. Why should it just stand like that? Come from nowhere, and then just stand like that, engine gone, before his own door and no other?

This is he. Here he is now. He made that reflex gesture that is always made, that the wielder-to-be of any weapon never failed to make yet. He knew the hammer head was there safe in his pocket, but one hand came out from behind him to touch it anyway, then slid back where it had been.

A door slab ground open, not a wall door but the curved, metal-sheathed door of a car, with its more resonant, crunchy sound. Then it was slapped closed again. Shoe leather scuffed across pavement, came right up to the door, silenced.

He could hear him breathe, through the door, he was so close. He probably couldn't, but his taut senses supplied the sound out of their own invention.

The doorbell battery, fortunately far behind him along the hall, clamored.

Marshall's hands came out from behind his back. He flexed them, to give them agility. He wiped them on his side, to dry them. He put one forward and placed it on the knob. Left it there like that.

The rearward battery clarioned again.

His wrist turned, and he tugged the door in, and he was looking at him, the man he was going to kill within the next few minutes.

6

He was shorter than Marshall. He was broader by a good deal. He was also older than he, not by so much perhaps as that he showed it more. He was balding, and there were already certain creases imprinted about his mouth and eyes that had become permanent, remained unaltered no matter what facial expression backed them.

He saw everything about him at a glance, Marshall. Things that were of no consequence, that he almost didn't want to know, that only intruded on the main issue—which was life and death. Life at this particular moment, death at another moment very presently to come. As when you're taking a snapshot of one certain subject, and background irrelevancies crowd into the print, doing away with its singleness of purpose.

Such as that he was wearing a tie of dark blue silk, with a very thin diagonal band of gold repeated on it at wide intervals. Such as that there was a mole on his neck, just down from the lobe of his left ear. Or such as that there was the top of a fountain-pen barrel affixed to the rim of his breast pocket by a ball-pointed clip.

There was an intentness to his eyes that boded ill. They somehow betrayed the fact that they were alert lest his vis-á-vis, Marshall, get away from him, elude him in some way. Though they were intent, they weren't still. It wasn't a passive stare. Their pupils vibrated, danced. They remained at dead center of the eye, but they reminded Marshall of that subtitle at the picture awhile ago, the way they quivered while yet standing still. As though, if you go over to the left, I'll go over to the left after you; if you go over to the right...

He waited for him to speak, Marshall.

"Good evening, Mr. Marshall?"

"Mr. Marshall."

"Mr. Prescott Marshall?"

"Mr. Prescott Marshall."

"I think I'd like to see you."

"You think you would?"

"I'm sure I would, Mr. Marshall. In fact, I've tried before."

Marshall repeated the phrase, without interrogation. "You've tried before."

Notice how watchful he is, afraid any moment I'm going to close him out? Notice how his eyes just went down to the base of the door, to make sure my own foot isn't down there as a wedge? Notice how they now went toward the inside knob, to see if I wasn't about to ram it closed?

"But I'm persistent. My experience has taught me to be so. I never give up."

"Never?" He thought of a line in Gilbert and Sullivan: Never? Well, hardly ever. But his mind didn't smile at it.

He was looking past him now, warily and dissembledly studying the terrain. The car was empty, he'd come alone. No one out there on either side of the walk.

"And, as you see, it's paid me not to—"

Not to what? He had to think back. Not to give up.

"—because I've finally run you down."

Marshall's eyes widened slightly, then drew back to normal.

He thought a sentence over, then said it. "Does that mean I've been avoiding you?"

The man smiled a little, for the first time. It wasn't friendly, it was a cynical half-smile. "In my line, I think most people do. I have to go out and nail them down. They're not going to come in to me."

He's becoming more broad by the minute. It's not an overt arrest, though, or it would have already occurred, the minute I opened the door. Blackmail, probably, the same as the woman. Only infinitely worse this time.

"I think we could talk over what I have to say to you more comfortably inside, Mr. Marshall."

"Well, then we will," said Marshall crisply. He drew the door back past himself full arm's length. He followed it back, still facing forward, like a soldier executing a rearward wheeling movement. "Help yourself," he said, dangerously reticent. Come in at your own risk.

The man came forward. "Your lady at home?" he asked tentatively.

"I'm here alone," Marshall said.

"Well, I think maybe that's better for our purposes."

Marshall closed the door, and locked it. Then he managed to get over to the room opening ahead of the man, by quick-stepping, in order to be there in time to indicate.

"Sit in that chair. That one there, where you'll have enough light."

It was so akin to an order, that the man glanced at him. But then he went over and stood before it.

"Shall I…?" He bent, offering to pick up the scattered sheets of newspaper.

"No, leave them there," Marshall said. "Just put your feet on them. We spilled something on the rug earlier."

The man sat down without further ado. Marshall sank into the diagonally confronting chair he had ready, knowing he was going to get up again in only a moment.

When I do, that'll be twice I've done it. Killed someone. Most people never do it even once. Strange, when it happens by accident, like the first time, you're so frightened, you think it's so terrible. When you've planned it ahead, like now, you're hardly frightened at all, you hardly think anything of it at all. I mean, as far as feeling guilty about it.

What are those papers he's taken out, and is looking over? Typed reports? Documents having to do with me? He has it all written down already.

"I have here a complete dossier on you, Mr. Marshall. That's a fancy French word I picked up, I find myself using it lately, dunno why. Well, in plain English, a file. You look surprised." He chuckled. "I already know more about you than you do about yourself, I'd like to bet. Well, when a man's whole future—you might even say his very life itself—is what you're concerned with, it pays to be thorough, that's the least you can do."

His very life itself, echoed Marshall.

The man began to read aloud, but in a curious mono-tone, as if more for his own sake, to refresh his own memory, than for Marshall's.

"Now, let's see what I've got on you so far," he said. "Prescott Marshall. Married. Age—twenty-six."

"Who told you that?" said Marshall with a visible start.

The man looked complacent. "Oh, I've been making inquiries. Here and there."

Marshall let go a deep, shuddering breath.

"You came out here in July of this year. You work for the Ponds Company, everyone knows who they are. Before that, you worked in New York, different type of job."

"Where'd you get that from?"

"That's my job. I've had my eye on you for some time."

Now. Do it now. Don't wait any longer. Beat him to the punch.

"Oh, well," the man said indifferently, "I have enough on you. The rest I can get from you your—"

Marshall was on his feet, after a pretended patting of several of his pockets. "Just a minute, I think I'd like a cigarette. I left mine over there in back of your chair."

The man was suddenly holding a package so close to him that it touched his midriff. "Here, have one of mine."

"No, I, uh, smoke Murad. That's my brand."

The man slanted his thumb down out of the way, revealing more of the package. "That's what these are. That's my brand too."

Marshall took one, it slipped through his fingers, he

lost it to the floor. "Slips don't count," joked the man amiably. Marshall took another, and as though it were immeasurably heavy, seemed to collapse under its weight back into the chair.

The man poked a lighted match into his face. He chuckled. "The condemned man smoked a hearty cigarette."

The man blew, his eyes went back to his documents again. "Now, you're going to die. You know that, don't you? Your number is up."

Marshall was scarcely listening to the words any more. The smoke tickled his nostrils. That gave him a better idea than the one that had just been so catastrophically thwarted. He pretended to sneeze. Made the sound that goes with it, one of the easiest of all sounds to mimic. "Ha-chew!"

"Good health," the man said inattentively, eyes on papers.

That's one thing he won't offer me, is his handkerchief.

He rose from his chair. "Just a minute. Get a handkerchief back here." The man started to turn his head. "Don't stop. I'm still listening."

The man obediently, and incautiously, reversed his head. The papers were before him, on his lap, anyway.

Marshall was behind the chair now, dead center. The man's head, over the top of it, was like an egg sitting in its cup, waiting to be cracked.

This is too easy, this is almost like something in a dream. I couldn't keep my hands down now if I wanted to.

"Go ahead talking. I can hear you."

His right hand went into his pocket, came out with the hammer head. His left into his rear pocket, came out with a handkerchief, the one he was supposed to have come back here to get. He wrapped the handkerchief deftly about the hammer head and its stalk, made it into sort of an impromptu blackjack.

"I'll come to the point. I guess you know why I'm here."

"I do. I know exactly why you're here."

His arm went up and back. His body arched. His heels cleared the floor.

In the middle of his next sentence, he'll be dead or dying. He'll never get to the end of it, be it long or short. This is the last sentence he'll ever speak, coming now.

"I want to interest you in taking out life insurance. I represent the Mountain States Insurance Company, 'Bloodhound Farrell' they call me, the way I track 'em down. Oh, they can't get away from me; I never lost a man ye— What was that? What happened?"

This time he did swing his head—and his shoulders—completely around in the chair. Marshall had lurched forward, down onto one knee and one extended hand, out past the chair, but a sideward direction from it.

"I tripped over my own feet," he said in a choked voice.

His hand was holding a bulgy-looking handkerchief, but it had not come unwound. He stuffed that back into his pocket, right while he was still prone like that, then rose, dusted the knee of his trouser.

"Didn't hurt yourself, did you?"

Marshall was out of breath and shaken, but there was a curious smile on his face—and in particular an expression in his eyes—that was almost one of dazed exaltation. "No, I feel all right," he said. Then, as though he liked the sound of that to his own ears, liked the feel of it on his tongue, he repeated it twice more, each time with increased intensity. "I sure feel all right. Boy, do I feel all right!"

Farrell looked at him a little dubiously, as though finding his behavior a little eccentric and wondering whether he would make such a good risk after all.

Marshall had stepped out of the room without a word.

He came back bringing a bottle and two thimble glasses, all hooked onto the fingers of one hand. He was sparing one leg just a trifle, as though it still hurt him from his recent fall or lurch.

"I want you to have a drink with me," he said ebulliently. It was a command, not an invitation.

"I came here to talk business."

"Just one," Marshall said. "I have to have just one drink. There are times when it's, when it's a sacrilege not to. Can't help it if you join me or not. Put those papers back in your pocket. My wife's waiting for me at the movie, and I have to get over there to her right away. You can look me up at the office some day, any day, if you want to talk business with me. But I'm giving you fair warning ahead of time, I don't think you'll get anywhere."

He filled the two small jiggers, handed one over.

"Good luck," Farrell said, crestfallen at the unpropitious turn the interview seemed to have taken.

"I know a better toast than that," Marshall said self-satisfiedly. "You won't understand it, but join me in it anyway. 'To the last sentence he ever spoke.' "

7

He slipped into his seat during the duration of another subtitle. It was so appropriate, it was almost uncanny; it gave him a start as he first raised his eyes to it.

> "NOW YOU SEE HOW LITTLE
> YOU HAD TO FEAR."

In the brighter pallor that flushed the theatre immediately after it, she turned and saw him sitting there beside her again, almost as though he'd never left her.

"Did I take long?" he asked.

"I was so taken up," she admitted, "that I lost track of the time. You missed the best part of it. Oh, it was so exciting."

It was exciting where I was, too, love, he confided to her ruefully, unheard. But it would have been considered too unbelievable to go on a movie screen.

"I think it's going to have a happy ending, though," she assured him.

It had a happy ending there where I was too. But when a movie ends, it ends for good. The other story, outside the theatre, that's never through, there's always more to follow. And you can't get up and leave your seat, for you *are* the story, you take it with you if you do.

"Did you get your wallet?" she remembered to ask after a moment.

"Yes," he said. But then he began to laugh. He felt his pocket. It was still empty. He'd left it back there after all, even the second time.

8

Marjorie's mother died in September 1915, quite unexpectedly. On a Sunday, the 12th of the month. The notifying telegram arrived the next morning, Monday, after traveling the night. He was the one who took it in; she was busy preparing their breakfast.

There had been no warning. She had been all right up to within hours of her death. A letter written by her to Marjorie, in which she expressly stated she was enjoying the best of health, had reached them only two days before, Saturday.

He opened it on the spot, the telegram. The fear

he had felt at sight of it and which caused him to do so
without waiting to give it to her, had nothing to do with
her, was a personal fear for and about himself alone. That
fear that was always hovering, so ready to pounce. A telegram was not a casual thing in 1915. What might this
one not contain; accusation, denunciation, warning of
impending arrest?

It was with a sense of relief that he read the actuality
of the message. It was good news by comparison, for it
was not the bad news he had dreaded so.

> *Mother passed away one this morning cerebral hem-*
> *orrhage. Delaying final arrangements pending your*
> *arrival.*
>   *Father.*

"Was that our bell?" she said, peering briefly from the
kitchen doorway. "Was it somebody for us?"

He had to tell her then.

He told her in the kitchen. Gently took the thing out
of her hand that she was holding, first, and then swung
over the kitchen chair toward her. "Sit down," he said,
and when she had, then he told her as best he could.

Her grief was restrained. She had never, he found
time to remind himself parenthetically, made a scene.
She was a true lady.

She wept quietly, and slowly her head went down until
she was looking over at the floor, that was all.

He brought her a glass of water, but she shook her
head. She even found time to whisper "Thank you." He
held her hand a little. He dabbed at her eyes a little, with
his handkerchief. There was very little else that he could
do; her affliction was within, and not on the outside where
he could reach it.

She even sat by him at the breakfast table, presently,
though without touching anything herself, and poured a

cup of coffee for him and saw that he had everything he wanted. (The wives of men, so close to ministering angels!)

And when he offered to stay home for half the day to look after her, she dissuaded him, with an ever-vigilant eye to his own best interests. "No, you go ahead to your job. You mustn't stay out like that." And even added, "I don't like you to see me like this."

Then when he was already at the door, she called after him: "Press, will you ring me from downtown as soon as you've got our tickets, and let me know. I'll begin our packing meanwhile."

He suddenly stood stock still there in the doorway, rooted to the spot. *Our* tickets, she had said, *our* packing. She expected him to go with her. As who wouldn't at such a time? He was her husband. What husband would let his wife make such a trip alone with her grief?

But how could he go? How did he dare? Go back *there*, of all places? That was forbidden territory. That was the nucleus, the focus, of all he had to fear, and all he had feared, for three solid months now. That was putting his head into the lion's mouth. To go there was almost like surrendering of his own accord.

"Press?" she was querying, from where he'd left her. "Are you still out there at the door?"

"Yes," he said, stirring to belated departure. "I'll call you up—later."

He completed his exit, closed the door.

No use. He knew he wouldn't make the trip back with her. He knew he couldn't.

It happened in your room, he told himself. In your room she died, in your room they found her. Even though you called yourself Prince, that Prince was you. Once they hold you, the landlady will be able to identify you with Prince, a half-dozen others in that home will be able to identify you with Prince. You become one with him. You become him. Don't go back within reach.

Keep away from New York.

He was at the railroad station by now. He was at the ticket window. He asked for it in the singular, not the plural.

"Ticket for New York."

The man gave him a chance to correct himself, had he wished to even now.

"One?"

He didn't. He wasn't a free agent in this; fear was buying his ticket, not he. "Just one. What afternoon trains are there?"

"There's a three o'clock, and then there's the Limited at five. That's an extra-fare train."

"Which one gets in first?"

"The Limited, of course. It beats the other's time by a full two hours."

"One for the Limited, then."

He kept his word, called her at once. Right there from the station.

He wouldn't tell her right now, of course. That she was making the trip without him. He'd break it to her swiftly, at the last moment, that was the best way. The way a surgical dressing is wrenched off, with one swift jerk, rather than peeled off by sparing degrees.

He'd tell her they wouldn't let him off from his job. Say that he'd had to cancel his own ticket, after having already bought it.

She came to the phone. Her voice sounded weak, but she was bearing up well. He asked her how she was, first.

"I'm all right, Press. I've got both the valises ready. It gave me something to do. The tickets, dear? Did you get them?"

He carefully kept all reference to number out of his

answer. "I did. The Five O'Clock Limited. It goes straight through with only one stop, at Philadelphia. It gets in at nine-forty-five, tomorrow night. Will that be all right?"

Yes, she assured him, the quicker the better. Then suddenly, at an unlooked-for tangent, she had asked him: "Are you at the office now? Where are you speaking from?"

For a minute he was going to lie, then (since there was no point to such a lie) luckily he told her the truth. "No, I'm still at the station."

"Oh, good," she said quickly. "Well, then you haven't heard yet. I already phoned Mr. Ponds, to save time. And to save you the embarrassment of having to ask him yourself. I told him what happened, that I'd lost Mother. He was very nice. He said they'd gladly let you off. You don't have to be back until the first of next week."

He had to swallow repeatedly, two or three times, unable to say anything.

"Press?" she said. "Press? Are you still there?"

I waited too long to answer, just then. I shouldn't have let that lapse creep in.

"Yes," he said somewhat shakily.

"What happened?"

"The darned cord tangled with the button of my coat-sleeve, I couldn't free it for a minute." He measured the distance between the two with his eye, saw that that could have happened.

"I can take the bags to the station and wait for you there," she suggested. "It's nearer to you from the office than coming out here and then going back downtown again."

He didn't want his own bag to leave the flat, at any cost. As though there were some dangerous magnetic impulse inherent in the train; that the nearer the bag got to it, the more danger there was of its being sucked into the train, and himself with it.

"No," he said firmly. "I'll pick you up at the flat. Wait there for me."

It was on his mind all morning—new york, New York, NEW YORK—it kept looming larger and larger, like a huge maw waiting to devour him. Its stylized skyscraper outline became the jagged teeth of the maw.

He couldn't eat any lunch. He sat there at the soup-stained tablecloth, alternately drumming his fingers on it and ploughing them through his hair. (The table-waited business lunch had not yet been supplanted by the waiter-less counter-served one, except in one or two of the large metropolitan centers.) The waiter would take each course away and bring the next without comment or remonstrance: the noodle soup, the beef stew, the apple pie—all for forty-five cents; probably attributing the trouble to the quality of the food and the perspicacity of this one customer over and above all the rest. Which was partially correct, anyway.

Marshall went back to where he worked and still couldn't conquer the problem.

New York, New York, New York. The Tombs Prison, the "Bridge of Sighs." The railroad ride up the banks of the Hudson to Ossining. The Death House at Sing Sing Prison. He saw only those things about it. It was a different New York; his own personal, private hell.

Three-forty-five came. Four. And still no solution. He couldn't cut his time any shorter. He had to get out to the flat where she was waiting.

His boss, Ponds, came by to say good-bye to him, put hand to his back.

"Sorry about your wife's mother, Marshall. I know how those things are; I lost my own mother-in-law summer before last, and I couldn't have felt forse if she were my own mother."

"But you didn't have to attend her funeral in a city

where you were wanted for murder," flashed through Marshall's mind.

"I can tell how you feel about it by the look on your face. Go ahead, you don't need to finish this up; it can wait until you get back."

Don't be so kind, Marshall thought morosely. The time'll be up quickly enough, as it is.

But he got his hat and shook Ponds' hand and left.

He went out into the late sunlight. It was a vivid day, the sun creating a sort of glow like a haze of canary brick dust wherever it fell, the shade-lines sharp and azure like unblotted fountain-pen ink. Every pedestrian walked in a puddle of his own ink, every awning and projection spilled a pool of it. The sky had been drained almost white by the loss.

An electric trolley came grinding by, the one he needed to take to get home. Sluicing majestically through the lesser shoals of horse-drawn beer trucks, grocery carts, flimsy tin Fords with their high, awning-covered backs, and an occasional privately owned Reo or Mercer, Stutz or Locomobile, jaunty with brass fixtures and ochre or ketchup-red body paint. Its overhead transmission-rod contemptuously spit turquoise sparks on these underlings as it glided along the air-strung conductor.

He wasn't in time, it was already too far past the proper stop for him to signal and to board it. He'd have to wait for the next.

Then suddenly, as simply as that and with no further effort, he knew what to do, how to keep himself out of the clutches of New York. He cut out into the middle of the street and started running after it. It wouldn't stop of course, it had its appointed stops, and the next was two whole corners away. But this was June, and it was already one of the open-sided hot-weather cars; the banks of seats running crosswise, and you just thrust yourself over the side into any given one.

Nothing was moving fast enough to be completely unattainable by foot, neither it nor its surrounding school. A short sprint and he'd overtaken the rear end of it, while the nearest drayman accommodatingly reined in his horses. A short additional run and he'd gained mid-section, so that he could allow for the loss of ground that would come when he aimed himself at it.

He flung himself toward the projecting vertical hand-grip that accompanied each seat-bank.

He was sick with fear, but he was even sicker with fear of New York, and the greater fear overcame the lesser one. Moreover, a voluntarily incurred danger is somehow always easier to bear than an involuntary one. He kept reminding himself he must stay clear of the wheels. God, he must be sure to stay clear of the wheels, and not lose a foot or a whole leg! Roll *out*, if possible, so that he wasn't caught and dragged by the undercarriage.

He got the hand-grip, and he got his inside foot, the right one to use, on the long trestle that ran the length of the car from front to back. He'd caught it successfully (as you always do when you don't want to; if he'd wanted to, he wouldn't have.) All that was left was the simple act of levitation.

But then instead of pulling his other foot up clear, he purposely left it down, used it for a brake along the ground. He deliberately let go the hand-grip, crossbarred both forearms to make a sort of frame or cushion for his head, so that his skull should not strike nakedly, then he let himself fall straight forward on his face, parallel to the car, onto the cobblestones.

The impact hurt him. It was like falling into a puddle of pain and sending up a momentary splash—not of water, but of bright white shock.

He heard a man, one of the passengers above him, give a hoarse shout of alarm. He remembered to roll away from the wheels. Then he came to a stop several body-spans over, but still face down. He was perfectly conscious. His body, in particular his bone-structure, was tingling from the rough usage he had given it, but he had done it well, he knew he had done it well, and his hidden face gave a smile of satisfaction to itself in the moment or two before it was unearthed from the padding of his arms and multiple sympathetic hands picked him up (to a still-flat position, not an upright one) and transported him up over the curb, and set him down there again.

They bade him lie still there until he had been looked at, and in the meantime people stood around him gazing down at him curiously. He didn't mind that. Presently a horse-drawn ambulance wagon arrived, and an intern bent down by him and made an examination. His leg was beginning to ache a great deal, particularly down below at the lower part. He not only didn't mind that, he was glad of it. The very place he had wanted it to be. You could still travel on a train with an injured arm; with an injured or useless leg it was an almost impossible undertaking.

She was all ready to go to the train, when they helped him home to his own door. He had purposely accepted the offer of a ride there in the ambulance (for she could hear its dolorous bell, and see the white jacket of its attendant, and it made the whole thing far more convincing), in preference to that of one of the bystanders who had happened to be a car-owner and had offered to bring him home in that. It would have been much less effective.

He was holding his one shoe in his hand, and hobbling one-legged with its owning foot hitched clear of the ground.

She was badly frightened for the first moment or so, and it was a cruel thing to do to her, he knew, make her pay that way for his immunity, but it had had to be done.

"I fell off the trolley," he said, with a sort of complacent demureness. "I was in too much of a hurry to get back here, I guess."

"It's only a bad sprain," the intern tried to reassure her. "He'll be back on it again in a day or two."

Marshall was sorry he'd given him the chance to say that; he would have preferred to make it a fracture, but now it had to remain a sprain.

"Thank you very much. I can manage now." He closed the door on him.

"You'll have to go without me," was the first thing he told her. "I won't be able to make the trip now, in this condition."

"But how can I leave you, like this? Who'll look after you?"

"You've got to go. It's your mother's funeral, it's not a thing that can be put off for a few days, or even just a day. You've got to be there by Wednesday. I'll manage; at least I'm not laid up in bed. You can leave word with the superintendent's wife; she's a nice woman, I'm sure she won't mind getting my meals for me and keeping the place in order."

She decided to, then; only because of the tragic event that was calling her. Nothing less could have made her leave him. A taxi was summoned, and the man came in and carried out her valise for her.

She kissed Marshall good-bye; he was now sitting in an easy chair, with his cotton-swollen ankle at adjusted height out before him.

"I'll start back right after the services. I've told Mrs. Sorenson, she said she'd look after everything."

"Buy some extra flowers when you get there, in my

name, as well as the ones we already ordered. Hurry, don't miss your train."

She kissed him again, ran, the door closed. A moment later it reopened in agitated haste and she came running back again. "Thank God, I just remembered in time! You must have the tickets. You were to bring them home, remember?"

Incautiously, he reached into his pocket, brought out the little envelope, handed it to her. It was a motor reflex, more than anything.

She opened it, looked. It only held one. The one he'd bought.

She stared, puzzled; first at it, then at him, then at it again.

"I don't understand," she said. "If you bought them before the accident—and you must have, because you phoned me to say you had—how, how could you have known you were only going to need to buy one?"

In the silence he was unable to fill, the taxi driver suddenly called in from the open doorway, where he had reappeared: "Lady, if you don't want to miss that train, we'd better get under way."

9

A man named Wise suddenly appeared at the office one day. At least, that was the name he was introduced around by. Ponds introduced him around, making no other comment, no other explanation, than just that: "This is Mr. Wise." Not another word.

There was no warning, no preparation, no explanation. The day before he hadn't been in the office, no one had heard of him, known he was coming. Then all at once there he was, had a desk, belonged there, was a full-fledged member of the firm. As suddenly as that. Moreover, there seemed to be no reason for it. No one was displaced, he didn't substitute anyone. No one had left just previously, he was just *added* to those that were there already. And to make this even less understandable, there had been less business lately, not more. Even before he showed up, there had been too little work to go around, rather than too much. This had been an open secret among them for some weeks; it might have been seasonal, it might have been temporary, but it had been actual.

To the others it meant merely a raising of the eyebrows, a secretive shrug of the shoulders toward one another. And then forgotten. But Marshall felt a shadow fall over him.

At the end of the newcomer's first day, when they first exchanged a few words, Marshall and he, as they both happened to come vis-á-vis going out the door, he said he'd been transferred from the company's Kansas City branch. It wasn't said in general; it was said to Marshall only, for Marshall was the only one within speaking range at the moment.

When Marshall asked Ponds the next day if the company had a branch in Kansas City, without telling him why he wanted to know, he was badly shaken but by no means completely taken by surprise to hear him say, "No. Never. And now that you mentioned it, I wonder why not. Might be a good idea to have one there."

The shadow deepened.

Next day, Marshall, unable to endure dwelling alone with his knowledge of the incriminating (as far as he was concerned) misstatement any longer—it had kept him intermittently awake during the previous night—sought to trap him into some sort of exposure. An exposure he shouldn't have sought, for he would have been the sufferer by it had he elicited it, but he couldn't resist.

They brushed elbows briefly in the doorway again, leaving.

"Where'd you say you were transferred from?"

"Detroit."

"I thought you said Kansas City."

"I couldn't have," Wise answered briefly. "The company has no branch there."

He's found that out since, Marshall told himself grimly. Just as I did.

"I was sure you said Kansas City," he persisted.

"If I did, it was just a slip of the tongue."

You don't make slips of the tongue like that, Marshall assured himself. There's no similarity between the two place-names. They're not even alliterative. You might say Portsmouth for Portland, Columbus for Columbia. You never say Kansas City for Detroit.

"I heard you," he said coldly. Though what was to be gained by forcing this admission from him, he didn't know.

"I was excited, I guess. My first day here, and all that. Tongue might have gotten twisted."

Still, was all Marshall could say to himself, a man *always* knows where he just came from, he never gets excited enough to forget *that*.

"You from Detroit, yourself?" he said warily.

"Not originally. Matter of fact, I was only there a very short time." And then just when Marshall thought he wasn't going to go any further, he threw away the match he'd just used and finished: "I came on from New York. That's always been my headquarters. Stopped off at Detroit first a spell, and then headed here."

Danger. New York.

They'd separated now. A trifle stiffly. Mutually stiffly.

And why had he used that word "Headquarters"? Of course it had had a capital, of course! That cold glint in his eyes for a moment just then had capitalized it. He hadn't said "home" he hadn't said "birthplace." Why "Headquarters"? Why?

Marshall glanced cautiously over his shoulder after him.

He was glancing covertly over his shoulder after Marshall.

New York. Be careful. Watch out.

He took that home with him. He had that to keep him intermittently awake through the night now, instead of the other. He'd exchanged a nebulous suspicion for a cold hard fact, that was the good all his tricky questioning had done him.

The week dawdled to completion. They had no further exchanges. The man might have found Marshall too bristly to take to him readily. And on Marshall's side were the towering cumulus clouds of fear and suspicion, rising higher and higher into the blue.

In his mind's eye, Marshall was already looking at him askance. And as a matter of fact, when the man passed too close to him once or twice, he did that with his physical eye as well.

Every afternoon when he'd leave, all the way home he'd think about him. Nothing but him.

He's been planted there to watch me. That's the way they do it, that's how they go about it. It's written all over him. It's a dead giveaway, any time you watch him a little without letting him see you, as I was doing this afternoon. He hardly does any work at all. Just fools around. He's not a bona fide member of the firm.

He'd still be thinking about him when he arrived home, when he kissed Marjorie.

"Oh, so-so. Just about average. No, not a very hard day."

He gives me a wider berth, now, than any of the others, that's another thing. He's chummy with everyone else, but he steers clear of me as much as he can. That gives away who his quarry is, inversely. That makes it obvious.

He'd still be thinking about him when they sat at the table.

"Press, what on earth are you doing? Not the salt, dear, the sugar. That's coffee you're drinking."

"I'm sorry. I must be in love."

"You wouldn't be with that coffee, if you'd gone ahead and done that to it."

He's a plant. He's working there under cover. He's been put there to watch me. They're not sure yet. Not sure enough. They want him to get more evidence than they have already.

A stinging pain went through his finger, and he whipped it loosely, blew on it, sucked it.

"Well, for heaven's sake. I strike the match for you, I hand it to you, and then you just sit there and hang onto it until it burns your finger! What *are* you dreaming about?"

"You," he said glibly. It was so easy to lie to her.

Does he report, at intervals? I wonder if he reports back to them? He must. He'd have to. That's what he's here for; that kind of job requires it. I wonder what he reports, when he reports. I wonder whom he reports to.

He was using the typewriter, that time today, and then he stopped right in the middle of what he was doing, remember? And I caught him looking right over at me. Sitting staring square at me, in a speculative sort of way. And then he dropped his head and went ahead typing some more. Maybe that was one of them, right then and there.

Would he do it openly, right in the same room with me? It wasn't office detail, that much he knew. It was something personal, private unto himself. He'd seen him fold and envelope it, he'd seen him put it into his inner coat pocket. Any office communication would have been turned over for mailing; they had a boy for just that. That wasn't his job anyway, Wise's, to write anything for mailing out.

So the pros outnumbered the cons; they did that with him every time.

In his mind, then, the next step after that, in logical sequence, was: If I could only get a look at what he's got in his pocket sometime, if I could put my hands on it, I might find out something. Something that would tell me who he really is, what he's really doing here, who it is he writes to.

He began to watch, no longer Wise but rather Wise's coat. The coat into which he'd seen that typed sheet go that day.

Approximately a week went by. A week made up of five torturing years, not days.

He kept watching his coat, kept watching his coat.

He saw his chance, one day.

Wise had left it over the chair, gone outside for something for a minute. Maybe to the washroom, or to smoke a cigarette in the hall (they weren't allowed to do that in the office). It was a warm day, anyway, they were all working without their coats.

There wasn't much time. He had to improvise rapidly. I'll say I—I needed a pencil, if he catches me. He could see one there, peering from the inside pocket. He took his own, pressed it point-down against his desk a minute until the weight broke off the point, then flung it aside, got up and went swiftly over to the coat.

No one was paying any attention. In boldness lay his greatest safety, except insofar as the coat's owner himself was concerned. Just a man stepping to a fellow worker's desk for a moment. He took it by the lapel and widened it from the semi-rounded position the chair back gave it.

The label would have been the first revelation, but this had already been imparted by Wise's own admission to him, robbed of any intrinsic value. "Saks and Co., New York." He already knew Wise came from there.

His fingers clawed down into the pocket. An envelope came up between them, sealed and addressed for mailing but not yet stamped. He unsheathed it only part of the way, just high enough for the address to clear the pocket's mouth.

> William MacDonald
> 372 Broadway
> New York, N. Y.

He let it fall back. He could hear Wise's steps outside returning to the door.

Wise's eye would have caught him still in motion—on the way back to his own desk—had it rested on him at the first moment of opening the door. But it was cast in a different direction first, and by the time it had glanced desultorily over where he was, he was already settled and still.

Wise picked up the coat and started out with it once more.

One of the others pointed up the act—though to Marshall it needed no pointing up—by calling out to him ribaldly:

"Hey, Wise, do you always take your coat with you when you go to the can?"

"Any objections?" Wise answered drily, and went on out with it.

He remembered just in time that that letter was in the

pocket of it, Marshall said to himself. He's writing to someone in New York. And he doesn't want anyone to see what he's writing, or get hold of it.

I should have taken it out of the pocket; I had time. I didn't have enough nerve. That was my one chance. Now it's gone beyond recovery.

If it's a report, I wonder how often he sends one? He must send them in at regular intervals. Once a month? Too far apart? Once a week? That would be about right. Today was Wednesday. I'll try again next Wednesday—if I last that long.

Wednesday came. He thought it never could, but it did.

He watched Wise closely; eyes never once directly on him, but not missing a move, a stir, he made. He waited to see if Wise would get up again and leave the room. He didn't. Things like that don't repeat themselves. Life doesn't repeat itself. He'd just been fidgety, wanted a cigarette; or else he'd been uncomfortable, wanted to leave the room. Today he didn't want a cigarette, he didn't want to leave the room.

Marshall tried to think of ways of getting him out of the room; couldn't. They were on an equality, on a par, he couldn't send him on an errand, send him with a message. He would have refused to go. Marshall could have invited him to step outside with him for a smoke, or downstairs for a coke, and that probably would have worked, but that would have defeated its own object, for then they would *both* have been out of the room together. And the coat, and the pocket, would have been even more out of reach than now.

He did no work at all, he sat there dully pondering. Now with his cheek pressed against the upturn of his hand, now with his forehead braced by both hands, interfolded. And it was getting late, and within another half hour it would be time for Wise to leave for the day, and if there was anything waiting in his pocket, it would go into the mailbox downstairs, beyond recall.

Suddenly, somewhere outside the windows, in the street below, some sort of blurred commotion became noticeable. Everyone in the office became aware of it at approximately the same time, as is the way with such things, after it had already been going on for some time and slowly but steadily mounting in intensity. Within moments of its discovery it had erupted into a climax of onrushing apparatus and shrilly clanging fire-engine bells. They all rushed to the windows pell-mell, and in an instant a line of headless rumps, three to a sill, was all that could be seen of them.

All but Marshall. He wouldn't have cared if the building itself were burning around him. He too jumped from his seat. But it was only as far as Wise's coat on the adjoining chair back that he went. And it was into the refuge of its inner breast pocket that his hand fled like a frightened bird fluttering to cover.

It was even riskier than the effort of the week before had been. Wise was right there not six feet away from him, all he had to do was turn his head. But Marshall, with the desperation almost of insanity, wouldn't let himself be deterred. And that was what he was, if only for those few fleeting seconds, insane to consequences.

His fingers found it, and they pulled it clear of the sheath-like lining. There it was again all but identical to the one before.

William MacDonald
372 Broadway
New York City

And yet he could be sure that it was a second, succeeding one, and not the original one that he'd glimpsed the week before, and which perhaps had been left unmailed and carried forgotten in Wise's pocket ever since then, because of a variation in the city address which had crept in: "New York, N. Y." and "New York City." New York was the only city in the country so great that it would overshadow its own namesake-state like that and keep the face of an envelope all to itself.

It must be a report. A man didn't write to another man once a week; not even to a male relative. Only in or on business. And his, Wise's, business was supposedly here where he was writing from, and not there where he was writing to.

The distance from where he held it now, back to where he had just taken it from, was a fraction of an inch, was less. The distance from where he held it now, out and over and around to concealment on his own person, was many inches, a whole foot and more, of circuitous, involved motion.

Again he was saved by something that, if it was not blind luck, must have been sheer genius of instinct. A psychic ability to guess an impending intention, even before it had been carried out.

Look out, something warned him, he's going to turn around. Here comes his head!

He had to jerk his hand back unaccompanied, even then he escaped detection only by the blink of an eye. The added length the letter would have given his whisked-back arm would have ensured betrayal in itself. There would have been that much more to put from sight. The whiteness of its color would have caught the eye that much quicker.

"False alarm," Wise was saying to him. "That little

haberdashery across the street, know the one? They're
already coming out again."

He took one added look for good measure, to make
sure he wasn't missing anything, before he finally abandoned the window sill altogether. But by that time
Marshall was already back at his own seat.

10

The name had branded itself behind his forehead. He
couldn't have forgotten it if he'd wanted to. And, oh, he
didn't want to, above all else he didn't want to do that! It
burned and ached fully as much as a literal, physically
applied brand would have, even though the searing was
from inside out and not from outside in.

He had to find out who William MacDonald was.
William MacDonald of 372 Broadway. He said the name
to himself when he was awake, and someone or something
else said it to him when he was asleep. It gave him no
leave. It became the printed heading on the newspaper
he was reading, it became the context of the store-sign
across the street (until he stopped dead in his tracks for a
minute, and saw that it really was "J. MacDonald, Men's
Tailor"), it became the entry in the ledger he was working
on at the office (until he stopped short and saw that he
really had entered that, and had to erase it). And once
during those few hours and days, as he was riding home,
he seemed to hear the trolley conductor cry it out, in
revery-shattering appropriateness. In an insant, white-
faced and almost fainting, he was standing beside him,
pulling at his coatsleeve and panting: "What? What'd you
say just then? What was that?"

The conductor turned and stared at him coldly. "Calm down, mister. I wasn't talking to you." Then he flung a pointing thumb across his own shoulder. "I was saying something to *him* out there. Is that all right witchew?"

And looking past him, Marshall saw that an opposite-bound trolley had halted alongside this one he was on, and their two conductors had accordingly been placed more or less abreast of one another. So, although no further explanation was given, he had to surmise what he had heard had been either a hail by name between them, or else an inquiry about a third conductor named MacDonald, for whom the second one was substituting on the daily run, perhaps because it was his day off.

Marshall turned and stumbled back to where he'd sprung from, aware that every eye in the car was on him, in gradations of expression from incomprehension to snickering amusement. His legs still felt weak when he finally got off that car.

The next day the obvious finally occurred to him, long after it should have. Or perhaps would have, had he been more in command of himself. A New York City telephone directory might give some clue, one of the classified that listed subscribers under their businesses and occupations. One of the ordinary kind would not do, for that might only give the name and address, both of which he knew already.

The next problem was where to locate one, here. Although the New York to San Francisco circuit had already been open since the previous year and one could now reach almost any city in the country by telephone, such calls were still fairly uncommon. There was little or no demand for out-of-town listings, at least not enough to make it easy to put your hands upon another city's directory. He tried several of the hotels first, and was told they had none. At last, and with considerable misgivings, he stopped in at the local main telephone exchange and approached the information desk.

"I have a name and address here, for New York," he said tremulously, offering the slip he had written out ahead of time. "Could you, could you—is there some way in which I can find out the number and the occupational listing that go with it?"

"We have a master directory here for New York City," the young woman told him. "I can have Information look it up for you, if the party is a subscriber to the New York directory." She handed the slip to a boy and sent him off somewhere. "There will be a short wait."

Marshall sat down fearfully on a bench and slowly rotated the brim of his hat between his two hands.

After what seemed like a far greater time than it must actually have been, the boy returned. Instantly Marshall jumped up and returned to the counter, almost leaning flat over the top of it. She returned the slip to him.

"Your party is listed in the New York City classified directory. Here is the complete information."

He stared at it for a moment, feeling as though the blood vessels in his eyes were about to burst.

"Do you wish to put in a call to this number?" he heard her asking him.

"No! No! No!" he gasped, eyes fastened to the slip as though he couldn't believe what he was reading. And then tried to modify it somewhat by mumbling half coherently, "Not just now—Later in the week—I'll be back…"

Horrified, he almost forgot to thank her, in the haste with which he took himself out of there.

Outside, he looked at it once more, before hurriedly stuffing it away out of sight in his clothing.

With the additions that had been made, it now stood:

"MacDonald, Wm....detective agency...372 Broadway..." and then a telephone number had been added.

"Well, you wanted to know," he told himself bitterly. "Now you do!"

11

Marjorie's news only added fuel to his already smoldering fears and disquietude, sent them sparking and flaming upward into full-fledged bonfire panic, like gasoline poured onto a bed of latent coals. News was too subdued, too casual a word for the tidings. Even to her, it was a dramatic crisis. To him it was a revelation of the direst import. He had the key to it, the explanation; she didn't.

He had unsuspectingly taken his usual short terminal walk down the sun-slanted russet-dyed sidewalk from bus-stop to their house. Up to that point, no warning. And then as he turned into the building, the first shock. Their flat-door wide open and a uniformed policeman loitering there. Not coming, not going, just standing there posted alongside it.

All the blood left Marshall's face and he could feel it puckering into a resemblance to a sucked-out lemon skin.

The policeman said to him: "You belong inside here?"

He couldn't muster breath to float the words from his mouth, but he nodded affirmatively.

The policeman took a little pity on his consternation. "Don't be frightened," he tried to reassure him. "Your wife'll tell you about it, she's in there now," and motioned him permission—or advice—to go ahead in without further delay.

Marjorie was standing there in their front room, talking

with an unknown man. He was writing something down (that recurrent little manual gesture that Marshall invariably hated so, dreaded so).

They both turned. "Here he is now," she said.

She ran over to him and held herself against him, as if seeking solace.

"What's happened? What's wrong?" he managed to get out. (Oh my God, is he here to arrest me? I can't get out past the door again, with that policeman by it. I shouldn't have walked in.)

"Somebody's been here," she said. "Somebody's been in here."

He didn't understand her for a minute. She realized that and repeated herself more clearly. "I mean, our flat was broken into. A burglar has been here. I went to the butcher about half-past three, to get some veal. I came back, and somebody had been in here while I was gone. I found it like this. Look at the way it looks."

Somebody had. It was obvious. It was not just her imagination, or a case of nerves. He could see that at a glance.

The front room was not too flagrantly disturbed. Even his practiced eye might have noted nothing amiss, but for her say-so and the presence of the stranger in it. One or two of the chairs were awry, that was about all.

"But wait'll you see the bedroom," she said. "That's a sight."

All the drawers were yawning out, almost to within tipping-over distance, from the bureau front. Their contents were stirred into a turmoil, and in several cases had fallen to the floor below. The clothes-closet door stood wide, and in there, too, several garments had slipped their hangers and lay in a muddled puddle below.

"You'll never know what went through me, when I first stepped in here and found this staring me in the face! I immediately phoned the police, and they sent this young man over."

A detective.

His feeling was that of being in the same small, cramped room with a shoulder-wide cobra, reared six feet or better on its tail and busily jotting a report in a notebook.

He had to choke back a yell of unadulterated horror when, in the course of his writing, the tip of the detective's tongue suddenly flicked out at the far corner of his mouth, then withdrew again.

"And the windows were all down, just as they are now?" he said to Marjorie.

"Yes, I can be positive of that, because I remember latching them all, the last thing, just before I left. There were some dark clouds over in the west, and I was afraid it might rain before I could get back. I'd just put up fresh curtains this morning."

"Then he, or they, got in by the front door. Either by using a skeleton key, or passing a strip of celluloid in through the doorseam."

"I never heard of that," she exclaimed wonderingly.

"It's something new they've got onto lately," the detective let her know grimly.

He readied his notebook once more, to take inventory. An inventory that proved barren.

"How about jewelry?"

She dropped her eyes momentarily. "I don't have any, except what I was wearing: my wedding ring and this little watch."

"Silver?"

"We only used this bone-handled set." She opened the lid of the chest to show him. "It's all in place. Nobody would want it anyway."

"How about money, then? Is that all accounted for?"

"I had my pocketbook with me under my arm. And Pres—Mr. Marshall doesn't get paid until Friday afternoon. Oh, wait—" she remembered suddenly, "I did have a dollar and a half in a baking-powder can in the kitchen. I let it accumulate in there to pay the milkman, at the end of the month. A dollar bill and a half-dollar piece!" She ran to look.

Marshall desperately wanted that money to be found missing. In order to prove this the bona fide burglary, that he was afraid in his heart it wasn't.

"They found it!" she called out alarmedly. "The lid's off the little can, and it's empty inside!"

They both hastened in there after her. Marshall's step was light; there was actually a smile of relief on his face, which he remembered to quench just in time.

"It was standing right here like thi— Wait a minute!" she cried sharply, and dipped down to the floor. "Here's the dollar bill, lying right under it, by my feet. The linoleum pattern blurred it."

"And here's your half-dollar piece," the sharp-eyed detective added, scooping up something that lay out before the stove.

"Why, they must have just turned it upside down and shaken it out to see what was in it, and then when the money fell out, didn't even bother picking it up!" She looked at the detective in amazement. "What were they after, anyway?"

Marshall's heart had gone down to his feet. He could have told them what they were after; *he* knew. But he didn't dare. Evidence against himself; documentary; papers of one sort or another. There was the proof of it right there; the disregarded money from inside that can. You didn't have to be a detective...

The real one acted fairly crestfallen, even resentful of the waste of time (and perhaps even of the opportunity to distinguish himself) that this expedition had turned out to be. "Well, I have to get back," he said somewhat brusquely. "If you can't report anything of value missing, Mrs. Marshall, then I'm afraid it becomes only a case of suspected illegal entry, and I doubt we can do anything much about that, since you didn't even actually see anyone in the place."

Marshall was glad to see the young plain-clothesman go. He even walked with him to the door to see him out (and chiefly to make sure the door was closed fast behind him once he *was* out).

Her disquietude ended with the realization that nothing was missing, nothing had been taken.

His only began there.

Nighttime was the usual time for burglaries. Why broad daylight? The answer was obvious. Because he himself wouldn't have been there in the daytime, would have been at night. *He* was the hindrance, not anyone else. His belongings were the objective.

And, now that he recalled, Wise hadn't been to the office that day. Had phoned in that he was ill.

What more was needed? It all hung together too beautifully.

With skin drawn tight over his cheekbones, and a feeling of rigidity to the walls of his diaphragm, he watched from the bedroom doorway while she moved about restoring it to its norm of orderliness.

She picked up a receipted gas company bill from the floor. Then a letter addressed to her from her father, of some time back, which she had been keeping.

"Wait a minute!" he said sharply, and strode forward. "You always had that in the original envelope it came in. I've seen it there several times. Now it's without an envelope."

"Here's the envelope, right here," she said soothingly,

picking something additional up. "They flew apart, I suppose, when it was tossed to the floor."

"It couldn't have come out of the envelope by itself," he insisted, almost palpitating with tension. "You don't open envelopes like other people, rip out the flap along the top. I've seen you too often. Look at this. You tear off a thin little sliver down the side, the short way." He tried to reintroduce the letter into the slotted envelope; it balked, warped. He had to shake the envelope, and pat the letter down into it with his fingers. "That was taken out deliberately, to be read over, find out what it said."

She gave a little laugh of complete incredulity. "What kind of burglars were those?" she demanded. "Taking time to read other people's mail!"

He knew what kind of burglar that—or they—had been. Not a burglar after money, after trinkets. A burglar after evidence.

A *police-agent* burglar.

Wise.

How ironical, he thought, to have had that young plain-clothesman here in the flat just now to investigate.

One detective trying to cancel out another's work, all unknowing.

12

Wise brought a camera to the office with him one day, at about this time. Marshall, ordinarily so alert to every nuance of potential danger, for once didn't think anything of it. It meant nothing to him. It was just a camera, and a camera was harmless. Knowledge of police methods, techniques and apparatuses used in the identification and apprehension of criminals was not very widespread among the public at large. And certainly a camera, to the average layman—and Marshall was still very much the average layman, in everything save conscience perhaps—bore in itself no intrinsic connotation of police processes. It was an idle-hour thing, a holiday thing, to be used at the beach, or on a picnic in the new Pierce-Arrow, or on the front porch steps on a Sunday afternoon en famille.

So he saw it, and remained unalarmed.

It stood there on Wise's desk all morning. It wasn't a Brownie box camera, it was one of the folding kind, an Eastman Kodak, one of the newer models.

The middle-of-the-day break came, and they all went to their lunches. Marshall left the office before Wise did. He didn't think a second time of him or of his camera. He went to his usual little tablecloth-restaurant lunching place, sat alone at his usual little table, ate his usual forty-five-cent "businessman's lunch," plus five cents for the waiter. Went back toward the office again. With time to spare, as was usual on other days as well.

It was a piercingly clear sun-gorged day. The sidewalk in front of the office building was flour white with hot-baked sunshine. People's shadows were India ink in intensity. He did now what he'd done many times before. Backed himself against the building wall and prepared to stand there and bask for the remainder of his leisure period, hands locked behind him, face tilted slightly upward to catch full effect of the benign solar rays. Some of the others did that too. To get the benefit of the sun in their faces they all had to stand facing the one way, outward to the street, and they did this. It was like an impromptu little line-up of three or four, strung along out there on the open sidewalk. Exchanging an occasional desultory remark (particularly at the passing of

some comely young woman) but otherwise not con-
versing overmuch. They had enough of one another all
day upstairs in the office.

Suddenly Wise appeared from somewhere, camera
expanded for usage and cradled within the bend of his
arm. Whether he had come out from inside the building
just then, or had come up to them from somewhere out
on the street, Marshall was not able to determine afterwards; he had not caught sight of him in time.

"I'd like to take a snapshot of you fellows," he offered.
"Shove in a little closer, so I can get you all in it together."

The others, nothing loath and smiling fatuously as
people usually do when an offer is made to photograph
them (for they think this implies they are considered
handsome), drew inward together shoulder to shoulder.
One smoothed back his hair, one corrected the knot of
his necktie, the third lifted one foot and surreptitiously
dusted off his shoecap by stroking it up and down against
the opposite leg of his trouser.

But Marshall, suddenly and belatedly, in that one
instant, knew full-fledged suspicion and wariness of the
camera. Of Wise's motive in using it gratuitously like this.
Where, until now, there had been none.

It's me he wants. He wants to get *my* picture. Wants to
get my face down on record. To send it off someplace,
maybe, for purposes of comparison and identification.

"Come on, Marshall; you too," said Wise, seeing that
he made no move to sidle toward the others.

"I'm not in it," he answered with sullen wariness, beginning to shift further over out of range.

"Sure you are. Why not?"

"Because I don't like…" He changed his mind about
saying that; it might lead their surmises too close to the
truth. He amended it to, "Because I take a poor picture."

"They're no raving beauties," Wise protested jovially.

"Why should yours come out any worse than theirs?"

Marshall had moved now, deliberately, so far wide of the rest that Wise could no longer possibly have encompassed him with the same lens. But yet as he looked he noted that (possibly because it was he that Wise was addressing and turned to at the moment) it was he that the camera was sighted toward and not the rest of them any longer.

This only inflamed his conviction. It's mine he wants! he told himself harassedly. Mine, and not theirs at all. Including them was just a blind. He'll mark an X over me, or run a circle around me, if he does take the whole group, and then send it on to—

"Cut it out!" he cried out almost savagely, and threw up his forearm protectively before his face, to ward off any impending snapshot.

"You're not afraid, are you?" somebody jeered.

What could he say then? "I'm not afraid. I just don't happen to want my picture taken. I'm not in the mood right now, that's all."

"All right, let him alone, I'll take the rest of you," Wise said, crestfallen.

Marshall, safely out of range, watched closely. He received a distinct impression that no exposure had been made, that Wise's thumb had not shunted the trigger at all, even though it had pretended to.

He turned, moved all around them in a wide circle, careful to pass behind Wise and camera, and started to go in the building entrance.

"Marshall," Wise called to him unexpectedly.

He turned his head inadvertently, unable to control himself in time. Wise was holding the camera up, and in that instant took the snapshot.

"Thanks," Wise said drily. "Got you that time."

A laugh went up at Marshall's expense. His first impulse

was to stride back, wrest the camera away from Wise, and trample it. He checked himself. Too drastic, too self-incriminating. Then they would surely fathom that he had graver reasons than just an unsociable mood for not wanting his picture taken.

He started again to enter the building, but was thoroughly frightened now. At the elevator he turned and watched for Wise. Had the latter remained outside for any length of time—such as would have been required to step around to some nearby drugstore to leave the film for developing—he almost certainly would have gone outside again, followed him, and perhaps made some desperate, last-minute attempt to impede or thwart him. Though what form it could have taken, he had not the slightest idea. But Wise—and the others—came in at his heels, so he could feel sure the roll was still in the camera, if nothing else.

They all went up in the elevator together. Wise now tried to make amends (probably for the reason that obvious discomfiture was still to be read all over Marshall's face). "I didn't really take your picture just now, Marsh," he said placatingly. "I was just kidding."

He's lying, Marshall told himself. He wants to throw me off guard. Showing that it's even of more importance to him not to have me think he's taken it (now that he has), until it has been processed and he can get a confirmation on the basis of it.

Wise replaced the camera on his desk where it had been all morning, and everyone went back to his work.

Marshall couldn't keep his eyes off it. Under their concealing lids they surreptitiously went to it again and again. His undoing, his destruction, he told himself, was lurking at this very moment in that harmless-looking slablike oblong box, so near at hand.

He mustn't carry that out of here with him this evening! He mustn't be allowed to take it beyond my reach, while it's got what it has in it! Once he does, I'm lost. But how? How?

Near three, Wise was suddenly called inside to Ponds' private office for something. The camera stayed there where it was.

Marshall was on his feet even before the closing of the intervening door had been completed.

He unobstrusively caught up the camera en route, while passing by, and took it with him over to the sun-slopped window sill.

There, with his back screening what he was doing from the others in the room, he opened the lid, expanded the shutter, as if he were about to take a picture of the emptiness outside the open window.

He peered down into the little red-glassed indicator slit. The numeral 5 was standing there. Meaning either (he could not be sure) that Wise had so far taken four shots and moved the film onward into position for the fifth ahead of time, or already taken all five and left the film in its last position.

He put his thumb to the lever, pushed it down, held it there as for a time-exposure, letting the sun go boiling in through the open lens, blanching the exposed film to a useless milky white.

Then he went back, and did it to 4, and 3, and 2, and 1. Finally, lest he be taken unaware again and Wise make another attempt at snapping him without his knowledge, he brought the film all the way forward to 6 and exposed that too. That was all there were on any commercial film roll, he knew; six exposures.

Then he closed the camera once more, took it back to the desk, replaced it there.

Pandora's box had been rendered harmless; it could be opened now and nothing would come out.

"He sure wanted that badly," he smiled to himself with grim satisfaction. "But not half as badly as I didn't want him to have it."

13

On Friday, that was two days before, that was the 20th. Wise was leaving for the day, around five. He'd just gone past Marshall's desk, without even an acknowledgment of departure. As though he didn't even see him there at all. Then suddenly, with hand already to knob, with door already open, with face already out the door, he halted, he drew his face back into view, turned it, said as if by haphazard afterthought:

"Say, do you like rowing, Marshall?"

Why did he wait until he was nearly through the door to ask me that? Why didn't he ask me sooner, when he passed my desk just a second ago? That was too premeditatedly unpremeditated. Too elaborately deferred, to be innocent. Why did he single me out to ask, why didn't he ask any of the others?

"Hunh?"

"I said, do you like rowing?"

"Rowing?"

If I say yes? If I say no? More time.

Wise was pleasantly impatient by this time. "I'm only trying to find out if you'd like to get out in a boat and take turns at the oars."

"Why do you ask?" Marshall parried.

"I'm looking for someone to go along with me Sunday."

No. Wants to get me alone. Say no.

"I don't know about Sunday." He shook his head pensively. "I don't think so." He shook his head again, finally attained the definitive refusal he'd set for himself. "No." And then he stared at Wise searchingly and said: "What about some of the others?"

"Already asked them. Can't get anyone."

Too thin. If he did, I didn't hear him.

Wise shrugged. "Okay, forget it. I'll go alone, then."

The back of Wise's head and the back of Wise's heel disappeared from the door slit.

Will he, though? Will he really go alone?

Someone else passed, on his way out.

" 'Night, Marsh."

"Say, Horton, did Wise ask you to go rowing with him Sunday?"

"Not that I recall."

Still someone else passed.

"See you Monday, Marsh."

"Rogers, did Wise ask you to go rowing with him Sunday?"

"If he did, I didn't hear him."

Two out of two. I'll try one more.

"Blaine, did Wise say anything to you about going rowing Sunday?"

"Yes."

Marshall sighed deeply.

"What'd you tell him, no?"

The answer he got was catastrophic. "Oh, he wasn't asking *me*. He knows I couldn't anyway, May's laid up with a bad ankle. What he said was, that he wondered if he could get *you* to go along with him."

Me. That shows. Even speaking to someone else, it was me, and no one but me, he had on his mind for it.

Will he go alone, though? Will he really go alone?

He may. And yet not be as alone as he seems...

14

And yet not be as alone as he seems.

"Help you, sir?" the sporting-goods shopkeeper inquired.

"Just looking. If I see anything, I'll let you know." And then he added, "Just forget I'm in here. I don't like to be hurried."

He looked at woolen lumberman's shirts, heavy, plaided, scarlet and blue. He looked at portable camp stoves. He looked at tin eating kits. He looked at—

He spoke again. He'd taken the long way around, down one aisle, and around, and then back along the other, instead of going straight across to it. "How much is this?"

"That's a hatchet for chopping kindling. Best there is."

"I know what it is. I asked you how much it was."

Then when the storekeeper had told him, "As much as that? I didn't know they came that high."

He put it down and strolled on, seeming to have lost interest in it. The storekeeper, however, having detected at least a spark of interest, if nothing more, assiduously fanned it for all he was worth to keep it from going out. It was the only one there had been so far.

"Wait a minute, let me show it to you. Just look at the cutting edge on it. Made of the best steel." He picked it up and followed him with it, to present it to close view once more. "They come in mighty handy, if you're ever on a camping trip—"

"I know they do. But that isn't really what I came in here—"

"Look, you shouldn't be without one of these. Do you do much camping…?"

When he came out of there finally, he'd bought—or rather, been sold—a hatchet. For chopping kindling.

15

Two hours later he'd reappeared there again. The hatchet still made the curious, flat, wedge-shaped parcel the storekeeper had bundled it into, with the aid of thick brown wrapping paper. The string hadn't even been taken off it.

Step two. Now to get what I really had in mind the first time.

The storekeeper lost a modicum of his affability.

"No, I can't return you the money on it.…I see that, I see that. It's not a question of whether it's even been unwrapped yet or not. It's sold, and once it's sold, it's sold."

They argued about it at desultory length, and without too great heat, as two men who are perfectly well aware that in the end they are going to compromise, but don't wish to weaken their bargaining positions by being in too great a hurry.

"No, I'm not asking you to lose money on it.…I can give you a credit against the purchase of something else, that's the best I can do for you. You see anything you like, you let me know."

Then he tried to help him along, by suggesting things that were priced a good deal higher than the original hatchet, so that their selection would amount in reality to a second sale over and above the first, rather than just an exchange.

"How about some fishing tackle?"

"I never fish."

"Do you do any hunting?"

"Now and then. Not too often."

"Could you use one of these?" The shopkeeper was offering it to him cradled lengthwise in his arms. "This is a beauty."

Marshall looked at it in surprise, as though it were the last thing he'd had in mind just then. "Well, but—"

"Go ahead, hold it a minute," the storekeeper said with treacherous persuasion. All men are attracted to such objects, drawn to them, can't resist fondling them if given the opportunity. "Just get the feel of it. Run your hands over it."

When he came out of there for the second and last time, the package he bore was much longer and thinner. But he wasn't a man who had bought a gun. He was a man who had had a gun forced on him, very much against his will, by a glib and crafty storekeeper.

Technique.

16

Slowly it got light. Never so slowly before. Never since the prehistoric gloom. Never since the first man waited, in the dim dawn of time, beside the first pool, to kill his first quarry—the first quarry who was of his own kind.

The lake surface, seen flat from this tree-shrouded height, went up the chromatic scale, passing from indigo through deep blue, through azure, through ultramarine, to the silvery sheen of broad daylight at last. No color at all, just the brightness of a mirror that borrows its reflections.

He never moved. Perfect repose. Utter inanimation. The waiter. The wait. In the cool, the shady place, up there, high above the lake. Only breathing, nothing else. Breathing, that necessity for survival. Waiting, that necessity for survival. Lying hidden, that necessity for survival. Everything he did—that necessity for survival. Survival, that alternate of death. Death, that alternate of survival.

He waited prone, belly to ground, lying on a mattress of broken-off fir and evergreen branches, a screen of them even before his face, with just two eyes to peer out through them. Two eyes, and later, death, when the time came. Death, lying beside him now, and later, death, when the time came. Death, lying beside him now, its burnished brightness marred by lampblack, so that no errant gleam of sun could strike it when at last it moved and reared and peered forth.

Down there below, on the opposite shore, two men came down the path to the water's edge together. Men the size of clothespins. One of them unlocked the boathouse door on the landward side, and they both went in and disappeared for awhile. Then the bigger double door on the lake side swung open into its two halves, and they were folded back out of the way. Then they came out to the end of the little pier carrying a rowboat between them. They let it down into the water, and carelessly slung a rope over one of the pier pilings to hold it. Then they brought out a second, then a third.

The waiter waited. The watcher watched. Only breathing, nothing else.

They were in and out, now, all the time, in desultory activity; sometimes one was out while the other was within, sometimes both were inside at once. One got down into one of the moored boats and tinkered with it for a long time, then climbed up again and went inside.

Death took nourishment. Under the branches, one hand moved slowly, down along his own person. He fumbled, took out a chocolate bar. He gnawed at it, keeping half the wrapper turned downward about it, like a cuff, in order to maintain a place for his fingers to hold onto it. When it was gone and only the empty cuff was left, he even finished up the crumbs that were left along the seams of his palms, dredging them up with the tip of his tongue like an anteater.

Then he dug a small hole beside him, with just two fingers, and buried the small banded wrapper of glossy paper and the inner wrapper of tinfoil, and covered them over.

Death of a chocolate bar. Death and burial of a chocolate bar. Death of a man? What was the difference? Death was death, always death.

A man was coming down the path alone, toward the boat-house. He was clothespin-sized, but his shape was the shape of Wise. His walk was the walk of Wise. His dark-blue suit was the dark-blue suit that Wise wore, and the flat straw boater on his head was the flat straw boater that Wise wore. He held a small square basket in one hand, with a handle-grip, such as might have been used to carry a lunch in. And under that same arm, pressed to his side, was an even smaller, flat shape that Marshall made out to be a book.

The watcher never moved. He only breathed; more quickly, but he only breathed, stirring the pine needles a little before his shrouded nose.

Wise went into the boathouse. Then he came out onto the pier with the other two men. They stood around for a few moments, in friendly, desultory fashion, looking now at the lake, now at the sky, now at the boats, nodding a little (he could see them nod).

Then Wise handed something to one of the boatmen.

The boatman put it away, handed him something back. Wise lowered his basket into one of the boats. Then he dropped his book down atop it. Then he clambered down into it himself, a little ungracefully but sturdily, just as Wise *would* have done such a thing.

He stood in it for awhile and stripped off his coat, and folded it lining-out, and placed it over by the basket. His hat he left on, perhaps out of regard for the sun; not the sun as it was now, but the sun as it would be later.

Then he loosed the boat and sat down to his oars. The two men, after watching his dexterity for a moment or two, went back inside the boathouse, one of them speeding him with a half-wave of the arm, as if bidding him to enjoy himself.

He was alone now on the lake, on all that silvery-gilt water. He rowed with the air of a man who enjoys rowing, with a long leisurely pull, lithely, without knots, without strain. And though he was far away, you could almost hear him exhale with deep satisfaction each time, as he rested at the moment of equipoise before starting his oars over and back to him again. A man rowing, not to get anywhere, but for the sake of rowing itself.

He stopped presently to undo and detach his necktie, place it with his coat. Then he opened his collar and stripped his sleeves up over his elbows. Then with renewed relish went back to his oars again.

A second boat was venturing out into the lake by this time, a young couple in it, she with sunshade held aloft. Then presently a third, this one with a man with his small boy in it. Then more.

Soon it was as though an ever-advancing flotilla were striking out from shore, fan-shaped, point foremost, but with the lead boat, the first one, still maintaining its distance. The fan-wise tracks they left on the glasslike surface of the water (which was being disturbed for the first time that day) heightened the impression of their number, made it seem greater than it was. There were in reality no more than half a dozen.

The phalanx formation was soon broken up, once the original impetus out from shoreline had been accomplished, and some of them just lolled about where they were, and others strayed off on circular courses of their own (perhaps because the rowers used more strength with one arm than the other) that got them nowhere. Only the lead boat kept going resolutely, clear across the lake to the far side, as if seeking privacy from its fellows.

The water was now like fluid brass with the rapidly mounting sun. It cast a phosphorescent yellow gleam even on the trunks of the firs and spruces that ventured down the steeply inclined slopes too close to it, and moved illusionary viscous disks about on the undersides of their overhanging shoots and branches.

The gemmed oars of the lead boat had stopped flashing by this time; its occupant had banked and rested them. He took up the book he had brought with him, reclined in the bottom of the boat so that his shoulder blades rested against the plank seat at one end of it, his heels were cocked against the one at the other. Concavely arched like that, only both extremities of his person were visible above the gunwale, even when looked down on from a considerable height as he was now; his head and shoulders at the prow, his feet and crossed ankles at the stern. In-between, he disappeared.

He held the book standing open on his chest, and leaning over somewhat downward, so that his eyes could properly focus on it without his having to raise his head; his hat, at the same time, he tipped far forward, almost to the bridge of his nose, to keep the sun out of his eyes.

The boat drifted gently and at random, whichever way the water willed it.

A promontory, running down from the height where death watched, its backbone fuzzy with the tips of little firs, thrust far out into the water, nearly across to the other shore. This in reality made two lakes instead of one, with just a slender channel to join them. On the one side of it was the large, main part of the lake, now dotted with all these boats; on the other, just a little basin, far more circumscribed, private, secluded, screened from view by the aforementioned spit or promontory. At the moment it was empty of life. And yet the *pull* of the water, apparently, was from the larger body, in through the needlelike channel, to this smaller lagoon. A tiered falls at one end might have had something to do with it. For the untended boat, slowly coasting the intervening peninsula, was being effortlessly but surely drawn toward the connecting strait.

Death just watched and waited, in position to command both sides at once. For on the one hand there were the many boats, and on the other there were none. None to give succor or to bear witness.

The prow slowly turned in toward the restricted little channel, and for a few moments, even from where death watched, it was as though the boat had been swallowed up, or had beached itself and gone underground. Then presently it began to peer forth on the other side, where solitude was, and then came out full-length, and floated there, cut off and alone.

If the reader noticed, he made no move to correct its course. It was perhaps better for reading here, away from all the others. It was also better for dying.

And now a new branch springs erect among the other branches, a branch that wasn't there before. A branch without leaf, without sap, without bend. Black, and foundry-hard, and with a little round malignant mouth at the end; and its flowering will be death.

The little boat floated nearer and nearer, resting bottom-to-bottom on another little boat etched in glass. The reader read. The black branch hung steady on the air.

Death cleared his throat a little, down low behind the gun sight, to be more comfortable. A very little sound it was, almost a cozy, disarming sound.

The little boat floated nearer, nearer still. The black branch traced it down the surface of the lake, like a surveyor's instrument, but shifting so very slowly it could not be seen to move at all.

Detonation.

Death's eyes shuttered and opened, and his head jerked back a little, making a blurred double outline for an instant instead of a single clear one.

The screening branches danced a little. And paled in smoke, and darkened again. The report seemed to come from the opposite slope. It was as though only the echo had sounded from here, the original had been over there.

In the boat no commotion, no violent jar, no dramatic alteration. Scarcely a sign of anything having happened. The occupant made a lazy half-turn over to the gunwale. Instead of reading a book, he was now peering down into the water alongside, as though trying to make out something at myopic range. One arm hung over beside his head and trailed in the water. The book had fallen in and slowly thinned into submersion, as though it were having the color gradually washed out of it. His hat had also fallen in, but that remained afloat, like a ribbon-banded lily pad. The boat continued placidly to drift.

Death got up and ran, bent low, head down, gun parallel to ground, but agile and swift, as death always is, cleverly lacing in and out among the shadowy tree trunks to quick-gained enshrouding disappearance.

17

The opening sweep of the office door, next morning, seemed to sweep all the blood from his face with it as though it were linked by some drainage tube to his own veins.

He was left with a paper face. Paper-white. Paper-stiff.

A dark-blue suit just like Wise wore. Stiff straw boater just like Wise wore. Wise wearing them.

"Hello, Marshall," Wise saluted him carelessly, striding by.

Marshall didn't answer. Paper doesn't. Paper can't.

"You don't look good," Marshall heard him say, from somewhere behind him now. "Why don't you get out more on Sundays? I told you to come with me yesterday. Didn't go rowing after all, though. Fellow talked me into trying my hand at golf with him, instead."

18

He was still in the act of hoisting hat to hook when her arms closed about him from behind, across shoulders.

She was overjoyed about something, that was obvious.

"What's the excitement?" he said amiably. He could sense that it was a benign one, nothing to cause him alarm, so he was untroubled by it.

"I have a surprise for you."

"What?"

But instead of telling him, she tested his face, stroking two fingers along it. "I want you to shave before you do another thing."

"Shave?" he said. "Now?"

She gave him a little forward push between the shoulders. "Right now."

On the bed, in the bedroom, he made a discovery. "Hey," he said. "That's my *other* suit."

"I know that, mister," she called in to him pertly. "You just climb right into it."

He came back to the doorway to ask her: "What's it all about?"

She clasped her hands together, almost in a form of benediction. "We've got an invitation!"

Mrs. Bennett, on the top floor, he thought patronizingly.

"Mrs. Bennett, on the top floor," he said patronizingly.

"That's no invitation," she said, tilting her nose, "living right in the same house with us. I mean a real invitation. From *outside*. To go *out*. You finish up in there. You'll hear all about it when you come out."

When he had, and had sat down to the table with her, he suggested patiently, "Now would you mind telling me?"

"Can't you guess?" she said happily.

"No," he said forebearingly. "If I could then I wouldn't be asking you."

"Your friend, Wise, at the office. We're invited over to his house. For the evening. For an evening of bridge."

A crust of bread was suddenly arrested midway down his throat. He finally dislodged it with a cough and a swallow of water.

"Well, it's all right to look surprised," she remonstrated. "But you don't have to look so stunned about it."

"*He* invited us over?" he said faintly.

"He didn't. She did."

"*She?*"

"His wife. Mrs. Wise. You act as though you didn't know he had a wife at all."

I didn't until now, he thought. And I'm still not sure he has.

Some policewoman, maybe, that's been assigned to work with him on it. On *me*.

She'd already jumped up from the table, meanwhile, after having touched scarcely a thing. "It's much more fun to eat at somebody else's house. And it's so long since I've done that. I'm going to start getting ready. I want to look my very best. Stay where you are….No, no dishes tonight." She'd gone on into the bedroom.

He took out a cigarette, forgot to light it. Kept it thrust under his over lip, like a thermometer taking the temperature of his thoughts.

I've got to get out of this. I'm not going there. I can't go there. It's like going to a—it's like walking into a police precinct house of your own accord and giving yourself up. It's like standing in the line-up for three solid hours. Only, with a bridge lamp pouring its light on me instead of a row of footlights.

She was twittering like a bird on the first day of spring in there, behind him. She was talking out of sheer happiness.

"It's so long since I've played. Press, when was the last time *you* played bridge?"

He tried to remember. "Before our marriage, I guess. At your house, wasn't it?"

"You sound so doleful about it. It's supposed to be fun. Oh well, the game is just the excuse, anyway."

You bet it is, he interjected bitterly. You bet!

"It's the chatting around the table, the little sandwiches afterwards, the 'Now you must come over and see

us' as you're leaving, the waving from the door." She
ended with a deep sigh, the sound of which carried even
to where he was.

Starved for sociability. Tired of loneliness, of exile.
When there's no fear, you love the company of your
fellow men and women. When there's no guilt, you seek
them out.

When there is...

She came bustling in, ready now, hands out before
her, adjusting something at her pulse. "I should have had
a new pair of gloves. Do I look all right? How's my hair?"

He shaded his eyes with his hand and looked down at
the table.

"I'm not going. I—call them up and tell them we can't
make it. Give them some excuse. Say I'm not well. Or
wait—I'll call them for you." He got out of his chair.

Her face was pitiful. All the animation had died. She
had turned white with disappointment. With a stronger
emotion than that, even; utter disheartenment, futility,
surrender before some mysterious inevitable, that she
couldn't fathom but that she couldn't escape either.

"They'll never ask us again," she said almost inaudibly.
"It was our one chance. To start making friends, to..."
Her eyes were on him in a supplication that was almost
haunting. He'd never seen an expression like that in
them before.

He was already at the phone. "Central, give me..."

She stood there a moment at his shoulder. "Press," he
heard her whisper, "don't do this to me." And then she
did an odd little thing; she let her hand stray in a tender,
sketchy way up the side of his arm, from above the elbow
to a little short of the shoulder and no higher. Somehow
he sensed its meaning perfectly, he was always so good
that way with her; it was not a bribe, a caress to induce
him to relent. It was quite the opposite, it was a little

gesture of forgiveness, ahead of time, for what she knew he was going to do anyway, for what she knew she couldn't dissuade him from doing. Then without another word she went on into their bedroom, and without latching the door entirely, allowed it to drift semiclosed after her.

A man's voice, Wise's voice, was suddenly sounding aggressively in his ear. "Hello? Hello? Who's there?"

"Is this you, Wise?" he said. "Just a minute."

He left the ear-piece dangling at the end of its cord, and went to the bedroom door, and widened it.

She was lying across the bed, face down. She sensed that he was looking at her, although he'd made no sound. She quickly raised her head.

"I'm not crying, Press," she quickly comforted him. "I'm not crying, really I'm not. Just—resting here a minute or two. I'll be out shortly and finish up those dishes."

He knew, though he couldn't see them from where he stood, that it was true, that her eyes were dry.

But the tears that never reach the eye at all, he thought sorrowingly, are the bitterest tears of all.

He knew a little braveness, then, for one of the few times in his life. Some men know a lot, and some men know very little; but when it comes to those who knew it very seldom, perhaps it's even a braver braveness than when it comes to those who know it often.

He turned without a word and went back to the phone.

"Wise," he said. "This is Marshall. I just wanted to tell you that we're leaving now, we'll be at your house in about half an hour."

19

They rang the bell, and then side by side they both went through a brief flurry of harried, last-minute fidgetings and adjustments, highly similar in performance, but each stemming from a totally different incentive. For her concern was for her appearance, but his was for his personal safety. Thus he worried at the knot of his necktie, and pulled and plucked at the cuffs of his shirt, and reshaped the fit of his coat collar across the back of his neck. Thus she loosened her hair in this place, tightened it in the next; drew her fingers across the top of her envelope-handbag, as if to shape it more concisely; fluffed at the frill that hung from the neck of her dress, to have it fall more fully spread out.

"Ring again," she said after an unendurable moment. Unendurable to him, at any rate.

Before he could discover whether or not he had enough courage to (and he felt that he didn't), it had become unnecessary. A woman of approximately forty-eight to fifty stood there, smiling welcome to them. She was fairly small in body, and considerably shorter than Marjorie in height. Her eyes were light, and though they were kindly and cordial at the moment, there was an impression of experienced wisdom in the configuration of lines about them, that did nothing to reassure him or make him think he had jumped to the wrong conclusion.

She's some sort of policewoman, he repeated to himself; she's never his wife.

Her hair was a mixture of pale gold and silver; the gold having evidently been a partially artificial assistance that had been discontinued for some time past now, but was not yet entirely effaced by the encroaching silver. She wore a dress of peach chiffon, with a string of pearls about her throat. She was totally lacking in that softness and fineness that were Marjorie's whole aura. Her movements were brisk, almost spasmodic. Too much so. The briskness of one who follows instructions in every move she makes, and need never falter, has them committed too well to heart ever to be in doubt as to what is expected of her. It was like standing too close to someone giving a performance on a stage, without yourself being in the play; being right up on the stage beside them, so that all illusion was lost, and every artifice stood out with unnatural, with magnified, clarity.

"Well!" she said too loudly. "Well! So here you are! Glad to see you! Come right in. We've been waiting for you!" And sought for, and lifted, and wrung Marjorie's hand. Too vigorously, too enthusiastically. "I'm Jeanette Wise."

"This is my husband," Marjorie said demurely. Her voice, he thought, was like a chiffon whisper after the other's ringing tones.

Mrs. Wise's look at him was too prolonged. He seemed to feel it across his whole face, like the slow tingling impact left by a slap. "Oh, I know all about him!" she said strenuously. Her eyes never left him. "From Bill," she added.

I don't doubt that, he concurred inwardly, with a sinking feeling.

"Well, come on in! Don't stand out here like strangers," she admonished. She slung her arm about Marjorie's opposite shoulder, marched her forward in advance of him.

He wanted to reach out and pull it off, from behind. What others had it rested on like that, he wondered; what shoplifters, and disorderly drunken women, and even worse? And the girl who had once entered the most restricted drawing rooms in New York, as an intimate and an habituée, was now going into this place, with that on her shoulder. Thanks to him.

Wise came forward.

"This is his wife, dear," Mrs. Wise said.

Even that minute turn of speech was detected by Marshall. She hadn't said "Mrs. Marshall" or "Mr. Marshall's wife." "His" wife. A pronoun like that was used when the noun it referred to was so well understood by both parties it needn't be repeated; when it had been recently and thoroughly the subject of discussion between the two of them. And this, you might say, was an involuntary continuation of the discussion, a postscript to it.

Last-minute instructions, last-minute outlining of strategy; and then: "This is his wife, dear."

Wise was considerate and cordial to Marjorie; scrutinized Marshall a little searchingly, Marshall thought. It might have been no more than the thought: Higher-class than you are. How did you happen to get her?

Marshall preferred to translate it: How much does she know about you? How much have you told her?

They shook hands a trifle restrainedly.

There was no one else there. There was to be no one else there. That soon became apparent. A bridge table had been set up, with four chairs about it. On it a deck of cards, a pencil, a score card.

Marjorie and Mrs. Wise had gone into a bedroom. They returned now, Marjorie without hat and gloves.

"Well, anyway, you found your way all right," Mrs. Wise proclaimed. "We didn't have to send out a patrol car."

Marshall's symbol of thought was a stunned exclamation point.

They had gone past that point, conversationally, by the time he recovered.

"—I said, 'Now Mr. Wise, now that I'm here I'm not going to live like a hermit, just you make up your mind to that.' (They love to keep you in solitary, these men.)—"

Why does her mind unconsciously run to illustrations like that? Notice?

"—So the first thing he said was, 'Why don't you ring up Mr. and Mrs. Marshall, have them over?'"

What more do I need? The first name he suggested to her. The *only* name he suggested to her.

"And, here you are," said Mrs. Wise brightly. "Shall we play a few rounds?"

They shifted over toward the table.

"You sit here, dear," their hostess said, tapping the back of one of the chairs. "And you can sit here, Mr. Marshall."

"No, let him sit here," Wise countermanded suddenly, "and I'll sit there."

Marshall studied the new position warily. With the lamp bearing straight down on me like a cone light, he thought. He's placed it right behind that second chair, notice?

But the two women had already settled themselves, and Wise himself preempted the third chair before he could get within sufficient reach of it, so he was forced into the position in spite of himself.

He turned his face slightly aside, grimaced.

"That light bother you?" Mrs. Wise asked. "Move it back a little, hon."

"We need it for the business at hand," answered Wise obdurately, and refrained from putting a hand to it.

"We'll cut for the deal," he added.

Marshall got the high card. He shuffled with a good deal of nervous trepidation, the tension he was experiencing expressing itself in that way: with shaking, over-active fingers.

But he had no sooner begun dispensing, than they stopped him again.

"To the left," corrected Mrs. Wise with a toothy smile. "Always to the left."

"You'll have to forgive Press, he's a little rusty," Marjorie apologized.

Wise turned his eyes on him. "Maybe he has something on his mind."

Why did he look at me like that just then? Always these double meanings, that he knows I alone get, and that he wants to make sure I get.

He completed the deal, he made his bid, the hand was played.

Another began.

His hands were so unsteady he fumbled, trying to assemble his cards.

"You dropped a card," said Mrs. Wise charitably. He bent to retrieve it, and the fan-shaped assortment in his hand tilted down as he did so.

"Don't let him see your hand," his partner quickly warned him.

Wise smiled with cold superiority. "*He* can't cover up. I'm on to him. He has no secrets from me."

Marshall shuddered momentarily. There went that look again. Why does he keep sending me that? Like a cat playing with a mouse.

"Dear, you're perspiring," said Marjorie compassionately, a moment or two later. "Don't take it that seriously." She reached up and dabbed at his forehead with her handkerchief.

No remark from Wise, for once. But he fairly cringed, waiting for it to come. Expecting it and not hearing it was almost worse than hearing it. When he stole a look, though, there was a tiny triangle of smile at the corner of

Wise's mouth, with Wise's protruding tongue-tip nestled in the middle of it.

"Why didn't you come back to me?" complained Mrs. Wise within the next few moments, after they'd lost another of the numberless tricks that kept going their opponents' way.

It was Wise who answered for him. "I had him worried. I've had him worried all night long." And his brows arched and his eyelids closed.

It was so ghastly appropriate that Marshall flattened his cards face-down against the tabletop, and just held them that way, with his hand pressed on them, for a long moment. As though he were trying to grind them into the table. What he was trying to do was get his breath to fluctuate evenly once more. He kept his eyes on the white scars that were showing over his knuckles.

How much longer can I stand this? Why don't I tilt the whole table over into his face, and spring up for the door? When every nerve in my body wants to so.

Marjorie, sitting there. I can't. I can't make her a hostage to fortune.

She saw him looking at her, and she smiled privately to him. As if to say, even though I play against you, I'm on your side. I'm on your side still.

But the game, he pleaded to her unheard, isn't cards. It's another game that's going on. A game that you don't know about.

Another round was dealt, and cards were sorted.

"Police!" shrieked Mrs. Wise comfortably, at sight of something within her hand.

"Don't call on them in this house," her husband admonished her with a good-natured chuckle.

It was as though they had some private joke between them.

"Why?" she retorted depreciatingly. "Are *you* afraid of them?"

Wise returned the innuendo.

"No," he murmured. "Are *you?*"

"Pretty late to be asking me that, don't you think?" she said almost sotto voce, to the accompaniment of a sly smile.

Wise cleared his throat warningly. As if to say, You've gone far enough now. Don't go any further than that.

Marshall got the nuance perfectly. They're of the police; and therein lies their little joke: Are you afraid of them? No, are *you?*

If I could only get out of this room. If I could only get out of this room.

He kept manipulating his bid each time, to try to force the play into his partner's hand; so that, conversely, he could free himself of table duty. Make his escape. No matter what she said, he doubled, tripled, quadrupled it, even when there wasn't a card in his hand to substantiate it. But Wise, almost as though he guessed his intent, and had set out with equal deliberation to hold him where he was, would stubbornly go him one better each time. Then his wife, losing courage, would drop the bid at last, and Marshall would be kept pinned down there where he was.

But then at last, as is likely to occur during almost any game, the cards suddenly descended with such freakish unevenness, that almost the whole of an entire suit was divided between himself and Mrs. Wise. And fortune was with him, for the original bid became hers, not his, due to the formation in which they sat playing.

He held his breath, waiting to see what Wise would do, after the bid had gone up to five.

"All right, take it," he said pettishly at last, after a long frowning moment.

And then, before Marshall could draw the first full

breath of anticipatory freedom, Wise suddenly nodded toward Marjorie. "Your play."

"No, yours," said Marshall quickly. He could feel his face paling in spite of himself, as if this were the most momentous thing in the world, instead of a trifling card-table regulation. To him it was, it had become so by now. "It was Mrs. Wise's original bid, I only seconded her."

"Oh, no it wasn't," said Wise with a vigorous shake of the head. "It was your original bid. You play, and she lays down her hand."

He was not only aggressive, he was almost threatening about it, Marshall thought. As if to say, I'm on to you. You'll stay here pat, or I'll know the reason why. Even if I have to falsify the progression of the game.

Marjorie suddenly spoke, in that soft, even voice of hers. "Mrs. Wise made the original bid. I heard her."

He didn't wait for any more than that. With a ripple, his assisting cards were suddenly strewn along the table face up and he was already on his feet, and his chair was back.

"Excuse me a minute," he said. "Guess I'll stretch my legs."

He turned and began to stroll casually away from the table, toward an open doorway he had had his eye on for some time past, that presumably led into a bedroom beyond. He felt weak from the long nervous strain he had just been subjected to. His backbone felt limp, as though it were a column of twisted rags. If I can only get in there for a moment, out of sight, away from his eyes; I'll be able to pull myself together. Not too fast, now; don't walk too fast...

"Murder!" ejaculated Mrs. Wise sharply, having just finished appraising the magnificent secondary hand he had left behind for her.

"Yeah," observed Wise glumly. "And there goes the

murderer." And he pitched his thumb over his shoulder in Marshall's direction.

Marshall stumbled slightly over the projecting foot of a chair in his path, and to maintain himself had to bend acutely for a second and lean upon the chair-arm.

Then he straightened, moved on into the adjoining room at a rusty, recalcitrant gait. The kindly partition was between him and them like a protective shield.

It was a twilight-dim bedroom, all in pearly gray tones. On one wall the opening behind him cast an illusory panel of pallid, straw-colored light. Within this, in purplish-gray, was a silhouette of Wise, profile-wards, as he sat there at the bridge table outside. It wavered a little about the edges occasionally. At other times it was steel sharp in outline. Every so often a monstrous, swollen sausage of a hand would loom up before him, deposit something on the table or reclaim something. Something that looked like a slab or a tile, though it was in actuality a playing card. Sometimes the silhouette would become satanic, and a tangled mass of thin snakes would issue from its mouth and nostrils and writhe upward to the top margin of the panel. Skeins of cigar smoke.

Marshall leaned across the beveled edge of a bureau in there, pressing against it as though he were using it to hold in his stomach, and he could feel a drop or two of moisture slowly part from his downturned forehead and fall off.

Their voices were as close as ever, sounded almost at his shoulder.

Marjorie's winning little laugh. "I thought you were holding that up your sleeve!"

And Mrs. Wise: "Does he know where to find the light? Tell him where the switch is, Bill."

Wise called in: "Need any light in there? Want me

to show you? It's right behind the door, as you go in."

"I've found it," he called back. They were helping him in what he intended doing. The illusory panel vanished from the wall as the light went on. But at least it would have warned him of Wise's approach; now he had no safeguard at all.

He put up his hand, gave the back of his head a couple of quick cuffs at a tangent, that started the hair awry.

I was looking for his comb, in case he comes in on me, he instructed himself.

He noiselessly slipped open one of the top drawers of the bureau, and it was lying there, in the first one he opened. He moved it, deposited it out of sight under the lining paper.

The accompanying brush to it. Handkerchiefs. Collars. A pair of suspenders, with the elastic worn threadbare. A buttonhook.

He stealthily closed it again. He opened the one below. Hers. Closed that again. He opened the one on the opposite side.

"Take your hands off that!" Mrs. Wise commanded with sudden sharpness. "That's mine!"

And Marshall jumped, and buckled, and died a little; but it was the cards she was talking about, in there.

The hand must be nearly over. They'd be through soon; he'd have to hurry.

A paper or two, written matter, in this one. Not much, but this was more like it, this was what he'd been hoping for. A celluloid pocket calendar, compliments of one of the local merchants. A Chinese laundry ticket, beetling ideographs inked on it. A rough draft of an expense account, left incomplete, penciled columnarly on the back of an envelope:

> 1 month's rental, furnished flat .... $35.
> meals, @ $1.50 per day .... 45.
> laundry, barber, and other supplies .... 2.
> telegram to N. Y. 0.40

That last item caught his eye, showed him it was no harmless household expense account. Showed him Wise was not working for this office, here, as he pretended to be, but for someone or something in New York.

A picture postcard, sent from somewhere called Sharon Springs, from someone called simply "Jim"; little more than simply exuberant greeting and then signature. But the greeting in itself—"Hello, you old flatfoot!"

Flatfoot; wasn't that what they called policemen? He'd heard that somewhere, that slang expression.

It hadn't been sent here, it had been sent to that last place, Detroit, and then he'd brought it on here with him, for some reason. Maybe overlooked in some pocket.

Nothing else. Nothing else written.

There was a dingy leather collar-button box there in the middle drawer. Why he looked into it, he didn't know. But it was as though his hand were led to it unerringly, without his being aware of the wherefore.

It held the collar buttons it was intended to. A stickpin or two, with a gaping hole where there had once been some semiprecious stone. A pair of cuff links. A scattering of pearled buttons lost from shirts and the like.

A metal shield, the color of silver blurred to a pewter drabness.

He picked it up and stared.

The coat of arms of the City of New York. And lettering, above, below, that read "Department of Police of the City of New York." And numerals.

He clapped his hands together over it, blotted it out.

As if hiding it from sight, covering it from his own eyes, would undo the actuality of its existence.

A plain-clothes detective, a member of the New York City police force! Evidence could go no further, proof could be made no more final than this. It was here, pressed tight between his own two hands. And he, Marshall, was right in the same house with him. His wife was playing partners with him, with the very manhunter sent to track him down, at a table in the other room.

He replaced it in the collar-button box, and shut the box, and reclosed the drawer, and heeled his hands to the latter, pressing desperately, as if to hold it shut by main force.

Then he turned from the bureau and, hand out to any available support that lay along the way, lumbered totteringly, as if dragging an iron ball and chain after him, into the adjoining bathroom.

He turned the light on in there. He opened a tap, and sluiced water from it along his forehead.

He opened the door of the chest next, and looked for a moment. Then his hand reached up into it, came down again. Now he looked at his hand, not the chest any longer.

He was holding a squat brown bottle in his fingers now, allowing the warning symbol of a death's head to turn slightly within his grasp from left to right as he revolved the bottle. That seemed to make it come more alive, somehow, that little flicker of movement.

He poured. But what he was reading wasn't there on the label.

He was reading the past. His own past. The flight and the heartbreak. The crumbling of hopes, the defacing of a marriage, the endless pursuit by shadows. He was reading the future. The aloneness of those who run counter to the pack. The waning of youth, the lessening of earning power, the misery and destitution inevitably bequeathed by lifelong rootlessness and vagrancy, the horrors of a derelict old age at last, supine along some gutter somewhere.

Words came into his mind.

I'm tired. Tired of fear. I'm sick of being afraid. I want *not* to be afraid any more. I want to know peace.

I want to go where there *are* no police. Where it's too dark even for the police to follow you. Too far even for the police to bring you back from.

Where I can be at last let alone.

There was a tumbler there, upside-down on the strip of glass shelf that stood above the washstand.

He took the tumbler and poured from the bottle into it. Then put the bottle back and closed the chest front. It wasn't his bottle after all.

The faucet was still running a little. He held the tumbler to it for a moment, and let a little run in. As though he were mixing a highball. The highball of death.

Then he raised the tumbler a little, and stood looking at it. As if no more than an onlooker, as if waiting to see what would happen next, waiting to see what he himself would do next.

His wrist loosened and turned, and the tumbler turned with it, and the courage of his death went where the courage of his life had gone, down a drainpipe.

Something made him turn his head slightly, and Wise was standing there, unguessed and unheard, in the bath-door opening, looking in at him. There was no expression to be read on his face. Or perhaps it was there, but there were no eyes sufficiently skilled to read it.

Marshall smiled at him a little. Or seemed to, though it was meant for his own thoughts, and not for Wise.

I wouldn't have had any luck even in that. If I'd gone

ahead and tried it, he would have stopped me or pulled me through.

"You have to let it run a little while, first," suggested Wise, amiably. "It comes too warm at first." Then he said, "Why didn't you ask me? I would have gotten it for you from the kitchen; it runs colder in there."

Marshall thought of the past, and thought of the future. "I'm not thirsty any more," he said with a sigh of fatalistic resignation.

"Come on back," Wise invited. "The ladies are waiting for us. You deal the cards next."

No I don't. *You* do. You still do, echoed mirthlessly in Marshall's mind. I just accept them as they fall.

Wise, about to turn, made a slight move of the arm, which Marshall anticipated. Marshall had suddenly shrunk back flat against the doorframe, with a minor but audible concussion from the woodwork. "Don't," he said faintly.

"I was only trying to give you the right of way," protested Wise, with bland astonishment.

"I thought you were going to—"

I thought you were going to put your hand on my shoulder. It's like being arrested already.

Wise gave him an odd little look, but he didn't ask him what he had been about to say. He took a step in advance. "Coming?" Then went on without waiting for the answer.

Marshall stood there a moment, alone. Sheltering hand bent into a cone over his eyes. He knew what he was going to do; what he had to do, what he couldn't keep from doing now. Suddenly he buttoned the upper part of his suit jacket, which he habitually wore open; and as if that weren't enough, held it gripped together with one hand.

Then he struck out, passed through the room where they were sitting, at an intent, undeterred stride, without

a word or look at them. Face pale, its muscles and tendons showing as in a plaster anatomical cast. In one
doorway, out the other. As if he were some stranger who
had suddenly lost his way and had to cut through the
room to get to the outside.

The woman who called herself Mrs. Wise was over at a
smaller table, across the room, back to him, putting some
sandwiches on a platter.

Marjorie and Wise were still sitting there, both
turned his way to stare from their diametrically opposite
positions.

He caught something that Wise murmured to her
in an undertone, as he went by. "—doesn't seem to
feel well."

He would have flung the outside door open then and
there, he had already arrived at it, but her voice halted
him. She had risen and come out to the room opening
after him.

"Press. We're waiting for you to...Press, what are you
doing?"

She saw something in his face. Anyone would have
who merely looked at him. She came quickly the rest of
the way, to join him. "What is it? Don't you feel well?"

"I've got to get out of this house, Marjorie. I can't
stand it. I've got to get out of this house."

"But what'll I say? What'll I tell them?"

"Hurry up, I've got to get out of this house. I can't
breathe. My chest—"

"Come in and say good night to them, at least."

"I can't. Don't ask me to go back into that room. I
can't."

And holding one hand open, close before his body, he
kept pummelling the other, clenched, into it, in some sort
of inchoate tensity that couldn't express itself in any
other way.

She'd gone back inside, momentarily. He heard her saying, "He's not well. I'll have to take him home....No, I don't; I never saw him this way before."

In the meantime, he definitely wasn't well. No pretense was necessary. A nervous chill had set in, and he was standing, face turned to wall, one arm stiffly out to hold himself against it, shaking spasmodically at recurrent intervals.

"Can I get you a little whiskey? Think that would help?" he heard Wise address him.

He couldn't bring himself to answer him. He shook his head, keeping it turned as it was. "Hurry up, Marj," he besought her in a smothered voice. "Hurry up."

"Yes, dear; just a minute," she tried to calm him. "I have to get your hat and my own things. I'll be right there in no time."

The two Wises stood puzzled in the inner doorway, he turned one way to stare at Marshall in the hall, she turned the other to stare after Marjorie on her flying errand within.

She came back to him at a veritable run.

"Say good night to them, at least," she whispered parenthetically. "You can't leave like this, without saying *good night* to them, at least." She was pretending meanwhile to adjust the collar of his coat at the back of his neck, as an excuse for directing her voice into his ear from close at hand.

They saved him the greater part of the necessity. They had come up closer by now.

"Good night, Mr. Marshall," Mrs. Wise said uncertainly. "I do hope you feel better. So pleased to have met you."

Wise, however, held out his hand toward him.

I can't do that, he warned himself. I'd better not try; I know I can't.

"Press, Mr. Wise is offering you his hand."

He had to look down, then. He had to pretend he was first seeing it. He allowed himself to touch it.

A sudden rigidity locked his spine, made of it a steel brace. A pair of handcuffs seemed to close around his wrists with a clash. He could even feel them pinch the flesh, the illusion was so realistic.

He could feel his eyeballs roll around in their sockets, and thought he was going to drop for a second. Marjorie must have thought so too, the way she suddenly brought her second hand up to support the first in its hold at his elbow.

Then she had him outside the door.

Then they were in the open, walking rapidly away side by side.

Presently she handed him his hat, which she had been carrying until now.

They came to where their homebound bus was to be met. He glanced behind him, to see how far they were from that house. They weren't far enough, it was still in sight back there, within the gloom.

He continued walking, on toward their home afoot, without waiting for the bus. Without a question, without a word, she continued along beside him.

She didn't ask him what it had been, what had caused it, what was its meaning. She asked him nothing. One of her greatest gifts was tact. That was her own undoing.

The only thing she said, when they were better than at the halfway mark on their return, was: "Feel better now?"

He looked up at the untrammeled sky overhead, he sighed, he nodded. Freedom felt so good.

"Yes," he said. "A lot."

She murmured poignantly, more to herself than to him: "They didn't ask us to come again." She gave a sigh, such as he had given in the bath doorway back there. The sigh of an enduring resignation. "I would have liked to have—somebody for a friend."

20

There was a surreptitious air of excitement about her. As though some special event were in the air; some portent that must be kept concealed until its due moment had arrived. With that quickness for nuances he possessed, he noted it right away. He was no sooner in the door, he had no sooner pegged his hat, than he'd detected it.

It was a lot of little things; it was nothing in particular, yet it was everything at once. She was smiling a little more; she was bustling a little more; there was more zest to her kiss. She'd changed the curtains on the windows. She had more lights lit. As on a party night, as on a Christmas Eve. And she herself burned brighter. Her color was higher, her eyes more glowing. The incandescence of some kind of joyous excitement was alight within her.

Why, she even had a special dish for supper, a Sunday sort of dish. Leg of lamb, with capers, and with roast potatoes.

She had their little slab-topped box-square Victrola going, as though she'd timed it so that the record should begin spinning just as she'd first heard his key in the outside door and not a moment sooner. Something gay, something jaunty; a new dance that had come out this year, they called the fox trot. The latest of the long line of animal and barnyard gaits and prances, and the last. "Hel-lo-o-o-o-o Fris-co-o-o-oh!" it greeted him raucously, like some sort of metallic parrot.

"What's up?" he said.

"You're home, that's what's up. Isn't that enough?"

She led him by the arm. "Now here's your chair." She even edged it toward the table for him as he took his stance over it. "Now give me your plate." She filled it for him. "Now eat your lamb."

"But won't you tell me?" he said. "I've got to know. This suspense is killing me."

"Tell you what?" she said. "You mean I'm not as nice to you as this on other nights? Why, what an unkind thing to say! And I thought I was doing so beautifully."

This went on through the whole meal, a teasing, a parrying, such as they hadn't known since their courtship days.

"Oh, please, that record," he had to say at last, after about the tenth consecutive salutation to San Francisco.

She jumped up and stilled it. "I guess I am likely to wear it out. I just bought it today. Seventy-five cents. Wasn't that extravagant? But they give you a package of needles free with each one. And it's been so long since we had a new record."

She even had his favorite dessert.

"I didn't do it myself," she added hastily, "because I can't do pies yet. But it's fresh; I got it at Mueller's, that German bakery around the corner from here. His wife does all their baking herself."

When they were through, he tried to rise. "I'll help you do the dishes."

"No, sit here in this other chair, over here." She led him to it. "Just smoke a cigarette. Here's a match."

She blew it out in that quaint, awkward way women still had with matches. Had to blow twice to make it go out once.

"Don't I help you other nights?"

"Tonight," she said mysteriously, "is tonight. Don't you move now. Be right back."

When she was through she came in and stood behind him a moment, let her hand stray through his hair. He reached out for her without looking, drew her around in front of him. There she sank down upon her knees in a docile crouch on the floor beside him.

"What is it? Will you let me in on it now?"

The phrase seemed to strike her mischievously. "Maybe I will 'let you in' on it. I'll think about it."

He waited.

"Well?" he said at last.

"Wait a minute," she commanded, "I want to get this right. You know, there's one time in a man's life when he has a hard time finding just the right words. That's when he proposes marriage. And there's a time in a woman's life like that too."

"Are you proposing marriage to me?" he chortled. "You're a little late, aren't y—?"

She overrode the interruption with a shake of her head. "We're going to have company."

He was startled, and altogether unpleasantly. He sat up straighter, as though a pulley controlled his motions and had just been given a violent jerk.

"Your father's coming out. Did you hear from him? Did he wire?"

She shook her head, hilariously.

"Somebody you've never seen. Somebody younger."

For a moment he knew a worse feeling, a deeper feeling, than the merely startled one just preceding; a hidden fright that she could not have guessed was there.

"How do you know?"

"I should know. I'm his mother. I will be when he gets here."

He caught her to him and hid her face against his breast, and she didn't understand it was a protective gesture, a warding off of an impending event. The way you hold someone close when you want to guard them against a threatened danger, that you may recognize but that they (perhaps) do not.

He reached down single-armed, without disturbing her, and picked up his fallen cigarette from the carpet and put it out.

His face was haunted. He was hiding the wrong face, hers, the blissful one, and showing the one that should not have been seen: pale and taut and stricken with dismay.

His tongue peered once or twice between his lips, trying to dislodge the words that would not come at first.

And when they did they were few and they were quiet-spoken, but they were strong and they were granite-hard with self-preservation and they doomed her.

"We can't. We may suddenly want to move on, from here to the next place. We must be free to go at a moment's notice. We can't be held down. For months and months we'd be nailed to one place. *It* would hold you, and you would hold me. It would be like a millstone around our necks. I couldn't stand it, I couldn't live through it. I don't want you to. *I won't let you….*When did he tell you? When did you find out?"

She didn't answer. She couldn't. Her heart must have been too busy just trying to keep on going.

"You're going to have to go to another doctor. With *me*. I'll find one. And I'll take you to him myself. Right away. Before—too much time has gone by."

Afterwards, he looked down and there was a tremendous circular damp spot, all over the left breast of his shirt. She was gone, but it was there. About where his heart was supposed to be.

21

She was a dutiful wife. She was a wife a Japanese or a Kaffir might have envied him. She was selfless. His wish was hers. No, not even that; she had no wish; there was only one wish, his, and she was the implement used to carry it out.

She sat there beside him on the cracked and peeling leather of the doctor's waiting-room divan. This other doctor, of labyrinthine inquiries and low-voiced confidences. A waiting room whose shades were drawn, behind windows that held no shingle. She made no scene, no whimper, she cast no pleading eye upon him. He held her hand in his, but whether to give her courage or to instill continued obedience, only he could have told.

They were alone in here. This was a place where patients came one at a time. And the very purpose of those who came here was to be thought alone. To be made alone.

The door opened and a nurse came out.

"The doctor is ready now."

Marjorie's face paled a little, but she made no other sign. She cast her eyes down thoughtfully, as if listening for him to say the word, the single word, the magic word, that would come now at the end, to free her from this horrid spell, to break this dark, untrue enchantment.

She couldn't hear it, for he didn't say it.

He tightened his grasp on her hand, as though he thought she might break and try to run away.

"Don't be frightened," he commanded her.

"I'm not," she answered.

"She's not frightened," the nurse repeated with pro-fessional patronage.

She came and claimed Marjorie by one arm, and he saw Marjorie wince and her eyelids flickered for a moment, but she didn't say a word. As though: this is my own ordeal; I can share it with no one; I can plead to no one.

"Did you bring the things you were instructed to?" the nurse asked him.

He produced a small valise that had sat until now on the floor between him and her.

The nurse took it. "If you left anything out, we'll be able to supply it," the nurse reassured him.

"I hope not," Marjorie said wanly. "I'd rather—use my own things."

"You go home now," the nurse dismissed him. "There's absolutely nothing to worry about. The young la— Your fiancée will be ready to leave by about, oh say, nine tomorrow morning. You can stop by then and pick her up. You'd better bring a cab. We have your telephone number, and if it should be necessary…" She didn't finish that part of it.

She put her arm about Marjorie's shoulder, to turn her from him and lead her in.

They didn't kiss, he and she.

She only said one more thing to him. "Tell her I'm your wife, Press. She said 'fiancée' just now."

"She's my wife," he said to the nurse.

"Of course she's your wife," the nurse answered blandly. "I know that. That was just a slip of the tongue."

"You didn't believe it, though," he heard Marjorie say to her, as they passed through the doorway. As though it were a point of honor to establish this. All else being lost but honor.

The door closed after them.

22

She didn't say anything in the taxi, going home the next morning. Just a quiet "yes," to his "Do you feel all right?"; a quiet "no," to his "Are you tired?"

She didn't say anything once within the house either. She only spoke when he spoke first, not otherwise; and then only to use those two words, "yes" or "no," as the case might be.

No more than that, that day, or the next, or the next.

Presently, as the days increased in number, added to a week and then to two, she began speaking a little more. A few words more, and without his having to solicit them first. But only a sparing few, no more than necessary. The things a woman must say around the house, to whoever dwells there with her. Things that are personal, and yet at the same time impersonal; things that are quite intimate, and yet are so abstract.

"Dinner's ready; you can bring your chair up now."

"If you're looking for a fresh shirt, there's one on top there."

"It's raining; we'll have to take a trolley instead of walking."

She didn't speak of *it* again. It was as though it had never been.

Yes, just once she did. Only once. When he first tried to kiss her again, her face turned quietly to the other side.

"I lost more than my baby, Press. I lost—my love for you."

23

The night was like purple ink. And it was as though the
bottle that had held the ink had been smashed against the
sky by some insurgent celestial accountant. For heaven
was pitted with its tiny, twinkling particles of broken
glass. And there seemed to be no one up there to sweep
them up. God's office was closed for the night. (*He*
thought so anyway, Prescott Marshall.)

The late-bound trolley that he'd just alighted from
curved off and went its separate way behind him, burning
bright as a blazing straw-filled crate on wheels. Even
after it was gone from view, the troughlike side street
into which it had disappeared continued to quiver and
ripple with upward-thrown orange-yellow reflections, as
though there were a touched-off gunpowder train slowly
coursing through it. And upper-story window squares
would suddenly flame up for a moment, then blacken out
again, but without the cause making itself seen.

He looked up overhead as he walked along, and gave a
slow, satisfied smile. A smile just between him and the
night.

The stars are in the sky, he told himself, and I feel
good. All's well with the world.

He quirked his head jauntily. The stars don't care what
you've done. The stars are on anybody's side at all. The
stars are on the side of the fellow who goes down—until
he goes down. Then after that, they're on the side of the
fellow who stayed up. And they'll stay there *while* he
stays up. Stay up, and they'll shine for you. Go down, and
they go out on you.

Look, I'll show you. He held out his hand before him, as if he were feeling for rain. Or as if he were showing it to them, letting them see it. See that, he said to himself, they don't even blink, don't even quiver. They keep right on shining a silvery blessing down on my hand. What do they care what my hand's been up to?

He began to recite a poem in his mind, as he walked along. But not poignantly, not with regret; contentedly, as one who has finally come to understand its true meaning.

"One thing is certain, and the rest is lies;
The rose that once has bloomed forever dies."

He nodded sagely to himself, in confirmation. That was all you had to know. That was the only thing there was to know. That told you everything, in just two short lines. All the rest was—what was that new word they were beginning to use in the war?—propaganda, that was it. All their churches, and all their religions, all their Good and all their Evil, all their stuff about the soul and about the conscience; that was just for children in Sunday school. There was no black, and there was no white. There was no sin, and there was no virtue. And just as there was no Devil, and almost everyone knew there wasn't, so almost certainly neither was there any...

You lived, you died; and that was all there was.

He took a last, deep, satisfying breath of the night, turned in at the doorway of his flat building. The night smelt good, it was a shame to go indoors and leave it: sweet, like clover, and cool, and a little bit damp, like things after a rain, but in a clean way.

But there'd be other nights, lots of them. He was the fellow that had stayed up, remember? Not the one who had gone down. He took out his latchkey and let himself in. Then he closed the door after him, but tried not to be too strenuous about it, in case she was asleep.

However, she must have been awake, for within a moment or two her voice reached him in plaintive inquiry. "Press?"

She appeared in the bedroom doorway with a wrapper already encasing one dimpled shoulder but not yet drawn up over the other. Her hair was what he had always thought it to be: even lovelier in disorder than when it was arranged for daytime.

She met his kiss passively, as she had been doing lately. Didn't reject it, but didn't return it.

"Did I wake you?" he asked.

"I was reading in bed," she said. "When you can't sleep, it helps to pass the time away. Mrs. Sanger, you know that nice little lady across the hall, she lent me a new book. It just came out. *Mr. Britling Sees It Through*, by H. G. Wells."

"I'm a little later than I figured I'd be," he admitted. He was undoing his necktie now.

She didn't comment on that. "How was the company smoker?"

"Some of them got a little soused." He took the links out of his cuffs and dropped them onto the dresser with a little metal splash. "That's always the way, at one of these stag business affairs."

"You didn't take much yourself, though, did you?"

"How do you know?"

"There was nothing on your breath just now."

"You can't think clearly when you do," was all he said to that.

"Would you like something to eat?"

"Don't trouble. Why don't you go on back to bed?"

"It's no bother. I wasn't asleep anyway."

They sat down together in a few moments' time at the

little oilcloth-topped kitchen table, he to eat, she to watch him. He was wearing a robe over his pajamas, now.

"This is sort of fun, coming back late and eating in the kitchen like this."

She smiled politely. As you would to a stranger at your table, who expresses appreciation.

"The walk gave me an appetite," he explained. "They held it way out at a place called Mr. and Mrs. Webster's. Outside town. Like a roadside restaurant. Combination farmhouse and eating place."

He was chewing enjoyably on a sandwich.

"The interurban trolley is supposed to stop close by there—I rode out on one—but I stood there waiting and waiting and no sign of one. Finally I gave it up and started walking toward town on foot."

"You didn't walk all the way in?" she protested.

"No. One caught up with me after about twenty minutes, and luckily I was able to stop it from where I was. So I jumped on and rode in the rest of the way from there."

"But some of the others had cars, didn't they? Why didn't you come back with one of them?"

"I didn't want to ask any favors," he said laconically. "Nobody else seemed ready to leave yet, and I was, so I just walked on out without a word. Besides, I wouldn't have trusted their driving; some of them were in a pretty bad way by that time. Arms slung about each other's shoulders, harmonizing; you know the stage."

When he'd finished, he lit a cigarette, took a reflective puff.

"This isn't such a bad town after all, it is?" he suddenly remarked, apropos of nothing.

She sighed.

He saw that she wasn't going to answer. "Anyway, right now it seems all right. I wish you could have seen the stars out there just now, when I came in." He blew a long, slow jet of smoke upward. "Peace of mind's a wonderful thing."

"Is it?" was all she said.

He tried to take her hand in his. It had moved by that time, just a moment ahead.

"What's been the matter between us lately?" he said softly. "There's such a distance—"

"I'd better wash off this plate and glass..."

He took them away from her, moved them out of reach.

"I kiss you, but—you aren't there. Just your face."

His eyes got a little brighter; dropping them for a moment, he put out his interfering cigarette with a few neat little taps.

She drew her wrapper a little closer together just above her breast, held it that way with fingers for fastening.

He raised his eyes to her again, from the extinguished cigarette. Hers went down, as by a counterweight. He reached out for her with both arms and drew her toward him. "Come here, closer to me," he said with smoldering laziness.

And drawing her down upon his knees, he enfolded her and put his lips to hers, in a prolonged kiss, that at last swept her head all the way over and back, out beyond the encircling rim of his supporting arm, his own pressed hungrily close to it.

"Now who loves you?" he breathed, when he had released her at last. "Who loves you now?"

Her face had become suffused with embarrassed color, and she tried to hide it by turning it away.

"Don't turn away," he said with throaty languor. "We're not single. What's wrong with a husband kissing his wife?"

He turned her face back toward him. He kissed her again, even more lengthily, even more ardently.

Then suddenly, piercing its way through the humming already filling their ears, a sharper, clearer ringing knifed its way to their attention. They could only gaze into one another's eyes, comatose, for a moment, without being able to understand what it was.

It came again, from somewhere beyond the darkened next room, stabbing its way throughout the stilled apartment, like shards of broken glass.

She pried herself from him, jumped to her feet with alacrity, as though she were only too eager to take advantage of the interruption. "Wait. The telephone. Don't you hear it?"

"Damn," he said languidly under his breath, trying to regain his hold on her. "Let it go. It'll ring itself out."

It sounded again. She escaped from him, went outside to it.

She remained out there by it for some time. It was not a wrong number. He could tell that she knew the person by the inflection she gave her voice after the very opening remark. He could, of course, hear every word she said, because of the total absence of any other sounds throughout the night-bound flat. Her remarks were somewhat disjointed, as any conversation is bound to be when only one-half of it at a time can be heard.

"Yes, he did. Some time ago....

"No, not very long. About half an hour....

"Why, I don't know. Shall I find out? Wait, I'll ask him....

"No, that's all right. He's not asleep yet...."

He had, however, gone into the bedroom by now, without waiting for her any longer in the kitchen.

She came to the bedroom doorway inquiringly. The light was on her side, he had left it dark in there. "Press?" she said, peering into the dimness.

He was already in bed, in a sitting position, knees reared in front of him.

"It's Mr. Wise's wife, Press. She's on the phone out there. He hasn't come home yet, and she's worried. She wants to know if he left when you did."

He was not only patently uninterested, but, perhaps because a mood had been destroyed, somewhat querulous. And, above all, extremely sleepy. He spoke through a yawn. "I left alone. He was still there when I came away. And plenty boozed." He raked his hair, collapsed onto his back, and let his knees deflate after him, more slowly. "Anyway, what does she bother us about it for? I didn't go there with him. Why doesn't she try some of the others?"

"She says she already has, she's tried them all, we were the last ones left. Nobody seems to have come home with him. She's beside herself, the poor woman."

"Well, what is he, anyway?" he growled blurredly. "A grown man or a child in rompers? Get rid of her and come to bed. I'm dead tired." He allowed his head to roll suddenly sideward.

When she returned, only moments later, he was already unfeignedly asleep, lips slightly parted, breath sandpapery, with that limpness of the entire body that only nature in its unconsciousness can bestow, that cannot be simulated. The deep, the dreamless sleep, of a mind at ease, of a conscience without flaw. Peace of mind.

24

He gave a peculiar convulsive start. Almost a cringing away of his whole body, a scuttling, lengthwise across the bed. Away from that touch upon his shoulder, that leaden hand of retribution that seemed to have fallen in his sleep.

A rolling, a floundering, as if blindly seeking to escape

even before his eyes were open. A warding-off, a suddenly arrested flight spasm.

"Press," she said, withdrawing her light-fingered touch. "I didn't mean to frighten you. It's only me. You'll be late. You'll be terribly late."

His eyes had opened now. "It felt so crushingly heavy," he said, glancing at her thin, supple hand.

"It's twenty after already," she urged.

He joined her outside, at the table, in a few moments. He was perfectly normal, now, perfectly casual, just as on any other day.

"Some day," he commented, noting its splendor through the window. "I feel sorry for anyone that's not here to see i…" He didn't finish that, as though it had just been a random thought anyway.

"Well," she said, "then they're someplace else, to enjoy it there. Everyone is someplace."

No, he thought, not quite everyone. Some are *no* place.

"What does the paper say, anything new?" he asked indifferently, but without bothering to take it up from where it lay.

"Splashed with blood," she said disheartenedly. "I hate to look at it any more. Those same old names, that once were so strange, staring you in the face day after day, until they ring in your mind. Douaumont, Vaux, Hill 304, le Mort Homme and…"

Splattered with blood, he repeated to himself. Then what difference does one added little drop make?

"I wish they'd move on a little, then we'd get a few new names at least," he grunted disgustedly. "Looks like they never will. Can I have a little more marmalade, please." After that they didn't talk about it any further.

She only made one passing reference to the events of the night before—the ultimate event, that is to say.

"Poor Wise," she said at one point. "I'll bet he got his, all right."

"He got his, sure enough," he concurred, albeit absently, without any great interest in what her remark had been in the first place or his agreement with it had been in the second.

"I've got to hurry, now." He threw down his napkin, kissed her hastily, and made for the door. This was the typical way in which businessmen, particularly suburban, were popularly supposed to leave for their work each morning. On the stage and in the comic strips they were always shown that way: taking their departure in a last-minute rush. As a matter of fact, he himself never did, other days.

"Don't hurry too much, it's not good for you," she counseled him from the doorway. "A few minutes more or less won't matter. I'll bet some of the others, like Wise, for instance, won't get in at all today."

He stopped dead in his tracks for a moment, flung her the oddest look across his shoulder, almost as though he'd heard wrongly, thought she'd said something other than she had; that sort of look. An absent, yet a quizzical one. Then, as if correctly translating it by afterthought, he simply nodded and rapidly resumed his way, rushing out into the biscuit-colored sunlight of the morning street, while powdered cornmeal seemed to sift over his head and shoulders from some canister held aloft.

Great as his haste was, he stopped once more out on the sidewalk as he encountered the building superintendent, who was coming the opposite way, and who would have passed with simply a good morning, and halted him by calling out his name, and turning back a stride to face him.

"Sorenson. You're just the man I'm looking for."

The man in turn came back a step. "You wanted to talk to me, Mr. Marshall?"

"You're going to have my flat on your hands. Don't start showing it yet, I don't want Mrs. Marshall disturbed, but you can consider this my notice."

"You leaving town?"

"Yes, we're going away."

"Where you going?"

"Can't say for sure yet. I won't know until tonight." He looked at his watch. "I'm late, I'll have to chase along."

He took his usual bus for the office, but he got off two stops short of his customary alighting-place and went into the bank. He consulted his bankbook, copied its bottom-most entry onto a slip, down to the last cent, and presented that.

The teller gave him that professionally hurt look they do at such a time. "Wouldn't you care to leave a dollar in? That would be just enough to keep the account open, in case you want to go ahead with it later."

"I won't have any further use for the account," said Marshall tersely.

He pocketed the money, threw the canceled bank-book into a waste receptacle on his way out, and went to his job.

He did his work, just as on any other day. He made no attempt to see Ponds, to tell him he was leaving. He made no attempt to write out a formal resignation. He was as a matter of fact more diligent and more continuously applied than most of the others, as if he were seeking to complete the greatest number of neglected details within an allotted length of time. A self-allotted length of time.

In general, there was an air of torpor about the office, no doubt an aftermath of the previous night's festivity. Yawns were prolific, and everyone was languid and supine. Wise had absented himself, but outside of an understanding grin or two toward his unoccupied desk, no comment was made on that fact.

Then, after two hours of this doldrumlike stagnation, at approximately mid-morning there was a little minor flurry of activity at the reception girl's desk, nearest the door, and two men were taken directly inside to Ponds' private office, without the usual wait, nominal as it was even at other times.

Marshall saw them go by. They looked at no one, they looked neither right nor left; simply followed her, and then went in and closeted themselves. And that was another thing; she had risen and personally ushered them to their destination, a thing she never did at other times, simply pointing out the direction from where she sat.

As when a stone has been dropped into still water, little outward-spreading ripples of bated rumor began to lave their way across the room and into its farthest corners, although their point of origin, the reception desk, was once more lifeless and still.

"Helen says they told her they're from the Police Department," Marshall overheard someone relaying from a neighboring desk.

He stopped what he was doing and put it away. He sat for a moment, without turning to look at the private office door, which remained inscrutably closed and silent, though more than one of the others turned and glanced around at it in a sort of ingenuous curiosity. The police, in 1916, were still to the average layman a fairly mystic, rather esoteric junta, more often heard of than personally encountered. At least, in their upper, non-uniformed categories.

"Did anybody do anything last night they shouldn't?" he heard somebody ask in a jeering stage whisper.

He got up suddenly, pale and quite intent, and walked out of the room and sought the washroom, across the public hall. There was, about the gingerly yet determined way he walked, his almost exaggerated preoccupation, and above all, his air of not brooking hindrance, a suggestion that he felt he was about to become ill.

He wasn't. He smoked a cigarette, and then another, and paced about a good deal. Looking thoughtfully down at the floor the whole while.

Just as he went back, they were coming out. He met them right outside the door, the door to the public hall, and had to cock his weight back upon his heel to give them passage. They brushed by him without a look or word, while the coat lapels of first the one and then the other rustled past his own, and then in turn he went in. He carried a palettelike impression of veinous high-blooded faces, seen too close to the eye for the features to be analyzed, stringy neckties, and teal-blue and cocoa-brown material, which, however, soon faded, for it had been seen at too close a perspective, almost a blur, to be long retained.

The excitement was very evident in the air by now, but no one could tell whence it was coming or what was continuing to generate it, now that the callers had gone. It was like an electrifying undercurrent, a tingling, that each one seemed to get from his neighbor and pass on in turn to the next. It was like a leashed waiting for something momentous that was to happen, though up to this point, nothing momentous whatever had happened. Two men, minding their business almost to the point of self-effacement, had passed through the room once, then passed through it a second time in the opposite direction. Someone had said that someone else had said that they were from the police. That was all.

There was on the surface no untoward sight or sound. Everything was as it had been before, half an hour ago. But everyone looked up too quickly at the slightest sound. A sound that at another time would have not even caught their attention; the scrape of a chair, the clearing of a throat, even the thump emitted by a closing ledger. And when there were not even such sounds, everyone looked around too frequently, as if in search of them. Marshall, for his part, sat more quietly than almost anyone else, head tilted downward. As if lost in thought. Or as if listening intently for something, that he alone would hear when it did come. Or understand when he heard.

Ponds hadn't been seen, nor even heard from, since the visit of the two men.

Noon came, and there was a general sortie for lunch.

On his way out Marshall took the trouble of accosting Helen Strom, as she was preparing to leave the reception desk.

As if on the spur of the moment, as if it only occurred to him now that he happened to encounter her, he asked: "Say, who were those two men who came in here about an hour ago?"

She immediately became animated, dropped her voice to an excited whisper; as if delighted at discovering there was still someone left to whom she had not yet related the incident. Inadvertently, of course.

"Oh, what do you think? They showed me some kind of a badge—quick, like this, you know—" She planed her hand edgewise. "I really didn't have time to see what it was, but isn't that the police, when they use a badge like that?"

"What would they want here?" He shrugged elaborately. He glanced around over his shoulder, as if just then discovering Wise's vacant desk. "I wonder what happened to Wise today; he didn't show up."

"He must be sick, after last night. Oh, wait a minute, there's Frances..." She had just then sighted someone more to her interest, of her own sex and occupational status, passing streetward along the hall, and left him without further ado.

He went on out to the street, behind the two.

He ate no lunch. He took a walk instead. A fairly lengthy, yet a rigidly circumscribed, walk.

He boxed the railroad station.

Suddenly, as if noticing this for the first time, he looked *at* it. Then went in.

He didn't go up to any of the various ticket windows, as you do when sure of your destination and the train you are to take. He didn't go over to the information desk, as you do when sure of your destination but unsure of the train you are to take. He went instead to the waiting room, as you do when sure only that you are going away. He sat down idly, as if choosing this place simply to rest himself awhile, simply to make the rest of his lunchtime hour pass more quickly.

Now and then the sepulchral-sounding voice of the announcer would blare out dismally, as if chanting a dirge for someone that was dead. Chanting a dirge in a vast hollowed-out catacomb.

"Train for Ogden, Salt Lake City, San Francisco."

He didn't skulk or hide. He sat there, rather, in an attitude of morose pensiveness, arms folded across his chest, head inclined to contemplate the floor, littered with peanut shells and scallops of orange rind and the glistening foil wrappings that had originally encased sticks of chewing gum.

"—Salt Lake City, San Francisco."

Arms folded across his chest, in an attitude of morose pensiveness, contemplating the floor before him, not seeming to hear anything, not seeming to be aware of anything that was going on around him.

"—San Francisco."

He got up suddenly, as if tired of loitering any longer. No more than that. Went to the ticket window now. As you do when sure of your destination and the train you are to take.

"Two for San Francisco."

"Pullman or day coach?"

"Day coach."

"Round trip or single?"

"Just there. Not back."

"That's thirteen...Twenty—six sixty."

"Thirty dollars."

"Seventy, seventy-five, twenty-seven, and three makes thirty. Better get a move on. It's pulling out in five more minutes."

"I'm not taking the one going out now. This is for tomorrow's train. Or maybe the day after. The tickets are good, aren't they?"

"Sure, any time within thirty days."

"Well, that'll cover it," Marshall said. "Any time within the next thirty days." And even after he'd turned from the window, he softly repeated it once more, as if for his own benefit: "Any time within the next thirty days."

He went back to the office.

There were people standing around the building doorway, on the sidewalk. Not just going in and coming out, but standing there at full halt, in a straggling crescent drawn around the outer side of the doorway. And all facing toward the doorway, as if waiting for it to give some sign. Beside its lintel stood a policeman, idle. And when their eyes sought him out, his eyes went up over their heads in a sort of vacant superiority.

Marshall quailed, and he wanted to turn and flee back toward where he'd just come from. But somehow he didn't. He only slowed gingerly, before he'd quite come up to them, and went over closer beside the wall, and lingered along there for a moment or two, body half turned so that you couldn't tell in which direction he actually intended going next, whether forward or backward.

Nothing happened. The doorway stayed as it was.

The people stayed as they were, with only an occasional shifting along their outside perimeter, when someone shorter than the rest tried to see over someone taller than he was.

Little by little Marshall drew nearer again, until finally the crescent had taken him into itself, he was one of them.

The policeman spoke abruptly, as if repeating something by rote that he knew was expected of him at fixed intervals, but without much hope of its being heeded.

"All right, now. There's nothing to see. Keep moving. Don't just stand here."

The crescent fluctuated a little, but remained intact, which was apparently all he'd expected of it anyway. His eyes went up overhead again, vacantly superior, as if preferring not to see this implicit disobedience.

"What is it?" Marshall ventured, of the anonymous shoulder beside him. "What happened inside?"

"I don't know. I heard somebody say there was an accident in the building. I saw them all standing here, so I stood too."

Nothing happened. The doorway remained as it was, the people remained as they were, the policeman remained as he was. The terrible hypnotic patience of mass-curiosity; that wears out the very stones of the street.

Marshall, after a courage-garnering moment or two, broke ranks, stepped up to the doorway.

"Where you going?" the policeman said gruffly.

"I work in there."

"All right, go ahead," the policeman said.

There was another policeman standing at the back of the entrance hall, beside the elevator grate.

The elevator came down.

A man in a white jacket got out. Then a stretcher with something covered lying on it. Then a second man in white behind it. They made an awkward turn with it, and the elevator was left clear.

Marshall got on. The attendant turned around and looked directly at him, for some reason. With some sort of curiosity or appraisal, he couldn't tell what it was. He could feel himself paling, all over again, and for a moment wished he hadn't come into the building and hadn't got on the car. He looked down at the floor and, if the attendant had intended saying something to him, that seemed to ward it off.

Marshall's body continued trembling slightly even after the pulsation of the car had stopped.

There were people in the hall, up there on his floor. Some of them from the other offices, a few, whom he didn't recognize, perhaps from other floors of the building. They were standing about in desultory twos and three, low-voiced, crestfallen in bearing. It was like the dregs of an audience left about after a play has ended.

He opened the door and went into his own offices.

He saw Helen sitting at her desk. She was crying quietly but with hysterical insistency, a balled handkerchief held pressed to her face. On the desk stood a glass of water someone had brought her. Untasted. Someone who hadn't had time to remain long enough, himself, to see that she drank it.

"Helen," he said in an urgent undertone, looking around as if to see whether he were being observed or not. "Helen."

She turned and raised bleary eyes to him, but she went ahead crying.

"Helen," he said. "Helen."

"Weren't you here?" she said, through the handkerchief and all. "Didn't they tell you yet?"

"Somebody down on the street told me an accident. Was it in here?"

"It wasn't an accident," she said, catching her breath manfully. "We were told not to tell anyone outside the office. They didn't want anyone except those of us who were in here to know, that's all."

"I've been—I've been away to lunch. I just got in this minute."

"You're lucky," she said. "I was right here at the desk. Just today I had to come back early from lunch. As a rule I'm the last one to get in, you know that yourself. I was the one who had to send out for them."

She held the balled handkerchief close to her face again; this time without further sobbing, rather as if nauseated.

"Mr. Ponds," she said muffledly. "He shot himself in there."

Marshall was leaning over before her, at the side of the desk, his palms spread paper-flat to its corners. His head went down a notch at this. The head goes down like that, with an abrupt dip, when one is stricken. But it also can go down like that when one feels a vast relief.

"I heard this crash through the door, and I thought the window-rope gave way or something and the whole sash came down, in there, like it happened that other time, remember? Right after that I got a call on the board, and automatically, I answered it. I heard his voice. He sounded calm. He said, 'Helen, send for the police.' Just like he was asking me to get out a file or something.

"I said, 'Mr. Ponds, what was that? Was that in there, where you are?'

"He said, 'Helen, don't come in here. Send them in when they get here, but you stay there where you are.'

"By the time they got here, he was dead."

Marshall didn't say anything, not a word.

"Wise," she said in a horror-stricken whisper.

Marshall didn't say anything, not a word.

"He wasn't one of us at all. He was an investigator, it turns out. A private detective."

Marshall just looked steadily down at the floorboards, palms flat to the top of her desk.

"He's been missing since late last night. They found him dead at about nine this morning, lying in the bottom of a ravine, halfway between here and that roadhouse where the beefsteak dinner was given. His head had been crushed with a big rock. They noticed the empty car standing up there all by itself on the road, that was what first called their attention. I heard them talking about it; they don't know if he slipped and lost his footing in the dark, and loosened the rock in falling, and it rolled down on top of him, or if he was pushed over and then the rock purposely sent down after him."

"But Ponds?"

"Mr. Ponds must have been the one Wise was sent here to investigate. Maybe he was doing something he shouldn't have all along with the funds. The head office— or one of the clients—got suspicious…

"I don't care," she said loyally. "Poor Mr. Ponds. I've known him since I was seventeen. I've been working here for him since I was sev—

"Sh," she warned suddenly, and turned her head away.

One of the plain-clothesmen who had been to see Ponds that morning had just come out of the private office, was coming toward them.

"You were asked not to talk this over with anybody, miss," he reminded Helen disapprovingly. "Your name?" he said to Marshall.

"Prescott Marshall."

"Take a seat, please. Over there. Don't talk to anyone. We may want to ask you a few questions, later on."

He didn't sit as he had, at that same desk, only that

forenoon. He didn't sit even as he had in the railway station waiting room.

He sat relaxed, indolent, at perfect ease. Rolling a little pencil back and forth across the surface of his desk, over and over again, under the fingers of one desultory hand. Letting it go just so far, and then recalling it toward him each time.

He lolled there, in a vacuity of patience that nothing could wear thin, no matter how long they might take to get around to him and then send him on his way.

25

Sorenson didn't keep his word.

There was a ring on their bell while they were still sitting at the supper table. Unguardedly, he let her rise to answer it. She was always quicker on her feet that way than he, anyway. Most women are.

When she came back to the room there was fright written all over her face. Fright of a sort he'd never seen there before, in just that way. Shock, as when the walls have suddenly crumbled all about you. As when the roof has suddenly come down upon your head. As when you suddenly find you have no home any more.

"Who was it?" he asked.

"There was a young couple standing out there," she said on quick breaths, with that chalky look livid on her face. "Sorenson was with them. He wanted to—he'd brought them around to look at our flat..."

He folded his napkin into meticulous quarters, then folded the quarters into compressed eighths. It seemed vital to get it just even.

"I told him to. We're giving up. We're going to San Francisco."

The fright didn't lessen. It wasn't the superintendent at the door who had frightened her. But he had known that anyway. It was this, now, of which the superintendent had been a harbinger.

She still couldn't breathe right. And she hadn't run, and she hadn't hurried. Just stepped out to the front door and back.

"Why? *Why*…? Why?"

"Oh, I don't know," he drawled. He was drawing invisible diagrams with the edge of his fork now.

"But you *have* to know," she contradicted him sharply. "This is something you *have* to know. And I do too."

"Well, it's hard to put into words…"

"But you must put it into words!"

"Sit down—"

"No." She remianed clutching at the back of her chair, slightly crouched above it in intensity.

"Ponds is gone now, and it won't be the same. Why stay on?"

"But someone will take his place. The organization won't be dissolved. The others aren't leaving."

"I know. But he dipped into the funds pretty deeply. It may fold, for all we know. Or they may cut down. Why wait for that to happen?"

She opened her palm, then clenched it to the chair again. "Well, why *not* wait for it to happen? It hasn't yet. Every additional week's salary you receive, is that much more. Leave *after,* but why before?"

"I'm tired of it here. I want to go to some new place."

"But you're not a child. You're a married man. You have me, you have a home. You can't just—just quit cold and move on, every time you tire of a place."

"Well, I'm me," he said absently. The diagram seemed

to require a deeper stroke, he shifted to the blade of a knife now.

"Yes, you are," she agreed, leaving her meaning hidden.

He didn't answer that. "Every young couple moves about at first, as we have, in the early years of marriage. Some a little more, some a little less. It's not so serious, it's not so sinful."

"No," she said firmly. "No, not as we have. Not suddenly, without warning, without reason, just"— She snapped her fingers for illustration—"overnight. One day no mention of it, no discussion; the next, all packed already, and on the train, and on our way. The refugees in Belgium and northern France had to do that in the summer of Fourteen; but there's no war here, why should *we?*"

"Sometimes you have to move, to better yourself," he said incautiously.

"No," she said again. "No. That doesn't fit our case either. In New York there would have been fifty-five a week waiting for you. And in a little while, my father would have given you the backing to open a brokerage office of your own. He said as much to you. Instead you never went back there. Not even to let me pick up my things. You came on out here—at forty-five. A year later you're back to fifty, still five short of what you would have been getting in New York all this time. Now, from here, you're ready to go on someplace else, where you won't work at all at first, maybe for weeks, until you can locate something. Is that betterment, is that advancement?"

He couldn't answer that. "You're getting all wrought up," he protested. "And you've just finished a meal. That isn't good for you. Here, sit down at least. Drink a glass of water."

She clung stubbornly to the back of the chair, as if it were some sort of a barrier between them, set up by him,

that she couldn't pass by in order to reach him as she
would have wanted to.

"No," she said wearily, "I can't sit down to this. I've sat
too many times before. When you tell me what it's my
right to know, then I'll sit down beside you again, where
my place is."

"What do you want me to say? We're going to San
Francisco. There isn't any reason. What do you want me
to say?"

She remained standing. "Be fair with me, Press, I've
always been fair with you."

"How am I being unfair?"

"Do you call this being fair, what you're doing to me
now?"

She left the chair at last, but she went across the room,
she held her back to him.

He shaded his eyes for a moment, in hopelessness.
"This isn't getting us anywhere. We'll be at this all night."

She didn't answer. She had one of their window curtains in her hands, was paying it off a few inches at a time,
seeming to study its edges as she went.

"All I can do is go back over what I've said before.
I thought there would be better opportunities in San
Francisco. I—I understand it has certain advantages over
here. I'm getting tired of it here, I'm getting stale. I—
well, I wanted to go there and try it out, that's all."

"All this comes at seven o'clock, on a Thursday evening.
On Wednesday, on Tuesday, on Monday, never a word,
never a warning. Even this very morning, not a sign, not
an indication. You paid the electric bill on Saturday, you
didn't tell them to discontinue. You even spoke to
Sorenson about putting in a new sink for me, because the
old one leaks. Why? For just the two or three days that
were left?"

She came back to the chair again. She didn't grasp it

any more; she let her forearms slump from across the top of it, hands clasped, in a sort of bitter patience.

"Why? Out of a clear blue sky like that."

He looked at the table before him.

"Either tell me the truth, or don't tell me anything at all."

How can I, he pleaded with her piteously in his silence.

She shook her head, at her thoughts, not at anything he'd said. "No. There's been something hanging over us from the first that hasn't been right."

God, oh, God! he cried out to himself. At last even you begin to feel it too.

"I don't know what it is. I only know it's something that's wrong, something that's bad for us. I've felt it so many times, and denied to myself that I did, keeping my head buried in the sand like an ostrich. Now, tonight, I'm going to face it, I'm going to look it in the eye, if I never did before."

His head went down lower, almost as though there were a weight on the back of his neck.

"And what have I to lose, anyway?" she went on. "I have very little left of anything. Very little, anymore. Yes, now I take stock. Now I add up the ledger. And what do I find?"

He'd closed his eyes.

"Is this all I am to have? This half life, this shadow life, this nothing at all? Is that what I thought marriage would be? Money doesn't matter, it isn't the lack of that I mind. I wouldn't give you two cents for it, I've never missed it a day since I married you! But there should be roots, there should be a foundation. We should be building something. I should feel I'm helping you build something. That's the only thing that helps to make the dreary, lonely days go by. And by the time I get it up so high, you come along and tear it all down again, and all my dreary lonely days went for nothing. Then you want to take me to a new place, and let me try to build some more, and then you'll tear that down in turn. And I have nothing. Nothing. Nothing. You won't let me."

A sob choked in her throat, but there were no tears.

It was no tirade; she spoke low and in a dulled accent, as if communing with herself, with him not there at all. It was all the more dreadful for that.

"You took me from my father and mother. Well, every wife must follow her husband, and I wanted to go with you. That's the marriage vow. But you made it into a permanent exile, you cut me off from them completely. No visits in-between, to break the separation; while she was still here, while I still could have enjoyed her. You kept me away, and now she's dead, and I can never see her again. She died without my seeing her alive again. For me, *she died the day I married you.* And that shouldn't be. I loved my mother.

"You took something else from me, Press, that I was meant to have. We don't have to name it, we both know what it is. And that's another face I'll never see." Her eyes blazed momentarily in accusation, her voice deepened to a curdled resentment. "Who are you, God? What right had you to do that to me?"

"Don't!" he whispered, and swerved his face violently aside. As violently as if he'd suddenly experienced an excruciating earache on that side, where she was.

" 'Don't.' It's so easy to say that. I never cried 'don't' to you. Maybe I've been in pain too as you are now. Pain that you gave me. I've spared you too long, Press. If I had pleaded 'don't,' would you have spared *me?* Will 'don't' bring back my mother? Will 'don't' bring back the baby I might be holding at this moment? Will 'don't' bring back New York to me, the years that might have been sunny and carefree but are spoiled now and thrown away?

Those first few years of marriage? You've smashed up all my hopes and dreams. I can almost hear something crunch now on the floor whenever you move around too much. It must be the sawdust, I guess, running out of their seams."

That night in Wise's bathroom came back to him, and he knew that not a word she said was untrue, not a word she said unjust.

She'd caught up. Just as she'd once caught up to him in love, so now she'd caught up in hopelessness and despair.

"Life isn't supposed to do that to you, what you've done to me. It's not that cruel. *You* are though! Life takes away from you, but it gives something back in exchange at least. For everything it takes, it's given you something else. If it takes your youthful dreams, then maybe it's given you money instead. If it's taken your money, then maybe it's given you love instead. If it takes your love, then at least, then at *least*, it lets you stay in one place, with the same sights and the same familiar faces around you, to help you bear it. Even the people in the shabbiest tenements on First and Second Avenue, they know that next year they'll still have that same roof over their heads. That they'll always be there, where they've always been. At least they're *home*, they're *home*, they're *home*.

"Everyone has *something*. No one has *nothing*. No one but me."

His head went down suddenly, into his wreathed arms. She gazed at him with moody tearless eyes, eyes that could not cry.

"That isn't the answer. You cry for a moment, I've cried for a year. You lift your head, it's over already. You light a cigarette, your eyes twinkle in the matchlight, now the matchlight's gone, and now the tears are gone already too. How quickly they went. What tears are those, that a cigarette can dry and take away? I wish I knew how to shed that kind."

"I must love you an awful lot," he said dully, "for it to hurt me so."

"Then think how I must have loved you."

"You don't?"

"I'm in pain. There isn't room for both at once. You only feel one or the other. Oh, are you blind? Have I been that good? Have I hidden it that well? Can't you see what you've done to me? Can't you see you've made our marriage a hell for me?"

She turned from the chair back at last, as if it had defeated her: the barrier that she had not been able to move.

"Because I thought I was a wife, but I wasn't. I was just a stranger living in your house with you, a stranger lying by you in your bed. 'Pack your valise, Marjorie. At five fifteen a train is taking us away.' Oh, you don't have to tell a stranger more than that. That's all a stranger needs to know.

"One time too often you've done that to me. One time too many."

She drew out the door, to go into the next room.

"Wait," he said quietly. He began to count out strokes with the lighted tip of his cigarette, into the hollow of a supper-table saucer, definitive, irrevocable, until it had been stamped out. "I'm going to tell you what you want to know, I'm going to tell you why it is."

She didn't offer to come back to him.

"Wait for me. I'll be back shortly."

She watched him rise from the table and move away from her, in the opposite direction, toward the outside door.

"Where are you going?"

"I'm going down to the corner a minute, to buy a

bottle and bring it back here. I'm going to try to tell you something, and what I'm going to try to tell you—I can't tell you sober."

"Does it take liquor to make you open your heart to me?" she murmured. "How close we must be to each other."

The outer door closed after him.

26

Sitting there alone, huddled disconsolate on a bare-backed kitchen chair, back to front, he drank it as though it were the bitterest of medicines. Gripping the tumbler each time with force enough to have shattered it within his hand, grimacing with an anguish that didn't come from taste, forcing the drink down, and then down again atop that, and then down once more, until it was all gone. The drink that was to tell his story for him, make his peace for him.

He stopped when he'd had three of them. Then he took the bottle and held it tipped over the sink, and drained it. Then he stowed it empty below on the floor, with a little swing and a thump.

He went into the bedroom. He didn't ask her if she were asleep. He knew she wasn't, she couldn't have been, after what had passed between them before.

"Marjorie," he said to her quietly. "Now I want to tell you what I have to."

She didn't answer.

He closed the bedroom door on the two of them, shutting off what pale light had been able to seep in from the outside. Then, alone in the gloom with her, he sought an armchair that stood off in a far corner, away from her,

away from their bed, and lowered himself into it with an
aching diffidence, the way a culprit does about to make
his supreme plea before a tribunal that holds his final
destiny in its hands.

27

The opallike tints of early morning, swirling cloudy gray
and milky white and flecked with bloodspots of rose and
crimson, flooding the room, found them as the night had
left them. He in an armchair that stood off in a far corner.
She in the bed, eyelids down, one cheek turned toward
him.

Both inert. Both with their eyes closed. Yet neither
one asleep. Unspeaking. Yet both so terribly aware of one
another, that every nerve ached.

She didn't ask me into the bed. That's why I've sat the
night out here like this, waiting for the word that never
came. I could have, I should have—but I wanted that one
word, as a token of forgiveness, at least of understanding.
That one word that never came.

She never said a word from the time my voice stopped
and the confession was through. As if she hadn't heard.
And yet I know she must have. I could hear the things it
did to her breath. How it quickened it at this point,
slowed it at the next; then took it away altogether. Then
brought it back again, but wounded almost to the death,
struggling for survival.

What good is it, speaking to her now? The time is past,
the time of forgiveness. What good is it, saying her name
now? For in the dark, there could have been two men
in the room with her: an unknown man telling her a
dreadful thing, and then her husband. But now, if she

hears her name and she opens her eyes, there can be only one.

I'll leave her alone awhile. I'll let her be. Then perhaps when I've come back, her fright will have calmed, her bitterness will have softened. Her horror will have lessened.

Then I'll say her name, and she'll say mine, and we'll find each other's arms. We'll be one again, as we were before. Not a dismembered two, on a chair in a corner, on a bed far off across a room.

He stood up, stiff and chill, and only after he had found his feet did he open his long-sealed eyes. Then he picked up his clothes from where they were and took them out with him and dressed outside. He didn't look back at her as he left the room, he had no need to. He knew her eyes had never opened, he knew she'd never stirred. He knew she knew he'd gone.

He took a sheet of paper, when he was ready to go, and wrote out a note to her and left it on the table where she'd find it.

> *Marjorie*—*We're taking the 5 o'clock train for San Francisco, so will you have everything packed and ready to go. I'll be back for you by around 4 at the latest. Press.*

Then he took his hat and he went out.

28

As he keyed the door and then swung it wide before him, the first thing he saw were their three valises, her large one and then the smaller one she also used and then his own, standing edgewise toward him in the hall,

all strapped and readied. And atop them, folded neatly
flat, his outer coat, which because of the season he had
no need for wearing now.

And when he'd gone beyond, into what until just this
morning had been their parlor—and now was just the
anonymous parlor of some flat—he could see at a glance
that the one or two accessories that were their own and
did not belong with the flat had all been taken up and
were gone from sight. The little things that had given the
room its savor, that had said, "Marjorie and Prescott, and
nobody else, live here; this room is theirs." The curtains
that had been on the windows; dotted Swiss, not very
expensive, maybe, but never limp. A runner that had
been across the table, to take some of the bareness away.
A small-sized Mexican serape that she'd had tacked flat
upon the wall, like a sort of miniature tapestry, in vivid
stripes of emerald, fuchsia and orange. That shallow bowl
for ashes that he'd picked up somewhere and clung to
ever since, of some kind of heavy green glaze. That was
about all, yet that was everything. All that was left was
mission furniture and a nondescript rug. The room didn't
belong to them any more.

He was gratified, but not unduly surprised. He'd never
had any real doubts but that she'd follow his behest. Even
apart from what she now knew, what was there for her
here and why should she want to cling to it?

He said her name then, as he'd told himself he would.
"Marjorie?"

And she answered it, from out of sight, as he'd told
himself she would. "Press? Yes, right away."

Just as though there'd been no revelation between
them last night. Just as though last night had never been.
Just as though today had followed yesterday, but with no
darkness—no double darkness—in between.

She came in from the bedroom the next moment,

already hatted and with handbag tucked beneath her arm, and seeing to the right fit of her gloves.

"I have everything done," she said, and her eyes fell on him for a moment without any strangeness, without any memory of strangeness, then went down to her glove buttons again. "Everything's put in the bags. There's only one thing, and you didn't tell me what you wanted me to do about that." She pointed. "That's that little Victrola over there." It had never played again after the night it had played "Hello, Frisco" so endlessly.

"I completely forgot about that myself," he admitted. "It's been down there on the floor so long."

"But the superintendent's wife—she was in here awhile ago—told me she's going to speak to him about it; she's always wanted one herself, and they might be willing to give us something for it."

"Oh, let them have it," he said with a dismissive swing of his arm. "It's too much trouble to carry with us anyway."

He turned away from it. He extended his arms, tentatively, toward her, and she didn't see them, though she was looking right at him.

"Press," she said, over and across them, "I'm not going to San Francisco, with you. I'm going to New York, without you. We're both going away, but we're not going the same way."

Three
New York Once More

I

Marjorie was modish again, as she had been in '14, that first year that Press had met her. She was in a coat very similar to one that he'd seen her wear at that time, even allowing for the changes a year and a half might have been expected to produce in the fashions. The dark green of bottle glass, with a chin-tight little collar of red-gold kit fox. On her head a toque of bottlegreen velour, a black aigrette standing up straight from the front of it, as from an Oriental sultan's turban. A tiny barrel muff hung from one hand, scarcely seeming to offer room enough for two to be inserted. The bottoms of her shoes were glistening patent, the gaiter part was champagne kid, studded all down the sides with jet buttons.

She was New York again. Using it as a descriptive noun. It stood out all over her, that vague yet so distinct cachet that only two places in the world have ever been able to give women, that patina, that reflection; so that one can say "She is Paris" or "She is New York," but one cannot explain why.

She was in the drawing room of the Seventy-ninth Street house, and the doors at the end of it had been closed to afford privacy. She was walking back and forth laterally, the short way—the room was longer than it was wide—as one does when engrossed, measuring one's own share in a discussion, thinking over carefully each answer given to each question, both before making it, and while making it, and even in retrospect, after having made it.

He was seated, grave of mein. Sometimes looking at her. Tapping with the rim of his eyeglasses, lightly, troubledly, against the arm of the chair he sat in.

The conversation had been going on for some time. It had started as a brief passing salutation, a look-in at the doors, on her way out. But now whatever expedition she had originally been on had been lost sight of, and the conversation had become the pressing thing, and not the sortie. As such things sometimes develop, reversing their own ratios.

"Then this is more or less of a separation?"

"I don't know how to answer that, Father. He's not here with me. Isn't every visit home that a wife makes without her husband, more or less of a separation; can't it be called that?"

"It can," he said shrewdly, "when she calls it 'home,' where she has come without him, and calls it merely 'that place,' where he has remained without her. As you've been doing, in nearly all our conversations."

She sighed wearily. "Oh, Father, you're in one of your lawyer moods."

"I'm in one of my being-a-father moods," he said ruefully.

The eyeglass rims tapped, the patent shoes twinkled restlessly across the floor.

"Marjorie, what is it you're keeping from me?"

This time she sighed without the spoken protest, as if to utter that further were merely a waste of time.

"I raised you. You grew up under this roof with me. I know that broken-doll look on your face. I know that I-fell-down-on-my-roller-skates-and-barked-my-knees trembling to your chin. I know that wounded oh-there-was-the-most-wonderful-boy-at-the-party-last-night, all-of-nineteen, and-some-older-girl-of-eighteen-came-and-took-him-away-from-me-all-because-he-thought-I-was-too-young expression deep in your eyes. I can't buy you a new doll as I used to, or give you a shiny fifty-cent piece to make your knees stop smarting, or buy you a new dress, so you can go back to the next party and win him back—and find out you don't want him after all. Time won't let me any more. Time is the enemy of fathers who have little girls. But I can do this—always this—to the end." His eyeglasses had dropped to the rug. His arms were open wide, straining to accept, to hold her close, in remembrance of past consolations. "Time won't take this away from me."

Her lips trembled, and with a melting motion, she started toward him, toward the sanctuary he offered; then checked herself, and turned her head aside, to avoid meeting the light of sympathy in his eyes, drawing her like a beacon.

"No," she murmured stifledly. "I know that place inside your arms too well. Don't make me weaken. I'm trying not to make a fool of myself. Help me."

"Is it foolish to open your heart to your father?" he coaxed.

Slowly, unwillingly, step by tremulous step, she came nearer. Everyone has to go to someone, at certain moments. No one can stand all alone.

"You wouldn't be Marjorie if you weren't loyal. *Be* loyal, among strangers, in the face of the world. Are you among strangers now?"

She was in them now. His arms closed tenderly, understandingly.

"What has he done to you?"

"Nothing, nothing…"

Then the sobs came, as she had foreseen, in that place of tenderness; the melting away of resolution and of bravery. They came in an anguished torrent, and she hid her face upon his breast, and he stroked her softly and

held her for awhile, and didn't speak till they'd ebbed
again.

"Tell me, and I'll understand. Not for you alone, I'll
understand for the two of you. Tell me, and I'll try to
help. Not you alone, I'll try to help the two of you.
I'm older than you are, than he is. Tell me, and I'll make
the skinned knee stop stinging, as I used to long ago,
remember? Remember how it was?"

"Father," she moaned feverishly, threshing her head
from side to side against the pillow of his chest, "you
don't know what you're saying at all! You can't. This is
something you can't. You can't understand *him*—in this.
You can't help *him*…"

"Something so terrible, so new," he murmured drily.
"The boy and the girl; so different from the boy I was, the
girl your mother was, not too many years ago. The same
sobs and the same soft hair against my hand and the same
bobbing head—and the same words that were said a
thousand years ago. 'Don't cry any more'—but of course
so different, so utterly different, from the boy I once was
and the girl your mother once was." And in tender irony
he touched his lips to the top of her head.

"Well, what is it, did he drink?"

"No. I've never seen him drunk. Never yet."

"Well, was it another woman, other women?"

"No, no. He never looked at another woman. He never
looked at anyone but me."

His caressing hand stopped, as a pendulum stops, as a
clock stops, bated.

"Instead of reassuring me," he said slowly, "you've
made me doubly anxious. I know you too well, it's more
than just a trifle. In other words, instead of being something less serious than those things I've suggested, it
must be something even more serious. But what can be,
what is?"

She tried to escape from his arms now, in realization that her last defense was down; threshing a little, trying to turn away.

"I had someplace to go. I think I was to meet Caroline—"

He held her insistently. "Marjorie, you're not leaving this room until you tell me why you left your husband like this."

She crumpled in his arms, as though all worn out suddenly, with the effort she had made trying not to tell him; went limp. Her voice was low, now, when it came, suffocating with its own horror.

"Father, he's a murderer. He killed a woman, right here in New York, the very day we were married. Less than—less than an hour before the ceremony. Father, for almost two years now I've been living with a man who's—wanted by the police. Who's a hunted criminal, in every sense of the word. I only found out the day before I came away…"

He'd drawn a single sharp breath, a breath that he never seemed to release again; no sound of its issuing from him, after the icy rustle of its taking in.

"You're sure?" he said batedly. "You're sure of what you're saying?"

"He told me so himself, in the dark, in our bedroom, that last night before I left him. He forced himself to gulp down some whiskey, and then he told me. He wouldn't have the light on, he wouldn't let me look at him. What else could it have been but the truth?"

"And they know?"

"Not his name, no. They know it was done."

"God of Heaven," he said bitterly. "And if you'd had a child by him—"

"He stopped that," she said exhaustedly, shoulders limp against him. "It nearly happened. But he stopped that. He took me to a—"

"Marjorie, don't!" He was holding his own head now. "I can't stand much more. Not all at one time. The little girl that I wanted so to be happy. The shining, clean little girl. It's like seeing you crawl out of a sewer, before my eyes, and stand up all covered with filth..."

"What's to become of me?" she moaned. "Oh, Father, please, you've always been so wise, you've always known more than I ever could; what's to become of me?"

"I could have forgiven—" he said bleakly, "no, not forgiven; I could have tried to understand, if it had happened *after:* once you were already his wife. Such a tragedy does strike occasionally, and when it does there's no foreseeing it, it's the will of Providence. But it happened *before;* he'd already committed it, and he knew he had, he must have. There was blood on his hands, and yet he cold-bloodedly, criminally, *bestially,* went to you, and stood beside you, and took you in marriage; less than an hour afterwards."

She sought to cover her ears with her own hands.

"Ah, no, my dear, the murder was not of this other unknown woman; the murder was of you, all your hopes and all your happiness. You're the one he killed. You."

"Help me. Help me."

"No, you were right, before. I can't help *him.* But I *can* help *you.* It's still not too late. I *can* help *you.* He must pay. For his two murders. The murder of an unknown young woman, and the murder of my daughter's whole life."

And stifling her sobs against his breast, and stroking her throbbing head with one hand while he held her thus, with the other he reached for the telephone and drew it toward him and said with a stony, inflexible determination:

"Give me the police, please....This is Barclay Worth, Nineteen East Seventy-ninth Street. Yes, yes, *that* Mr.

Worth. I have a confidential matter to impart. Will you send someone here to my house, please?...Nature? Homicide—"

"No!" Marshall yelled wildly. "Marjorie, stop him! Don't you hear what he's doing? Don't let him! No!—NO!"

And rising full-height, he flung the entire bottle across the room at his father-in-law, trying to stun him, so that he would drop the telephone. Trying to reach him—from that faraway town to New York.

The bottle smashed, and like corrosive acid, its contents seemed to wash away, to eat away, the whole fabric of the scene before his eyes. The canvas it had been on peeled back on all sides, in a great spreading circle, into its implicit frame. And behind it was revealed another, waiting there all the while and only coming to life now, at his signal. Just as one fresco covers up another. But in this case of fresco with movement, that suddenly begins to quicken with latent motion, held arrested until now, only after its full surface-area has been revealed, and not while the exposure was still going on. A still life suddenly thawing, fluxing at every line.

"That's enough of that, now!" a barman shouted, and came running toward him full tilt, sawdust spraying at his feet, apron flapping at his thighs.

A man jumped up from the table, and came for him from the other side. "Give you a hand here, with this," he panted. Another man sprang up somewhere in back of him, and closed in on him from there.

He was manhandled, violently flung this way and that, in a sort of rolling casklike progress toward the door.

A man was standing there, erect in his seat, against the opposite wall, still shaken and white in the face, eyes popping, crusts of broken glass glinting on both his shoulders, like a sort of crystallized dandruff. Up the wall a space, not too high aloft over his shoulder, a dark stain was sweating downward-trickling tendrils of varying lengths. Like a huge spider crushed and oozing against the plaster.

There was a hubbub of excited voices on all sides.

"Did you see that? Barely missed him!"

"And for no reason at all. Out of a clear blue sky."

"Go on, get him out of here, bartender. That's the idea. There's his hat, too."

The two wings of a milkily opaque glass door slapped together, cutting the noise off short. There was sudden silence, and his chin struck the ground.

Just over his shoulder a dreary array of bulbs, some of them showing gaps like missing teeth, spelled out the letters "The Rocky Mountain Café."

And prone there in the gutter, in the muck and in the rainpocked swill of the street, he still kept crying out "No! Marjorie, stop him! No! No!" and beating time to it with his hand against the ground.

2

On the intimate little dance floor at Churchill's, a trifle below street level at Broadway and Forty-ninth, the undulating grass-skirted line of "Hawaiian" hula girls wriggled slowly off into the wings, describing imaginary loops with their limp wrists held aloft before their faces.

Everything was Hawaiian in the entertainment and nightlife world this year. That was the latest rage. In their wake the band struck up an explosive cacophony intended for general dancing.

Everyone got up, and the tiny space was inundated. Within a moment, nobody could move any more, but the way they danced now, they didn't have to. The women

just shook their shoulders and bosoms—the shimmy—
and the men just stood still and held onto them.

He and she, however, stayed on at their little table,
with its intimate shaded electric lamp glowing upward
into their faces. Dancing was for when you were happy.
And though her eyes were bright—too sparkling bright,
in the lamplight—that didn't come from happiness.

He shifted his chair a little closer, so that she could
hear him above the clattering cowbells and heehawing
trumpets over there across the room. He poured her
more champagne.

"Then I do have a chance? I must, or you wouldn't be
here in New York. I must, or you wouldn't be here at this
table with me."

"I have to be someplace, so it might as well be here,"
she said pensively.

"I do have a chance."

"Don't ask me that now."

"I will ask you it, but don't answer it now. Don't answer
it. I can wait. Time is on my side." He poured some more
champagne.

"I shouldn't drink so much. I never have before."

"You're not drinking too much. And if you do? You're
among friends."

She said it over. "I *am* among friends. Among friends
at last. You don't know how good that sounds. To be
among friends. There's no more worry, there's no more
fear. I am safe now. It was like a nightmare. But the bad
dream is over. I am awake now." She raised her goblet.
"And I hear music. And I hear laughter. And I see a friend,
across the table from me."

She drained it, and seemed about to shiver, but she
didn't.

"Oh, it's so good to be with a friend. So *good.*"

He swallowed some of his own, but with an asperity.

"What did he do to you? What was it? You have that year stamped all over you. Oh, not in your looks, but I can see it in your eyes and hear it in your voice. What went on, all that time, out in that place where he had you?"

"Don't ask me to tell you anything. If I did, it would be the champagne telling you, and not I. And you wouldn't want to hear it from the champagne, you'd want to hear it from me."

"I'd kill him if he hurt a—a hair of your head!"

She gulped her champagne down almost voraciously, this time using both hands to the goblet stem. "Oh, my God. My God. Don't use that word. That's the one word you shouldn't use. Don't let me hear it. Just when I was beginning to forget a little."

"So you don't like that word," he brooded. "Who does? I don't either." He tilted his glass. "I never have. For a year now, I haven't. Your year and mine."

She was suddenly staring at him transfixed, her lips afraid to ask what her eyes so plainly did ask.

"Maybe this is the champagne telling *you*, now. *My* champagne telling *you*, instead of yours telling me. Telling you there's nothing for you to tell. No need." He turned his head briefly aside toward the jangled clatter. "Yes, play louder, louder still. But she's going to hear it just the same. I can't keep it in any longer. Maybe I know, Marjorie. Maybe I understand. Maybe there are three in on the secret, and not just two."

Even the lamp couldn't tint her face now, nor the champagne flush it any more; its whiteness overcame both of them. "What are you saying? I don't know what you're trying to say!"

"I know. I've always known. That's what I'm trying to say. I've known ever since an hour afterward."

"And yet—"

"Yes, 'and yet,'" he agreed sorrowfully. "Those 'ifs'

and 'buts' and 'and yets.' Short little words, but they cover so much ground. Would I stick a knife in your heart? Is that what I felt for you then, and what I feel for you now? No, I was the chum, the pal, the game loser. The little gentleman. That's me all over, Marjorie. The loyal friend who kept his mouth shut." His fist banged down in heavy contradiction. "The God-damned fool, you mean. Who could have had you a year sooner, but wouldn't hit below the belt."

She couldn't say anything. She wasn't looking at him now any more, she was looking at the past. Down at the bottom of her goblet where the champagne froth was. Not the past that had been, perhaps, but an alternate past, that might have been.

"For what?" he went on. "For who? To see you as you are now? To miss you as I have, to want you as I do, to be lonely as I am? Does one man do that for another? God didn't make us that way, and God was right. Why shouldn't I have my happiness, when it's right out there in front of my arms, and all I have to do is reach? What am I, an angel or a saint? No, I'm what I said before; a fool, a God-damned fool."

"And I am too, I guess," she sighed.

"But your eyes were closed, and mine were open."

"How did you come to…?" It wavered, and it stopped; as though she weren't really interested any more, at this late day; it was just a reflex question.

"I was the best man at your wedding. I went back to his room that day. I'd seen something I didn't like, when I'd been there the first time, to pick him up. I didn't know what it was myself, just something in the atmosphere. The way he took a drink with me, the way a burning cigarette on the edge of a table nearly sent him into convulsions. A cigarette that had lip rouge on it. I didn't know why myself, but I went back. *I found her there.* And I helped him. Or was it you? I—saw to it that no one else would find her there. Don't ask me what I did, it doesn't matter now any more."

"And I don't want to know it anyway. My heart has too much to carry already, it's heavy as lead. He told me the part before, in that faraway town one night. And every hour since, I've wished he never had."

"And now I'm here, and now you're here. With it. But he isn't. We make a peculiar threesome."

"What'll I do? Oh, Lance, what'll I do? I'm afraid to go back to him. And even if I don't—I'm still not free of him."

"Don't do anything. Just be you, be Marjorie." And low so that she scarcely heard, "Let others—do it for you."

They were somnolently silent for awhile, and then she said, "I'm drinking too much. What have we been talking about? It's gone now, but—I'm afraid I'll remember."

"I'm drinking too much too," he said, draining his glass. "And I'm afraid I'll forget."

She saw him push back his chair and stand.

"Will you sit here for a moment? I want to get some cigarettes."

"But you have some right there before you."

"Another kind of cigarettes. A *much better kind.* Just sit here. And remember—always remember—you're with friends. And no one will ever hurt you again."

He closed himself into the booth.

He could still see her sitting there across the room from him. Still see her in all her lovely, downcast, heart-quickening desirableness. It made him want to cry out in anguish, he wanted her so. It was important to keep looking at her. It was important to keep her like that before his eyes, the whole time, and not turn them to what he was doing.

The coin chinked home.

"Spring three, one hundred," he said quietly above the

glass-dimmed roar of the jazz band, worshiping her with his eyes there where she sat, lonely, lost, waiting to be claimed, across the room. A Madonna in an evening gown, an angel baffled with champagne. His hope of heaven, his religion…

Marshall swung a random, spindly bar stool by its long legs and the glass door of the booth shattered, and it pelted all over the man inside, so that he had to throw his arm across his face to ward it off. The jazz squawked off-key, as though every instrument were a chicken and their necks had all been wrung at once, then floundered in its death throes, and beat the air a little with crazed wings, and expired. The dancers thinned to isinglass cutouts— you could see right through their bodies—and then even that thinned, and they were gone. The little table lamps went out all over the room, as though he'd inadvertently damaged a master switch and the current was slowly failing.

"No you won't!" he panted. "You won't say a word! I'll see that you don't! I'll kill you first, myself, if I have to!" And he went for Lansing's throat with both his hands, and seized it, and tried to pull him away, out of there.

Then he was torn loose, and pinned back against the wall, by the shoulders, by the arms, held there flat against it and all spread out.

Only his head inclined away from it a little. Then a fist swung, and crashed into it, and it ricocheted back and smote the wall, and for a minute he would have dropped, but they still held him up.

"Get a cop in here," a voice ordered. "Are you all right, sir? Are you all right?"

Lansing came out of the booth still with an arm shielding his face. Then as he took it down, it seemed to wipe his whole face off with it, like some sort of curdling magic. And in its place was another face, older, and ashen with fright, lined, and rather flabby, and balding at the temples.

And when he looked at her, through the blood that was coming down over one eye, she was gone too. She and the little table, the little lamp, the goblets of champagne.

A policeman came in and stood there before him, listening to them tell it. Nodding, head inclined judiciously.

"I'll pay for it," Marshall blurted out terrifiedly. "I'll pay for it. I'll pay double for it. Only, for God's sake, let me go free. Don't let him take me with him. Don't let them lock me up, put me in jail." And he tried to take the policeman's coat-sleeve and pluck at it pleadingly.

"That's up to you, are you the owner here?" the policeman said to one of the men. "It's whatever you say; do you want to press charges?"

The owner squeezed his chin to a thoughtful, graduating point.

Marshall fumbled, brought out money, all the money he had on him, held it in palsied readiness in his hands.

"How much does one of them booth windows come to, about?" the policeman asked dubiously.

"Twenty dollars, say," the owner estimated. "He said double, though."

"And what about you, mister?" the policeman said to the man who'd been in the booth. "Did he hurt you in any way?"

"No," the man stammered confusedly. "No. Just gave me a bad fright for a minute. I saw him swing it and I threw up my arm in time. I—I was just about to call my wife, tell her I was kept over, I'd be a little late. But I think maybe I'll change my mind, go home after all…" And he turned and scuttled off.

"Give him twenty-five dollars," the policeman growled to Marshall. And he did it for him, took it out of his hand and handed it over to the owner. "And get the hell out of here, and don't let me catch you around again, here or anywhere else!"

Outside, the flanges on the corner lamppost said "Pine Street" and "Third Street." But he could still hear the ghostly music from Churchill's, all the way at Forty-ninth Street and Broadway.

3

The biggest, the heaviest hand in the whole world was on his shoulder. Bearing down, clutching him. An earthquake of a hand, shaking him. Shaking the whole world with him. Making the room he was in, the place, wherever it was, vibrate and throb and jiggle; clatter loosely and strain at the seams.

He'd always known that some day such a hand would find him out, descend upon him. For years he'd dreaded it in anticipation. He'd always known how it would feel. And now it felt just as he'd known that it would feel. The feeling of sick helplessness that it gave, he'd lived that a thousand times before.

The hand of Nemesis, it must be. The hand of reprisal, at long last. The hand of the punishing law. What else could be that heavy, that insistent in its claim?

His eyelids fluttered, and he instinctively tightened the double-armed overlapping clutch in which he held his coat, hugging the bottle that nestled upright on the inside of it, slanted against the pit of his arm.

"No," he rebelled automatically. "No. I haven't done anything. Let me alone. Go away."

His eyes darted about, and he saw that he was surrounded, that he was in some sort of a police trap. They were on both sides of him. For, outside the window, a man, slowly going by, was pointing directly in at him, with an extended centrally focused forefinger that slowly moved along as he, Marshall, moved along. Grim-eyed, lantern-jawed, elderly, with whiskers and wearing a tall hat with stars around its band. "I want you!" he scowled, and his speech, strangely enough, instead of being audible took the visible form of lettering.

"All right, son. All right, son. Now how about it?" This time the speech was audible, and no lettering appeared. Marshall swung his face to that side, and looked up the forbidding blue serge uniform to the face that topped it. This was elderly too, and whiskered like the first, but it was less grim than the other, there was something more humane about it. The headgear was different too, instead of the starred top hat it had a rather slouchy kepi with a visor to it.

"How about what?" Marshall quailed.

"Have you got a ticket or haven't you?"

Marshall shook his head; not in negation, but trying to clear it, to get the word in and absorb its meaning. "What kind?" he mumbled. "Ticket for what?"

"This is a train, boy. You've got to have a ticket to be on here. I don't know what you're doing here, I don't know how you got on—I must have missed you the first time I came through—but if you haven't got a ticket, you're coming with me."

"Train!" said Marshall, terrified, shooting his eyes this way and that. "What train? What train is this?"

And he saw that though the hand wasn't shaking him any more, just resting heavy and inflexible on his shoulder, the creaking and the throbbing and the shuddering still kept up. The man with the starred hatband outside the window had long ago lost pace, fallen behind. There was, now, a capped figure in wooden shoes wielding a stick, with the legend "Chases dirt."

The conductor was looking at him half in compassion, half in complete disgust.

"This is the train for New York, son."

And he spaced each word and said it again, slow, as though he realized himself what a terrible, what a shattering thing he was saying; although he couldn't have.

"This, is, the, train—that, takes, you, to, New York, son. Now, do, you get it? All, the, way, to, New York."

Marshall's neck jerked abruptly, almost as though a noose had lighted about it and a trap had sprung under his feet, as if he had been hanged while sitting down; and his face went down toward his chest, and he heeled his hands to his eyes.

"New York," he winced, like a man who has just incautiously caught a glimpse of hell and seared his eyes with it. "New York."

"How'd you happen to get on here, if you didn't know that?" the conductor asked him curiously.

Marshall uncovered his eyes again, and looked at him helplessly. "I've been wanting to do it. I guess I went ahead and did do it, without knowing it." And scouring his hair with his hand, he mumbled to himself, "Been having so many of these bad dreams, lately. But every time one ends, I'm back in that faraway town again."

"Well, we carried you this far without payment; I'm afraid you'll have to come back rear with me, hear what they're going to say about it." And the restraining hand, which had relented for the time being and quitted his shoulder, poised itself to descend once more.

He kept watching it askance, with a sort of horror, his neck acutely twisted to do so. As if that in itself, the return of that hand, would be the sum total of calamity.

"Wait," he said. "Don't. Can't I—can't *you* sell me a ticket?"

"Can if you've got the money to pay for it," said the conductor drily.

"How much will it take?"

"All the way to New York, day coach all the way." The conductor was looking it up, to make sure. "Forty-four seventy-five."

He fumbled with his money so hectically that it seemed to sprout up loose between his two hands, and several bills jumped to the floor between his feet, and over the seat to the aisle.

The conductor helped him retrieve them, helped him count a part of it. "Take your time. Don't want you to lose any of it now. I've got twenty-two here."

"And I've got thirty here!" Marshall discovered ecstatically.

"You've got a ticket, son," the conductor nodded magnanimously.

Marshall exhaled deeply and went limp against the seat back.

The two wings of his coat had come apart, and the bottle lay semirevealed, coddled against his shirt.

"Reckon I understand how it all came about," the conductor remarked shrewdly, without appearing to lift his eyes at all. "Here's your ticket, son. I'll have the change for you next time through. Sure you want to go there, now?"

"I have to do this till the dream ends," Marshall told him with the utmost simplicity. "Just follow it through, sort of."

"Better let me have that, I'll get rid of it for you," the conductor whispered, and winked, and smuggled the empty bottle up under his own jacket.

"Can I get another?" Marshall asked him with desperate urgency. "Where can I get another? I can't make it—I'll never make it—without another bottle."

"Probably get yourself one in K. C., we'll be in there in another hour and there's a forty-minute layover in the station."

"I don't want to get off. I'm afraid I'd never get back on again. Can't you get it for me? Here, I'll give you this. You keep what's over." He crushed a bill into his hand.

"Well, we ain't supposed to. It's against the regulations. But you seem to be in some kind of mix-up. And you don't 'pear to be the loud kind. Stay out in the vestibule, where nobody'll notice you, and where I can keep on eye on you. Don't go into none of the cars where there are women and children. When you take a swig, take it from under your coat, like you've been doing. I'll try to slip you one while we're standing still in K. C."

"Thanks," Marshall whispered fervently. "Thanks."

"I don't aim to preach," the conductor told him half sorrowfully, "but it's a shame, a young fellow your age. Better think it over, when you get to New York."

"When will the dream end, this time?" Marshall asked him, with a sort of pleading concern.

"What dream, son?"

"The dream that I'm on the train, the train to New York."

"Grand Central, son. Lower level. 'Leven 'clock tomorrow night."

4

The train had died. Every train dies at the end of every journey. The train was dead now, and lying in its coffin: the station.

Its passengers were gone. The platform was empty, and the cars were drained of all life, and their lights were for the most part already turned off. Just here and there, for safety's sake, one had been left on. Wanly revealing empty seats and ghostly passageways.

The friendly conductor knocked on the door. "Better come out of there now, son. Have to be getting off."

The door opened and Marshall came out, looking very pale.

"Everybody's off already," the conductor said. "Thought maybe you might have fallen asleep, or something."

"I've been awake since Harmon," Marshall said.

"What'd you do with the bottles?" the conductor asked him.

"I slipped them under the leather seat there."

"I'll have to get them out of the way," the conductor said. Then he looked at him. "Can you walk?" he said.

"I'm not drunk," Marshall said. "I tried hard enough, but I'm not drunk."

He started down the empty aisle, pawing the seat tops one by one.

"Here, let me give you a hand," the conductor said. "You're my responsibility until I can get you off of here. That's the last time I ever—"

"Thanks for everything," Marshall said.

When they came to the lip of the vestibule, just before the top step, Marshall drew back involuntarily, and bunched his shoulders together as if he were cold, and defensively turned up his collar in back.

"This is it," he said.

"This is it, all right," the conductor agreed.

"It smells sort of cold," Marshall said. "It smells like a tomb."

"Go 'head, it won't bite you," the conductor chuckled. "Don't take so long; I've got to be on my way too, you know. If you didn't want to come here, why did you come here?"

"I thought it was just another dream," Marshall said. "But the joke's on me."

"No, you ain't drunk," the conductor said caustically. "In a different kind of way, maybe."

Yes, I'm drunk, Marshall thought. Drunk with fear.

The conductor armed him down the steps of the narrow, chutelike car exit. "Up that way," he indicated.

"I know," Marshall agreed. "Up that way. New York."

The conductor watched him straighten himself, get the feel of the ground.

"You all right, now? Think you'll be able to make it, now?"

"I'm all right," Marshall said. "Sure, I'm all right."

The conductor watched him take the first steps, like a father anxiously watching a child just beginning to learn to walk.

"Know where you want to go?"

"Yes," said Marshall. "I know where I'm going."

"Well, good luck," the conductor said, with a downward slice of his arm, as though he were a dispatcher sending the train off.

"Wish it to me over again," Marshall said, without turning his head. "You can never have enough of that."

He went up the long platform, all alone. As you go through life—all alone. Without any baggage, without even any outer coat, with nothing, just a long shadow spilling out behind him. As you go through life—without any baggage, with nothing. Looking so small, so lost, between the long rows of empty, blinded cars. As you go through life—so small, so lost.

He went up the ramp—to meet New York.

5

It was nighttime in New York when he came out of the station. He looked up and the sky was black over the town, like a lid crammed down on a smoking cauldron. No stars, no anything like that. Stars over New York? They knew better than to waste their time over such a place. It had its own, crawling like gilded lice all over its serrated scalp.

It was too late to go to her tonight, too late to go to her house right now, from the station. He was her husband, and she was his wife, but it was too late to go to her house, to seek her out tonight. He'd only frighten, shock, or maybe alienate her. And then the way he looked, sleepless from the train, clothes unchanged, liquor still in his bloodstream if not in his brain. Tomorrow, the first thing tomorrow; tonight, a bed some place. Any bed, any place.

It was so big, so cavernous. It gave you vertigo. Shoals of lighted taxis went by, like regimented fireflies executing precision maneuvers. And their horns went squawk, squonk, squonk, squa-a-awk. An El train flashed across the air like a flaming concertina, the next block down, at Third, with a sound like somebody playing the kettledrums.

He didn't even know how to walk any more in crowds; he'd lost the New York knack. He kept trying to give way, as you did in other places. But as he did that on one side, he kept colliding on the other. He was buffeted along.

He shivered. It was so big, it was so dangerous. He couldn't stay here very long. He'd have to get out again as quickly as he could. Tomorrow. Maybe tomorrow he could persuade her to start back with him. Take the night train back with him to—to—to where it wasn't New York.

Just this one night. He'd have to shave first, he'd have to do something about his clothes. He'd make himself look good, then he'd go to her....

There was one right across the street, the Belmont, but he couldn't go there. He walked east a block, and then up a couple, and found one there, on Third Avenue, and bought a room for a dollar. The kind of place where they gave you a key and let you find the room yourself.

"Davis," he put down for a name, in their book.

He locked the door on the inside first, before he even put on the light. He struck a match, and found the tap, and found a tumbler, and filled it and drank from it, without caring whether it was foul or not. (It's not half so foul as my insides, it occurred to him.)

Every few minutes, regularly, the whole room seemed to burst into flame, as an El train roared by right on the other side of the windowpane. And then the fire went out, and the room was still uncharred.

He took off his coat and his shoes, for the first time since leaving that faraway town.

Then he pulled down the shade, and he sat there peeping out at the side of it. Peeping out at New York.

The enemy, the bad place, the trap.

The mouse was within the trap, but it wasn't caught yet. The way out was still open behind it.

6

How strange, he thought, to deck yourself out like this for a wife of two years' standing. As though she were a strange sweetheart you were courting.

Some people, he realized, might have thought it
pathetic, pitiful. He didn't. He thought of it as good
strategy. He was, he intended, using the only weapon he
really had, her love for him. And to help that along all he
could, he had to make its object, himself, as attractive to
her as possible. She had to see him as she first had seen
him, not as she last had seen him.

He kept feeling his newly razored cheeks, as if to make
sure they were smooth enough for her. He traced the
back of his neck, to make sure the man had trimmed it
just right.

He took out his handkerchief, and though he had only
just had his shoes shined, he dusted their tops off all over
again.

He bought a new shirt. He even bought a new tie.

"No," he said to the salesman's preferred selection,
"no stripes. My wife likes solid colors, in a man's tie. And
I'm wearing it for her."

He put on the new shirt right there in the haberdashery, behind a mirrored partition. He put on the new
tie. He came out with it left loose and had the salesman
knot it for him. "I never was very good at that," he said.
"She used to do it for me. Give me a good one, that'll stay
in place."

He bought her flowers; two dozen fresh young roses,
just beginning to open.

There wasn't anything else he could think of, to make
her love him more.

Then, outwardly confident, inwardly trembling and
agonized, he hailed a taxi and got in.

"Seventy-ninth, just west of Madison," he said. "I'll
show you the house when we get there."

7

They still had the same servants, apparently, as during his courtship days. He recognized the man who came to open the door, Cochrane, but if the man recognized him, he made it difficult to determine.

"Good afternoon," he said neutrally.

"Is Mrs. Marshall in?" Marshall asked. He couldn't move past him as unhesitatingly as he'd intended to, because the man wasn't adroit enough in getting out of his way.

"Mrs. Marshall?" Cochrane acted surprised.

"My wife," said Marshall, a trifle impatiently. "You remember me, don't you?"

"Yes, of course, sir," the man said drily. "But Miss— Mrs. Marshall isn't staying here at the house with us."

The roses went down like a flag about to be lowered in defeat.

"She isn't? Well, where can I find her? Where *is* she staying?" As a suspicious afterthought flitted through his mind, he gave it voice. "Are you quite sure of that? Or were you just told to say that?"

The man took no umbrage. "I'm quite sure, sir. She visits here quite regularly, but she has an apartment somewhere downtown."

"Could you tell me where it is?" said Marshall, choking down a rising resentment at what he took to be a premeditated evasiveness.

"Mr. Worth would know, of course, sir..." the man said uncertainly.

"Well, is he in?"

"You missed him by half an hour. He's gone to his club. I could ring him there for you, sir, and find out. Shall I do that?"

"No," said Marshall with asperity, "don't ring him. Don't ring anybody at all. There must be somebody in this house that knows my wife's address. Or is it just because you're not sure she'd approve your giving it out to me? I happen to be her husband, after all."

"No, sir," said the man guilelessly, "it isn't a question of that at all. It's just that I don't happen to know it myself, and Mr. Worth isn't here at the moment. I'll see if Mrs. Davis knows, or one of the others. Would you care to step inside and wait?"

"I'll wait out here where I am," said Marshall stonily.

He didn't want anything to do with her house. He only wanted her.

Cochrane reopened the heavy iron-grilled glass door after several moments and offered him a card.

"Mrs. Davis found it for you, sir. It's on Fifty-fourth Street, she has the exact house number on here. The telephone is—"

"I don't need that," said Marshall, curtly turning away. "I'm not a stranger."

8

There was a myopic moment in which the whole world was a blind, white-painted wooden panel. Nothing more than that, before his eyes. And his heartbeats seemed to swell and throb against it, playing the part his hand and the knocker should have played between them. While he held his hat in one hand, the paper cone of flowers poignantly head-down in the other. Suppliant. Abject.

Knowing that this was the turning point of his whole life. That nothing that had gone before had counted as this did, that nothing that would come after would count as this did. Praying, Give her back to me. Let me have her back. I can't go on without her.

Then he heard her step draw near. Then the knob turned. Then the blind wood panel fell away. Then the whole world was her face, there close before him. The most beautiful world any man could see. The complete world: the sun, the moon, the stars, all in one. The shield against loneliness. The buffer against weariness. The balm against pain. The face that in every man's life is a little glimpse of God, perhaps the only one he'll ever be given. The face of the girl that is his wife.

So familiar, yet so strange.

The soft lips he'd kissed a thousand times, but parted taut as he'd never seen them before. The eyes that had wept for him, smiled for him, planned with him, hoped with him, but startled now as he had never seen them before, too much of their whites showing.

Her breath faltered and she couldn't find full voice. She whispered. "You're in—?"

"I'm here in New York."

"Oh, Press," she breathed. And yet it could almost have been taken for a crushed remonstrance.

"Won't you open your door?" he pleaded. "Won't you let me come in?"

She swept it instantly to its full width; but that came after his plea, not before. "Of course I'll let you come in," she said. "When wouldn't I want you to?" But it was said half sadly, he thought, rather than happily.

She closed it.

"Let me look at you," he said tenderly.

She stood there to let him look.

"You haven't changed," he said yearningly. "You

couldn't; you were so perfect already. Have I?"

She dropped her eyes, then raised them. "No," she said. She didn't smile with it. Was that a victory? He wondered.

"Why did you do this?" He gestured. "Come down here."

"I didn't have to hear the questions that—they didn't ask," she said reticently.

So she hadn't told them.

"It's not bad, at that," he said. He hated it.

"Sheila Abbott was giving it up. I don't know if you remember her or not. She was one of the bridesma—" She stopped a second, then said, "I took it from her the way it was."

He went over to put his hat down, on a sort of Louis XVI commode she had there, light-blue lacquer and gilt. He picked a piece of paper up, then put it down again. "Lansing, Rector—," it said, and then some numerals, in her writing.

He tried to make himself sound casual about it. "Have you been seeing much of him since you're here?"

"Not much of anyone," she said tonelessly. "He called once, and I promised to call him back, and—that's been there ever since." Then she said with a sort of wearied gratitude, "He's a tactful sort of person. Doesn't make himself obtrusive. I've always liked that about him."

But the paper shouldn't have stayed there that long, he thought. Well, in San Francisco, it won't make any difference.

"Here," he said diffidently. "I brought you these."

She unrolled the paper from the flowers, and they flushed out, umbrellalike, spreading in her hands.

Then she took them rather quickly to a table and put them down on that, without offering, he saw, to put her face close to them and smell them.

"Why are you looking at me like that?" he said.

She didn't answer. But then he knew without her telling him. The color. He hadn't thought of that. They were red.

He closed his eyes in the pain she'd just given him.

She seemed, when next he looked at her, at a loss, oddly restrained, even awkward; a thing he'd never yet known her to be, with him, with anyone.

"I'd like to—I don't know what to offer—" she said. "I don't keep any liquor here, as Father does at home. As a matter of fact, there aren't even any facilities for making tea. I've been having to take my meals out. But wait, I think there may be some of Sheila's left-over cigarettes in one of these boxes. She's been taking up smoking, you know, lately..."

He shook his head, not in negation, but harassedly, almost distractedly, giving it full swings from side to side.

"How can we *sit* here like this! How *can* we! Like two strangers in a room, offering each other tea and cigarettes, and a hundred thousand miles away! What's happened?"

He jumped up and darted over to her, and caught her two hands in his two, from where they had lain, at her sides.

"Marjorie, take me back into your heart. Open the door. Oh, not that door of wood. *The* door, the door between us. I'm outside, I'm in the rain..."

And on his knees before her, like a worshipper at a shrine, he sent up his appeal.

"I'm cold, I'm hungry. Look at me; I'm the boy you loved, I'm the boy you picked. Look into my face, and tell me that I can't come in—!"

"Oh, I was afraid of this," she said, half to herself, "I've been dreading it, I knew it was going to come sooner or later. Don't," she begged him. "Don't. You have my pity already. Pity for you, and pity for me. Get up. I haven't anything else left to give you."

She strove until she'd drawn her hands away and freed them. And deftly moved herself away from him, withdrew.

He was left there stranded, with nothing to kneel to any more, nothing *near* enough, ludicrousness added to his abasement.

He rose at last, lamely.

"What am I going to do?" he asked her. "Without you? What?"

"Can't you see? Why must I tell you? You've come this far. You're here now. Go the rest of the way. Go to *them*."

"To *them*?" he said aghast.

"What other way is there to end it? What other way *can* it end? Isn't it better than going on like this? Why didn't you do it in time, why didn't you do it long ago, while you still had my— Press, there is only one right in this and only one wrong. It *has* to be paid for, it can't be kept hidden. Tell them the story as it happened. As you've told it to me. That this girl hounded you, up to the very day of your marriage, threatened your whole happiness. They're only men, they're only human, they'll be lenient. They may agree to a—to a second-degree count. It was unpremeditated, it was in a fit of passion. And even if they punish you a little for it, Press, that punishment ends, this kind never does. You've asked me what to do, and now I've told you. We'll help you. We'll stand by you. Father will get you a good lawyer. We won't turn our backs on you. I can't promise you love any more, Press. But I can promise you not to make any final decision until you're freed of this terrible thing, until it's out of the way. And I *can* promise to respect you." And very low she amended, "Which is something I don't do now."

He kept staring at her with something akin to horror.

"A second-degree count?" he whispered. "You don't know what you're saying at all. I can't hope for that, I can't, don't you understand? I didn't tell you all of it that night." And he groaned abysmally. "Do I have to tell you *everything?* Do I have to stand here naked before you? The girl wasn't the only one. There were two more after her. That's why we left so quickly. A man in a boat, I never knew his name. Wise—that was me…"

She seemed about to double up momentarily, as though a violent pang had assailed her in the stomach. And her hand, pasted palm-out across her forehead, added credibility to the illusion.

She took a staggering, nauseated step or two that brought her to the commode, and held her hands clamped tight to the forward edge of it. She looked down intently.

Instantly he saw his mistake. Instantly he saw what it had done. Instantly he saw that he had lost her irrevocably now, pushed himself beyond the pale. That if there had been a chance before this, now there was none, no chance at all. And frightened—he had always been so quick to take fright—he tried to hold her to him, where she was and as she was, to keep from losing her. And she in turn, taking fright from his fright, abandoned him even quicker, receded all the more and with an added haste. As a frantic beating of the water, in attempt to reach an unmanned boat, sends the boat even further off.

Not physical as yet, this play and counterplay, still of the reason; still spiritual, the bonds that he tried to reaffirm while she severed and escaped them.

"Don't come to me now with flowers," she cried out in a hurried frightened voice. "Don't come to me now with kisses. I didn't marry *you.* You're not the man I was married to. He died in the dark, in our bedroom that night, in the faraway town. Or else he never lived at all, only in my own imagination. I was married to a ghost, an illusion. How can I go back to *you*? There never was a *you*, as I thought you were. You *kill* people."

"It isn't true, it isn't true. *Now* is the lie, *then* wasn't. You knew my arms, I knew your kisses and you knew mine, I knew your body and you knew mine. You can't tear yourself away from me now, you're tearing the living flesh apart."

And went to her and took her in his arms and turned her to him.

"Words can't change it, can't change us. There aren't words in the whole world strong enough. Give me a chance. Look, I'll show you." And with throbbing lips, found hers, and tried to hold them. And failed, and tried again. "Was our love a lie? Was our love an illusion?"

"No, don't. For two years you drugged me that way, with those lips. The drug's worn off, I can see what they're bringing me now. They're not bringing me kisses. They're bringing me the smell of death."

And then he sealed the kiss. And with it sealed his own fate.

It was the spark to the tinder of her hysteria. He had pushed her too much. He had frightened her beyond recovery. In a moment he didn't know her. She was rabid. There was nothing there to reason with any longer.

"Murderer," she panted, straining to tear her face away. "Don't come near me. You're all covered with…I'll call the police!"

And now it was his fright that kindled itself from hers, and they were both lost.

He sought to seal her mouth with his hand.

"Stop, Marjorie. Marjorie, stop. I'm your husband. Look at me. Don't say those things…"

And now she had reached the point of screams, he could feel them blasting hot against his hand, and if he

took his hand away they would wing out. He couldn't
hold them much longer, couldn't hold them much longer.

There was a better, an easier place, to stop them, further down.

His hand shifted.

His love story came to an end.

9

Lying there now, side by side upon the floor, like lovers in
a vain embrace. Speaking to her, pleading to her, making
his love to her, without avail. One-sided love to a sudden
indifference, where there had never been indifference
before. Her face had an absent-minded expression;
drowsy, dull-witted, dead.

"Let me hear your voice again. Just say one word, just
say my name. 'Press.' I can almost hear the echo of it
now. Ah, call me 'Press' again, call me 'Press.' " And
putting his ear close to her recalcitrant lips, seemed to
drink it up privately from there. "Louder. Louder than
that. So that I can be quite sure. I know you said it just
then, I heard it in my heart, but say it beyond all dispute.
Say 'Press, you didn't hurt me.' Say 'Press, you should be
ashamed, now help me up.' Louder, louder than that. I
can't hear it well yet.

"Let me see your eyes again. Look this way. Look at
me, look at *me*. What do you see over there? Turn them,
turn them to me. Make them warm again. Make them
dance again with those little specks of sunny stuff that
used to be in them. Oh, I can't stand it without your eyes,
Marjorie."

And taking her hand, as if teaching it, as if reminding
it, caused it to caress him, drawing it lightly, lingeringly

down the side of his face. And put it to his lips and held them to it, on this side, on that, now back again. But his kiss didn't warm it any, nor cause it to stir in response.

Indifference; indifference for all time, for all eternity now. Never again to change.

He stopped and looked at it, her hand.

"You took it off," he said in tender accusation. "You shouldn't have, you shouldn't have."

And rising, left her for a moment and went to look for it. And found it soon, almost as though he'd known, in a little trinket box within a bureau drawer. Came back with it, and knelt beside her, and in a ghastly repetition of their wedding vows, the living marrying the dead, replaced the wedding band upon her finger. Where it once had rested in such bright hope and promise, such trust and faith and selfless devotion. And tears of the irreparable streaming from his eyes, repeated once again the words that made them one.

"I, Prescott, take thee, Marjorie, to my lawful wedded wife…To have and to hold…To love and to cherish…In sickness and in health…Until death do us part…

"And *beyond*— And *beyond*— And *beyond*—"

And as his voice swelled toward agonized screams, he had to stifle it with the back of his hand, until blood had joined the tears that coursed down it.

Then he had to leave her at last. For there was nothing there. Nothing that heard nor heeded, nor cared nor loved. He'd been trying to marry himself to empty space.

Alone. Alone now, in the dark. Forever alone, forever in the dark.

Never again Marjorie.

And staggering, swimming through mazes of pain and fear, like someone breasting a tide while he treads erect on his feet underwater, his after-life began.

To the telephone. Remembering another time, long ago. Someone who had helped him. Memory is long.

Took the piece of paper. Spoke from it to the telephone.

And then Lansing's voice, out somewhere in the world of light.

"Hello. Who's this?"

"Prescott…Marshall."

"Press! When did you get in town?"

Trying to come up through the layers of fog and darkness, to reality, to the upper world, where that voice was; like a drowned man's body trying to come up to the surface of the water from its smothered depths. Looking at that empty place over there. At that empty face that he knew wasn't there. Warning himself, craftily, 'I must not tell him, or he may not come. He may not come alone, and to help me he must come alone.'

He said with slow care: "I…have to…see you." And took a breath between each word or two, to see the next pair through.

"Why sure. I'm working right now. But look, how about us having dinner tonight?"

The fool. He thought it was just a plea for sociability.

He looked at her and closed his eyes in woe. She shouldn't look so clear, so plainly seen, in a place where she wasn't any more. It was like a decalcomania pattern left on the carpet, in her own exact image. Too exact. It had to be erased.

"It can't wait…until tonight. I have to see you…now. I have to see you…quickly."

"You sound…Are you in trouble?"

No answer, so the stupid voice tried to provide one, out of its own scant fund of knowledge.

"Look, Press, if it's money— Why don't you let me know now about how much you could use; that way I won't have to come out, and then make an extra trip back to the office again to get it for you. I'll bring something right with me, if you'll—"

"Don't stop to bring any money. Just come to me."

"All right, I'll go down and jump in a cab, that'd be the quickest. Now, where do you want to make it? Where'll I meet you?"

"I'll be waiting for you," said Marshall with haunted simplicity, "outside the door of Marjorie's apartment. You'll find me there. All by myself."

10

Afraid to go back inside again, and yet afraid to go away and leave the place, he stood leaning there against the outside of the closed door, in a state of erect collapse. A hand desperately pressing against the doorframe on each side of him, as though to ward off intrusion, discovery, just by being there.

He was like that when the top of Lansing's head slowly came up above floor level, over by the stairwell. He greeted it with an infantile whimper of delight. The way a lost child greets someone who has come to retrieve him. He'd never been so glad to see anything before, as the top of that other man's head. No sight of Marjorie, in all the years he'd loved her, had ever been as precious, been as dear. The instinct to live is greater than the instinct to love.

And then Lansing's shoulders, and then Lansing's back. Marshall was panting with eagerness, the way a puppy does when its owner has returned within its confused, limited ken.

A cartoonist would have drawn, for his eye sockets,

brief circumflex accent marks, they were so creased, so elevated, in delight. They could have stood for crying, they could have stood for laughing; they stood for rapture.

Lansing made the turn of the banister and then saw him.

"Press," he said in surprise, but no more than casual, conversational surprise, as when any two meet unexpectedly, anywhere at any time. And went on over toward him, hand extended. Reached down and found Marshall's, and clasped it in one-sided greeting. "Press," he said again.

Marshall's lips opened and closed, twice, over idiot silence.

"What is it, can't you get in? Does Marjorie know you're out here?"

All Marshall could do at that was give his head a mute, shuddering shake and let it dangle over remorsefully, chin to chest.

Lansing edged him a little out of the way, to gain clearance.

Then suddenly he'd done a horrible thing. A simple thing. A thing that was both at once: simply horrible.

He knocked on the door. Knocked on the door of the dead.

Marshall's features shriveled, as though a needle had gone into him somewhere.

He put his hands up and found his ears with them, to keep the sound out. Lansing had already repeated it just then.

"Don't," Marshall pleaded, in a broken whisper. "She can't hear you." He spiraled around and pressed his brow against the wall, arms hanging down now at loose ends beside him.

Lansing shot him a look, his hands went for the knob. The door crunched and he'd gone in.

Marshall rolled back again, the other way around, face

outward to the stairs, and stayed that way. All loose in the joints, and yet remaining upright.

His mouth was shaped into a curious wizened scowl; the grimace just preceding tears, but the tears never came.

He couldn't look in. He couldn't seem to turn his head and look in, to see what Lansing was doing in there, although the opening was just at his shoulder.

Finally Lansing was beside him again. Had come out to the threshold again. Marshall didn't look to see what his face was like. He only knew that it was there, somewhere a little rearward of his own.

"Who did it?"

Marshall's lower lip bubbled. The wizened grimace continued. The tears never came.

"You?"

The lip kept flickering. Like a loosened lip borne down by the weight of the words on it. But no words came.

No words were needed.

A hot, windy little gust, as from an unheard sob, fanned past Marshall's deadened cheek. From a sob that hadn't been his.

"I don't know what to do," somebody whispered forlornly, close by. "I don't know what to do." And it must have been Lansing, for it hadn't been he.

Then, blurredly, a figure moved out past him, turned to go toward the stairs. His eyes followed it inanely for a second or two, as though not understanding what it was, or why it moved, or where to.

Then, as if at least the first of these had been recalled to him if not the others, he spoke to it.

"Lance," he said, benumbed. "Where you going?"

"Downstairs, to the street," Lansing said. "See if I can find someone. A policeman."

"Don't," Marshall cried out sharply. That at least had

penetrated, that word. "Let me get out of here first, at least."

He made a sudden bolt, came up against Lansing's arms, flounderingly. Lansing's arms were suddenly a rigid, inflexible bar across the passage, from wall to stair rail. He recoiled from them.

"There's no way out, this way."

"The street! The street's down there!"

"There's no way out, this way."

Marshall took a faltering, rearward step.

Suddenly he turned and plunged the other way, toward the ascending arm at the other end.

He wasn't quick enough. Fear is quick, but there must be some things that are quicker. Again Lansing was before him, breast to breast, again his arms were locked like steel from side to side.

"Nor this way either."

"The roof! The roof's up there! I can go over it—"

"Nor this way either."

"But what other way is there? W-what are you doing to me?"

"There's only one way out, for you." His eyes flicked to the door, beyond which no one lived now. "In there."

Marshall turned and saw it, and then he turned again, and tried to cling to Lansing's coat revers.

"Lance, let me get out, let me get out! In Christ's name, let me get out!"

"I am. I'm trying to. But you won't."

"But that's just a room, in there. All closed up. It has no—"

"That's the only way out, for you. The only way there is."

"I don't know what you want me to—"

Then suddenly he understood. And all his fears of years and years came to a head on his face and burst like a great white pustule, and he was nothing but a mass of rotten, tainted fright.

"I don't know how—I don't know how to go about it…"

"She didn't either. You showed her."

"I was your friend…" He had instinct enough to use the past tense, at least. "Don't you remember, I was your friend—"

"You looked like a man. How was I to know? You would have fooled anyone. You even fooled her." He was past the point of even raising his voice, Lansing.

"I can't—cold like this. Oh, give me an hour more. An hour to—to get used to the idea. Until tonight, at least. Tonight, only until tonight."

"It's night already. You've made it night for all of us. For her. For you." And almost inaudibly he added, "And for me."

"I don't know how," Marshall moaned. He shrank away from him, sidling his back along the wall.

"It's easy. So easy." Lansing moved toward him. His hands went out. Marshall shrank still farther, but their reach overtook him. But Lansing didn't strike, or throttle, or offer to assail him with them. Instead, like a friend trying to help someone with the details of his appearance, he did something with the knot of Marshall's necktie. Slid it downward, until suddenly it had disintegrated, there was no knot any more. Then drew the tie out from under its ensconcing collar, until it had fallen, in a woolen puddle, into the hollow of his own hand, held below to catch it. And then he pressed it, coiled like that, into Marshall's hand. And taking the boneless fingers, closed them over it, so that they had to hold it, had to keep it, whether they wanted to or not.

Then he gave him a parting salute, gave him for gesture what was his due; said farewell to him in the way that he esteemed him. He wiped his own hand slowly down his side, as if to cleanse it of the soilure of the touch it had just been forced to meet.

Marshall was looking down at the tie now in horror, as though he held a snake there in his grasp, and couldn't let it go.

"I'll be down at the door," Lansing promised him in a leaden voice. "I'll stand there, and I won't go away. I'll never leave that door. And in five or ten minutes, I'll come back up here again. I'll come back up here, with a policeman. You can meet him—any way you want. That's up to you."

"Five or ten minutes is such a short time—to live—" Marshall whispered brokenly. "Such a *little* time…"

"It's five or ten minutes more than she had," Lansing reminded him. And then he added, with a contempt that was both lethal and yet at the same time almost detached, "What do *you* want to live for, anyway? *I* wouldn't, if I were you."

He walked away from him. He made the turn of the rail. He started down the stairs.

Marshall never moved.

Heavy, broken, dull of heart and of purpose, Lansing went down, step by slow succeeding step. Like a man going nowhere, like a man going to meet the empty years of the rest of his life.

"God forgive me," Marshall breathed with a shudder.

"No *man* ever would," Lansing answered bitterly.

Their eyes met for the last time; from below to above, from above to below.

Marshall never moved. The stray end of his own necktie dangled lifeless from his frozen fist.

Sight was exchanged between them for the last time. And then each died, for the other, and was gone.

Lansing's head disappeared below the floor level.

Somewhere up above him, unseen, a door closed with

a sudden fling of finality. As if it were never going to open again. Like the door of a life, suddenly closing on it, ending it.

Lansing went on down, step by lifeless step, into the barren, bottomless future that awaited him. Without love, without hope, without Marjorie.

11

The policeman came down to the street door for a moment, afterwards, and looked out at him, while he was waiting for his superiors to arrive and take charge.

"You were right," the policeman said to him. "I didn't believe you, but you were right. There's two of them up there, both dead. A woman lying on the floor. A man hanging by his necktie from the clothes rod in the closet."

And that's what it boils down to, thought Lansing, nodding to himself. A woman lying on the floor. A man hanging in the closet. Just a woman. Just a man. Any woman. Any man. As though they never knew each other. As though they never loved. How can the dead love the dead, anyway?

"What a hell of a thing to do," the policeman said.

Why call it that, wondered Lansing. What is hell, anyway? What an earthly thing to do, why not put it that way?

The policeman took out a pencil and a little notebook. "Did you know them both?" he asked.

"Yes," said Lansing, "I knew them both…"

I loved her from the time she was fifteen. From the time there first was any love, I loved her. You don't have to say "love" and "Marjorie," use separate words. Both words were always she to me.

I loved her from the first few kid parties we went to together, the stiff little dances we danced in each other's arms. She was so pretty then, a pink bow in her hair, a pink sash at her waist. How did she turn into that thing that's lying upstairs there now? Is that what little girls become? Is that what the little boys who love them can look forward to?

I loved her too much. That's the whole story. *My* story.

I just stood by. All her life, I just stood by. Waiting for her to turn my way. And she never turned. He came along. I just stood by. I saw him take her away from me. I just stood by. Now she's dead upstairs. And I'm still just standing by.

Because I loved her too much. Too much to try to take her away from the happiness I thought she had found.

When you love a little, you can be brave, you can be selfish. You come first, the loved one second. But when you love too much, it makes you a coward. You're afraid of hurting the thing you love.

He didn't kill her, I did. I killed the one I loved.

"...Yes," he said to the policeman, "I knew them both."

"Stick around," the policeman told him. "They'll want to talk to you when they get here. I've got to go back upstairs."

"Yes, I'll stick around," Lansing promised. I've stuck around all my life. That's all I've ever done, is stick around. I guess I can stick around the little while longer there is.

He stood there alone, by the doorway, in the dusk. Dead already. As dead as they were upstairs. All three of them were dead now; the triangle had been solved. Only, his was the kind of death that doesn't show. His was the kind of death that takes years, it is so slow. The death of the heart.

Far off somewhere, down on the next block, an organ-grinder was playing in the twilight. The wistful, lonely

notes seemed to come from some other time, far away
and long ago; as though they had been sounded years ago
and only found their way to earshot now, lost all the while
somewhere in between.

His head slowly drooped forward, and his buried heart
in its grave seemed to say the words over to itself, echoing
in its emptiness.

> *"Vilia, oh Vilia, I dream of the past,*
> *You were my first love and you'll be the last."*

Postscript

In a railroad flat on Third Avenue in the Eighties, Mrs. Timothy Meehan was suffering from one of her recurrent headaches. She sat at one of the old-fashioned, tall, narrow, curved-topped windows, elbows planted to sill, one hand holding in place a wet cloth pasted lengthwise across her brow, beside her a bowl of cold water (or at least as cold as could be hoped for in the jungle heat of a New York July) in which a replacement for the first cloth lay soaking, waiting its turn.

Below her, through layers of tropical miasma, were visible the latticed roadbed and tracks of the Third Avenue Elevated Railway, half again as high as her windows, and under that in turn, hidden in a subterranean dimness that never saw sunlight the tracks of the Third Avenue trolley line and the chasmlike street.

Tim Meehan was motorman on one of the latter's red and yellow electric surface-cars, and that incessant deafening disturbance going on all about her within the room right now, now toddling, now falling, now squalling, was his firstborn. With another already well on the way. And scant hope of any merciful pause or slackening in the immediate years to come.

"Well, they'll all be legal, anyway," she had a habit of consoling herself.

She swerved abruptly, lashed her hand downward and rearward, and was rewarded with a deafening cataclysm of noise. "Keep away from me now, can't you see I've got one of my headaches!" Then resumed her frontal placidity.

Cabbage was reeking from the kitchen coal range, and damp wash was steaming from the indoor clothesline that garlanded the rooms, and an El train was thundering by, shaking the whole window-embrasure that framed her and driving nails into her already-throbbing skull, and the very tar in the asphalt down there was softening up with the heat so that people left footprints in it.

Life wasn't a bed of roses.

It wasn't even a bed of the cheapest common field daisies that you picked for nothing.

But Tim Meehan's wife Leona was practical, had a lot of hard common sense. Always had had. This hard practicality, this common sense, had once almost been her undoing. And now, perhaps, it was her salvation.

"Still, it's better than the other way. It's better than the way I was going on."

That other way, it gave her the shudders to think of it, even now. It was only at rare intervals that she did, and they were becoming rarer all the time. These headaches brought it back, for they were its inheritance. They were the only link, any longer; the only link between two people who were not the same. The person she had once been, and the person she was now.

That had cured her once and for all, that knock on the head. That had knocked all the wildness out of her, and knocked some sense in, all in the one fell swoop.

That had cauterized her, that had immunized her to all further adventure.

She'd never, not to her dying day, forget how frightened she'd been, coming to her senses in the smothering dark, all buried-under with old clothes, on the inside of a closet (fortunately she'd been able to wrench open the door, after a terrible moment or two of resistance), left for dead on the floor.

And then hysteria, panic, when she'd floundered out of there, only to find herself locked in, in a strange room; head ringing, eyes blurred and scarcely able to focus. Claustrophobia, though she would not have known what the name was. (Even today, she wouldn't go into a closet; she let Tim hang her things up for her.) All the preceding weeks of disdain for him, lack of respect for him, sweated out of her now on the cold exudation of her terror. He was Bluebeard, he was Jack the Ripper. He'd only left the door locked on her like that because he intended coming back later, either to dispose of her remains or to finish the job of killing her as soon as he found that she was still alive.

She'd pounded frantically, like a wild thing, like a trapped thing, on the door, fearful of his return at any moment, until at last the landlady had been roused, and came running with passkey, and let her out.

Freed, she'd fled by her without a word, bolted past her before she could be stopped and questioned, like a rabbit on the run, she was so scared. Gone tumbling down the stairs, sobbing and heaving and with her head splitting, and out into the open, the blessed open. To be seen around there no more.

All that night she'd lain quivering and cowering in her own bed, with the covers pulled up over her head, afraid of all the nameless ogres and assassins rolled into one that have ever terrified women since the beginnings of time.

Two days later she'd had to go to the hospital for the first time, because of the dizzy spells that were assailing her, and forcing her to stop whatever she was about and lean for support against the nearest wall or shopfront or lamp post. A concussion, they told her. And how had she come by it? She'd fallen, she told them reluctantly, and

CORNELL WOOLRICH

struck her head. She didn't say how, and she didn't say where. She never again, to anyone, said how or where. Far from signing any complaint, her dread now was of ever accidentally encountering him once again.

They'd kept her coming back for treatment for months afterward. Finally they discharged her as cured. There would be, they warned her, violent headaches for a considerable time. Then eventually these too would lessen and would disappear, over the course of years.

Funny, how good came out of evil.

It was on one of these periodic visits to the hospital, riding a Third Avenue trolley, that she'd first met Tim Meehan.

Three months later they were married.

She hadn't trusted herself to wait any longer than that.

Here came another train, on the uptown track this time. She'd better get in before it gave her headache, now tapering off, another violent stirring-up.

She rose wearily from the window.

The kid was crying, and the damp wash was crisscrossing the room, and the stew was smelling up the place, and the flat was like a furnace, but still it was a lot better than the other way, than the old way. She wouldn't have changed it back again if she could. She was safe now, and her adventuring was through.

A whimsical chuckle escaped from her, as she pulled the blinds down on her revery. Probably for the last time, probably for good.

"I wonder whatever became of him, that young fellow?" she mused idly. Idly, and fleetingly, and without really wanting to know.